Desert
Soliloquy

LIBBY GRANDY

Cover photograph by Gordon Wolford

ISBN-10: 1475196725
EAN-13: 9781475196726

DEDICATION

For Fred,
my supportive, loving husband

PROLOGUE

The sun sank behind the black, jagged tops of the far mountains across the desert floor. The red-orange sky faded to melon and finally, the palest rose. Darkness descended. The silence was complete. She waited.

He held his hand in front of his eyes. He could not see it. The sweat of fear beaded his face and drenched his clothes. He was trapped in a world of darkness, without a glimmer of light.

CHAPTER ONE

Charles opened his eyes and stared into blackness. He swallowed the bile rising in his throat as he fought to control the panic threatening to overwhelm him. Where was he? He maneuvered himself into a sitting position. Every bone in his body ached, and he could feel a large lump on his forehead. Somewhere behind him he sensed a wall. Pushing with his hands, he slid backwards an inch at a time. When he reached the dirt wall, he leaned against it and waited for the pain in his head to subside and his mind to clear.

The last thing he remembered was climbing into the passenger side of his Maserati.

Good Lord, he thought. What happened to Stephen? Is he here, too?

"Hello?" he called out. "Anyone there?" Hearing his own voice only deepened the silence.

To calm himself, he focused his mind on Caroline, visualizing her lovely face. Was she waiting for him at Odessa?

Dizziness and nausea overcame him. Small rocks were scattered around, and he began clearing a space to lie down again. Reaching farther out, his hand touched something soft. He jerked back.

What the hell!

He reached out again. It felt like canvas. A bag? He pulled it toward him.

Shaking from suspense and hope, he explored the outside until his hand found an opening. He reached inside.

"Oh, my god!" He wrapped trembling fingers around the flashlight. A beam of light illuminated the inside of the knapsack.

Tears he had refused to shed his entire life began to run down his cheeks.

She lifted long, dark hair, streaked with silver strands, off her neck and anchored it high on her head. It was late evening, but the air was still hot and dry. Dipping a cloth into the porcelain washbowl, she patted cool water on her face and neck. Deep brown eyes stared back at her from the mirror attached to the dresser.

Another day and no Charles. Had he changed his mind? Why wasn't he answering his cell phone?

This was not like her ex-husband. He was always prompt. Since their divorce ten years ago, she'd missed that quality in the men she dated.

On the other hand, there had always been a part of Charles's life that he kept secret, even from her. Periodically he would go off on some mysterious venture, unconcerned if it inconvenienced anyone else. Had that happened again?

How long should I wait? she wondered. She looked around the bedroom. Like the rest of the house, it was spotlessly clean. Soft, lace-trimmed sheets were on the bed. An elegant crystal hurricane lamp sat on the antique dresser.

Caroline suspected the room looked very much the same as it had a hundred years ago, although the lace curtains at the French doors were obviously new. She opened the doors and stepped onto the front porch.

Walking across the sandy street, she looked out over the unobstructed view of the valley. The small, stucco house sat at the far end of an old mining town, halfway up the barren, craggy mountain. The desert floor below stretched for miles before reaching the mountains to the north. A single asphalt road ran east and west through the center of the valley.

What am I doing here? Why did I ever agree to come to this isolated, abandoned town?

But, of course, she knew why. Charles had promised a unique surprise if she met him, and she was curious about her ex-husband's life these days. She hoped this unusual get-together would answer some of her questions.

As the sun sank lower in the sky, Caroline looked toward the mountain behind her. Dilapidated buildings lined a sand-packed street. In the 1800s, there had been stores, a barbershop, jail, smithy, schoolhouse and several saloons in the booming mining town of Odessa. Charles had left a detailed history of the town for her to read.

She had been fascinated by the historical document, especially in regard to the family that once lived in the house where she was staying. In 1876, a young woman named Jessica had married the owner of the General Store and managed to raise five children in the small house. From the moment Caroline arrived, she had sensed a loving presence.

Each night, she slept peacefully in the bed where Jessica's children had been born. She used the old dresser for her clothes and had stared into the wavy mirror, tracing the fine lines that had begun to appear now that she was in her fifties. Had Jessica done the same as the desert stole her youth?

The sun had almost disappeared below the horizon. Caroline walked back to the house, choosing the second set of doors leading from the porch into the parlor. In this room, the original Victorian-style furniture was well preserved. Blue cotton drapes hung at the windows and a threadbare Oriental rug covered the middle of the hardwood floor.

She walked through the room to a hallway that led past a small bathroom to the kitchen. A week's supply of food stocked the kitchen shelves and the propane refrigerator. She lit the kerosene lamp on the table and made herself a ham sandwich. Arranging cheese, crackers and fruit on a plate and pouring a glass of wine, she carried everything out to the front porch.

Sitting on a wooden rocker, she ate her supper, watching stars appear one by one, until the sky was full. There was a familiarity about the place that filled her with a quiet peace. If only Charles were here. She closed her eyes and pictured the face of the man she had once loved so deeply.

Caroline!

Startled, she turned toward the mountain.

CHAPTER TWO

The road stretched endlessly through the flat, empty desert. In the distance, dark mountains were silhouetted against a ruby-red sky. Kate had crossed the Nevada state line and was now into the high desert of California. She wondered how far it was to the next town.

In the twilight, a lavender mist spread across the desert floor, leaving only darkness and a sudden cooling of the dry air blowing through the car window. She had turned off the air conditioning. The wind whipped her short, curly auburn hair.

Her mind was quiet for a change, and she savored the blessed absence of memory, of pain. Her sense of timelessness deepened. Kate had never seen the desert before. She'd only known green forests and rolling hills, but she loved the stark beauty of this strange new world.

She glanced at the speedometer and slowed down. No reason to hurry, she thought. No one's waiting for me. Tears filled her eyes as the reality of her aloneness returned.

The tears made the road in the distance unclear, and she squinted to see something up ahead. She focused on the growing black dot, realizing it was a car and that she appeared to be rapidly gaining on it. The reason soon became apparent. It was lying on its side just off the shoulder of the road.

Oh, dear God, she thought, is the driver all right?

Stopping beside the overturned car, Kate jumped out and ran to look inside. Empty.

"Thank heavens!" she said aloud. She stared at the wrecked car, and painful memories came flooding back, red and black memories of that dark night, blood everywhere, the flashing red light of the police car. Her therapist had explained post-traumatic stress disorder to her, but she knew it was more than that. The memory and her aloneness—they were her penance.

Seven months had passed since the accident, and well-meaning friends couldn't understand why she didn't get on with her life. She was only twenty-three years old, had enough money to live wherever she chose, do whatever she wanted. Except have a life with her husband, Danny, and their unborn child who also died that awful night.

Kate walked back to her own car. Leaning against it, she looked up. Billions of stars now filled the sky from horizon to horizon. The air was so clean and clear she could see stars behind stars. She picked out two of her favorite constellations, Cassiopeia and Andromeda. The Pleiades twinkled overhead, and Venus shone brightly near the horizon.

The silence was soon broken by a rustling, a stirring. The desert was coming to life.

A quiet peacefulness filled her mind. She didn't want to lose the feeling and stood, unmoving, until the chill of the night air finally forced her back into the car.

She pulled the seat belt around her.

Stop!

Kate gripped the wheel, tightly.

The instruction had been clear, but there had been no sound. No voice. Just an inner command. She waited. Sweat glistened on her forehead although the night had turned quite cool.

I need to get out of here, she thought, reaching for the key. The engine caught, sputtered then stalled. Kate tried again, grinding away. Finally she gave up. The comforting silence of moments before now held a different ambiance.

Listen!

She sat very still. Out of the darkness came a sound she recognized, the same sound she'd heard when she held her dying husband in her arms.

Grabbing a flashlight from the glove box, she stepped out of the car and pierced the darkness with the light. A rabbit leaped out from behind a cactus. A snake slithered away.

Kate cleared her throat and called out, "Is anyone there?"

She heard the low moan again. It came from the right, and she slowly walked in that direction. Memories stirred within her, and she began to tremble. Something moved in the darkness ahead. Was it an animal?

She swept the desert floor with the beam of light.

A figure under a mesquite tree moved, turned over and looked at her.

Kate awoke, clothes damp from the morning dew. Her body ached, and she groaned as she sat up. The sound of her own voice brought everything back. Jumping to her feet, she looked around. The surrounding desert was empty. No one was under the mesquite tree.

Had she dreamed it? Her heart began to pound.

I must have passed out, she thought. I don't remember anything after seeing...Danny. That's why I fainted. The man looked just like Danny.

The sound of a motor drew her attention toward the road where a man was hoisting the abandoned car from yesterday onto a tow truck. He obviously hadn't seen her, and she started running, waving her arms and calling out.

"Oh, thank God, you're here. My car won't start. Can you help me?"

The startled young man turned around. "Where the heck did you come from?"

"The Toyota's my car. I stopped last night to see if anyone was hurt and then.... Uh, I was just looking around and...." Kate didn't know how to explain to this stranger that she thought she'd seen her dead husband.

His intense scrutiny was beginning to make her uncomfortable. "Could you please look at my car?" she asked.

He walked over to the Toyota, climbed in and turned the key. The engine immediately turned over and caught.

Feeling foolish, Kate said, "It wouldn't start last night!"

"Where are you headed?" he asked.

"To the first place I can get some gas."

"Follow me."

Without another word, he got into his truck and took off. Kate had to rush to get into her car and catch up to him.

Mike checked periodically in the rear view mirror to see if the small blue Toyota was following him. Why did he feel so irritated with the young woman driving it? Then he knew. She reminded him of his ex-wife. But why? Laurie was tall and blond. This girl was petite with curly auburn hair and freckles on an upturned nose. Definitely not his type.

It was the eyes, the clear, light green eyes, with the same vulnerable look. He'd spent the past year trying to forget those eyes, as they conjured up too many painful questions. Had Laurie remarried? Had the baby come? Did it look like the son of a bitch who had once been his friend?

"Damn!" Mike said, hitting the steering wheel.

A half-hour later, the two vehicles pulled into a motel parking lot. Kate didn't want to deal with the unfriendly stranger again, so she watched him pull around back and waited until he was out of sight before leaving her car.

The motel was one long building with gas pumps in front. She hurried through the front door. The man behind the counter had to be in his eighties.

His monosyllabic replies to her questions made her wonder if the men in this part of the country could talk. Yes. He had a room. Yes. He could provide food. No. He didn't take credit cards. His name? Malcolm.

She paid up front and wearily followed him to a small, clean room, then showered and fell into bed.

It was late afternoon when she awoke. She couldn't believe that she'd slept all day. She got up, splashed water on her face and thought about the night before.

Combing unruly curls, she addressed the pale face in the mirror. "You were abducted by aliens, Katie-girl." Her image didn't smile back.

Maybe supper and being in the company of people will make me feel better, she thought.

At the front office, Kate found no one to ask where the dining area might be. A door at the back of the room, however, had a sign over it that said *Food*.

She peeked in and saw three men sitting at one of the tables: the motel owner, the tow truck driver and an older man, probably in his late fifties, who smiled at her. Relieved to finally see a friendly face, she walked in and sat next to him.

"Hi, my name's Katherine. People call me Kate."

"Josh," the man said. He had tanned, craggy features and thick gray hair. His handshake was firm and comforting.

Kate began to relax. She breathed in a delicious aroma and turned to Malcolm to ask if she could have some of the stew simmering in a crock pot on the table. He filled a large bowl and placed it in front of her, along with a basket of homemade bread.

"Are you driving out here alone, Kate?" Josh asked.

She nodded, greedily eating in silence, ignoring the curious stares of the men. Finally satisfied, she pushed her bowl aside and accepted a steaming cup of coffee from Malcolm.

"I'm sorry. I'm not usually so antisocial, but I was starving!"

"So it would seem," Josh said. "When was the last time you ate?"

"Yesterday morning, but it seems a hundred years ago. So much has happened since then."

The men waited for her to elaborate.

When she didn't, Josh prompted, "Like what?" His eyes had turned cool and appraising.

"I, uh, it's complicated. You see...well, I saw this overturned, empty car by the side of the road. And then I heard something."

Josh was listening intently.

"I walked into the desert and under this tree was a man."

"You saw a man? Was he alive?" The look on Josh's face changed from curiosity to excitement.

"Yes. He was moaning."

"He was hurt?" Josh asked.

"I guess so. But I really don't know. I'm afraid I fainted at that point. And when I awoke this morning, no one was there."

The tow truck driver jumped up, eyes blazing.

"You didn't tell me about this when I saw you!"

The fierce accusation took Kate aback for a moment. She suddenly felt angry, herself. "I was confused, and you weren't very friendly. Since the man was gone, I thought you'd probably just think I was crazy."

"For God's sake, there might be a dying man out there, and we're sitting on our butts watching you eat Malcolm's stew!" With that, he stomped out of the room. Josh shrugged apologetically and followed him.

Kate was stunned. Why hadn't she thought of that? Tears that were always close to the surface these days filled her eyes. She felt an awkward pat on her shoulder. Malcolm stood silently beside her.

"I'm sorry," she said, wiping away the tears.

"People see strange things in the desert," he said. "Don't worry yourself so. Not yet, anyways."

"But I may have caused a man's death! He probably crawled away somewhere and was out in the heat all day. How hot was it?"

"Not bad, maybe a hundred or so, but he wouldn't get far if he crawled. You'd seen him in the morning. If he walked away, he can't be too bad off."

Kate desperately wanted to believe that, but she was feeling worse all the time. Jumping up, she ran to the door and saw the angry young man climbing into his truck. Josh stood on the passenger's side. She ran up to him. No way were they going to go back there without her!

"I'm sure you don't want me to go along, but I need to know if that man is okay." Before he could answer, she continued, "I'm the only one who knows the exact spot." She pointed toward the driver's side of the truck. "He knows the location of the wreck, but I never showed him the tree where the man was lying. Let me go with you. Please!"

Josh opened the passenger door and helped her inside the truck.

The sun was low in the sky when they pulled out of the motel parking lot. Kate sat between the two men, staring out the dirty windshield. Josh reached over and patted her clenched hands.

"Stop feeling so guilty. You had a bad fright. No wonder you fainted."

Kate looked at him. He was such a kind man. Not like the one behind the wheel who was racing through the desert like a madman.

Josh asked about her trip across country, and they talked until she realized the truck was slowing down. Was this the place? It all looked the same to her. As soon as they stopped, however, she recognized the small tree off the side of the road.

She pointed it out and waited in the truck while the men headed toward the mesquite tree standing alone among the sagebrush. They walked around the area, apparently scouring the ground for footprints. She watched them as the sun sank slowly below the horizon, giving the desert floor a rosy hue. Finally, they separated and walked out into the surrounding desert.

Watching them go, Kate whispered, "Please, God, don't let me be responsible for another death." The desert seemed to blur and disappear as the twilight faded into darkness. Tired of waiting, Kate got out of the truck. She could see the flickering beams of the men's flashlights as they continued to search. The stars in the night sky seemed near enough to touch. Her nerves quieted.

The lights moved closer, and voices broke the silence. "I don't understand," Josh was saying. "The footprints should still be there. Hers were. But where were his? Did you see any prints except the girl's?"

"Not a one. And the ground around the tree should have shown some signs of a body lying there. I could tell where she lay when she fainted. What the hell is going on here? Was the girl just seeing things?"

When the men reached the truck, Kate climbed back in and debated whether or not to mention the hallucination about her husband. Heading back down the desert road, the two men talked over the top of her head. Kate felt invisible. Finally, she interrupted.

"Excuse me," she said to the driver, "but do you have a name?"

The blue eyes softened for a moment in amusement.

"Mike," he said.

Kate turned back to stare straight ahead into the path the headlights cut through the darkness.

"Josh," Mike asked. "What do you think? Could there have been a man out there?"

"Maybe. We'll know more tomorrow when the State Police have time to go over a larger area. Guess someone could have gotten to him during the night but seems like Kate here would have heard something. Unless...."

Josh stared at her questioningly.

"What?" she asked. "I told you I fainted. That's all I remember."

"But you didn't wake up until morning. You know how cold the desert gets at night?"

"Maybe she was on something," Mike said.

Kate opened her mouth to respond then closed it, too mad to say anything for a moment.

When she did speak, it was directly to Josh.

"No, I was not drunk or on drugs. I was dead sober and scared. I'd driven twelve hours straight and hadn't eaten." She took a deep breath. "I guess I should tell you what frightened me. When the man turned and looked at me, I thought it was my husband."

"You're married to Charles Laughery?!"

Kate frowned. "Who's Charles Laughery?"

Trapped in the close confines of the truck, she began to feel uneasy. After all, she didn't know either of these men. Yet, here she was in the middle of nowhere with them.

"He's the owner of the wrecked car," Josh said. "The State Police ran a trace on the license plates. But let's start over. You say you thought it was your husband. Where's your husband supposed to be?"

Kate bit her lip. In a small voice, she said, "He's dead."

Josh stared at her then asked, "You thought...you believed you were looking into the face of your dead husband?"

She nodded.

"How long ago did he die?"

"Seven months." She hesitated then decided it might help to talk about it. She was just finishing as they pulled up in front of the motel.

"I lost both my husband and baby that night," she concluded, "and I just can't deal with the thought of any more death. I hope Charles Laughery is okay."

Charles wiped the sweat from his forehead with the back of a dirty, blood-caked sleeve. He'd never known what cold sweat was until now.

He touched the knapsack on the ground beside him, started to reach inside then stopped. No, only when fear inched its way to terror would he turn on the flashlight to regain his sanity.

Who did this to me? he wondered. *And why leave me enough water and food to survive for a while?*

Of course, he was grateful for the supplies. When his emotions began to run amok, he turned on the flashlight, checked his rations and calmed down. Only then could he focus on finding a way out. And he would get out. He was not going to die alone in the dark!

Other men have.

Charles began breathing slowly and deeply, calming the fear that was beginning to build again. He refused to acknowledge the voice in his head that condemned him to death.

Light, he needed light. He reached for the flashlight, turned it on, and pointed it at the pile of rocks that reached to the ceiling, the result of an old cave in. Someone had dug through and then resealed it.

He knew where he was now. There were many large, dug out shelves like this in the Odessa Mountain, areas where miners had slept and eaten. They had survived for weeks in these places, but the only way out was the tunnel that was now blocked.

Somehow, he had to get through that wall of rocks. Grasping the flashlight, he rolled onto his knees and waited a few seconds until his head stopped spinning.

He crawled toward the nearest wall. Reaching it, he pushed himself upright until he was standing then shone the light over the walls and ceiling of his prison. There had to be an airshaft somewhere, but only solid rock appeared in the beam of light.

Holding onto the wall, he moved around the shelf to the caved-in area.

He laid the flashlight on the floor and began pulling one rock after the other from the towering pile, carefully at first, methodically, then faster and faster. A sense of panic set in, and he worked furiously until exhaustion forced him to stop. He looked up the wall of rock.

He hadn't made a dent in it.

CHAPTER THREE

Caroline stood at the edge of the rocky cliff, gazing out over the valley and sipping her coffee. The sun was barely over the horizon. She turned to look at the town of Odessa. It must have been exciting to live here when it was a thriving mining town. Where the mountain sloped upward, she could see the entrances to the silver mines.

Why had Charles bought this old ghost town?

Was this one of his hideaways when he needed to escape from the pressures of his high-powered business life? When they were married, he would often go away for periods of time. Unlike his business trips, he would return refreshed and full of energy. Had he come here? Why hadn't he shared this beautiful place with her?

She often wondered if their marriage might have survived if Charles had not been so secretive. Or if they had been able to have children, a sorrow she still carried in her heart.

After the divorce, their paths seldom crossed, and her social life changed dramatically. Although she occasionally shopped on Rodeo Drive or attended a fundraiser, more often she stayed in her cottage in the hills above Los Angeles, painting.

Charles often asked her to paint his friends, but their faces were too closed, too tight and unyielding. Only his face interested her, and she had painted his portrait. It hung in her studio at home.

Caroline's cell phone rang. She grabbed it from her jeans jacket. "Charles?!"

"It's Adam, Caroline. They said you called looking for the boss. I thought he was meeting you at Odessa. He hasn't shown up yet?"

Her heart sank. If Charles's trusted assistant, Adam, didn't know where he was, something was very wrong.

"No, he hasn't. I've been here two days, and I'm really getting worried. This isn't like him. Do you have any idea where he might be?"

There was a moment's silence.

"No, I don't," he finally said. "I've been trying to contact him, too. Normally, we don't bother Charles when he takes off for a few days, but there's a problem only he can resolve, so we've hired a private investigator to locate him. The guy's staying at a motel not far from where you are. He says Charles was last seen in Vegas."

"Vegas? He hates Vegas!"

"I know. My guess is he just stopped there to spend the night before driving on to Odessa. I'll tell you what. Let me continue to work on this, and I'll give you a call as soon as I know anything. Okay?"

After she hung up, Caroline felt better. If anyone could find her ex-husband, it was Adam. Charles's assistant was the brightest, most astute member of his staff.

Maybe this private investigator could help her. She looked in the direction of the low-lying mountains to the east. The motel must be that way. She'd traveled from Los Angeles in the west, and there were no motels for at least thirty miles.

Getting into her Ford Expedition, she drove to the bottom of the mountain and turned left at the asphalt road. Five miles farther, she pulled into a motel parking lot.

Caroline found no one in the front office, but loud voices came from an adjoining room. "It's beginning to look like Laughery was kidnapped. I think we should...."

She ran around the counter and through the door.

"You think Charles has been kidnapped?" she cried out.

Four people turned to look at her in amazement. Then a pretty young girl rushed over to her. "Oh, dear, we didn't mean to frighten you. We're not sure what happened to Mr. Laughery. Are you a friend of his?"

Caroline fought to regain control of her breathing. "I'm sorry. I was so startled to hear you talking about Charles that I just ran in here. I used to be married to him. My name is Caroline Laughery."

She hesitated, looking at the curious faces, then continued. "I received a phone call from him last week asking me to meet him at an old silver mine that he owns not far from here. I got there two days ago, but he never showed up. He hasn't even called. His assistant in LA said they'd hired an investigator, who was at a motel close by."

A tall, attractive man stuck out his hand. "That would be me—Josh Logan," he said, gently taking her arm.

He introduced her to the sweet-faced girl, Kate, and the young man, Mike, then turned to an elderly gentleman, who jumped up and offered his chair.

"I'm Malcolm Long, ma'am. Your ex-husband and I go back aways."

"You know Charles?" Caroline asked.

"He stopped by a couple times a year, and we had us some good talks. He liked to hear stories about the old days around here. He used to say to me, 'Malcolm, that mountain's still full of silver, and it all belongs to me.'"

"That sounds like Charles. Although I'm sure it would cost more to get the silver out than it's worth in today's market."

"Yep, that's for sure," Malcolm said.

"Well, I can understand that Charles would enjoy coming to this area but where is he now? And why are you speculating about a kidnapping? Please tell me what you know."

Kate glanced at the others. "I'll start." She began with finding the abandoned car and ended with seeing a man under the tree.

"Do you think it was Charles?" Caroline asked.

"No, the man was young. I'm so sorry that I can't be more helpful."

Josh Logan picked up the story.

"My sources tell me that your ex-husband was traveling from Vegas on his way to see you. He spent one night there then left the Bellagio with another man. They headed this way but obviously never made it.

"Yesterday morning, Mike towed his car in; that's when he ran into Kate. Later in the day we went back to the location where she saw the man but found nothing, not even footprints. The State Police are having the surrounding area thoroughly searched, so I'll leave that to them. But I would like to see this mining town you say Laughery owns. Would that be all right with you, Ms. Laughery?"

"Please, call me Caroline. Of course, you can see the town. I want to help in any way I can. I need to know that Charles is all right."

"I'm sure he is," Josh said. "I've located people who have been gone much longer than a few days. We'll find him."

He pushed back his chair and looked at Mike.

"Coming?"

Mike nodded.

"May I go along?" Kate asked. Josh suggested the two women ride together, and he and Mike would follow.

As they drove up the mountain road, Josh thought about the woman who had appeared out of nowhere. She had a serene, quiet beauty—like the desert he loved so much.

Josh smiled to himself. This case just kept getting more and more interesting.

He looked over at the young man next to him who stared silently out the window.

"You know, Mike," he said, "I think you'll get a kick out of seeing this old mining town. It doesn't take much imagination to put yourself back in time when you're in one of these ghost towns. Men used to come from all over the world to work the mines. I don't know how they did it. Spending days inside a mountain isn't my idea of a good time."

"It wouldn't bother me," Mike said. "I used to explore caves back home."

"And where would that be, son?"

"Don't call me son!"

Josh brought the truck to an abrupt halt.

"Let's get something straight, Mike," he said. "I don't know what your problems are, and you don't have to tell me. But you do have to speak to me with respect."

Mike turned away and stared out the window. "So you're a P.I. You never mentioned that fact when we met."

"That's what the 'private' in Private Investigator means, Mike."

Neither man spoke again as Josh continued to follow the women. The road ended half-way up the mountain on a large plateau where the remains of the ghost town stood.

Josh parked behind Caroline's SUV in front of a small, stucco house. When he stepped out and looked across to the valley below, he was stunned. The view was magnificent! The sight touched some far memory, something....

Caroline walked over to stand beside him. "Wonderful, isn't it?"

Josh looked into the deep brown eyes...so beautiful. He raised his hand to touch the lovely face but caught himself before completing the gesture.

"Come inside," she said, "and see what Charles has done with the place. He kept it as authentic as possible."

Caroline walked them through the house, beginning with the parlor that looked like a miniature Victorian living room. Josh could see that a great deal of effort had been made to replicate an era as well as make the house comfortable. A short hallway led first to a tiny bathroom with a claw-footed bathtub and then to a well stocked kitchen. Charles had clearly planned to spend some time here with his ex-wife. The tour ended in the bedroom.

"I love this house!" Kate said to Caroline, standing at the French doors leading onto the porch. She pushed them open. "Can we look around? Maybe there's a clue somewhere in this old town that will lead us to Charles."

"Of course, just give me a minute to put my hair up."

Josh watched as Caroline stood at the old dresser, brushing her long dark hair upward, retrieving loose strands. The nape of her neck was slim and inviting.

Josh felt himself flush. Get a grip, man, he admonished himself.

"Okay," Caroline said, "let's explore before it gets too hot."

Josh followed the others outside and through the town, listening as Caroline gave a history lesson on Odessa. He could easily imagine what life must have been like here in the 1800s.

At noon, while Caroline made lunch, Josh sat in front of what had once been the town saloon. Across from him stood the remains of a livery stable and blacksmith's forge. The stable was missing its roof. The building next to it had burned down and only the foundation was left.

Does Laughery plan to renovate this place? Josh wondered. Or was he keeping it as some kind of sanctuary, away from the stress and strain of modern life?

What would it be like to own a whole town, deserted though it might be? Or to have a woman like Caroline for a wife?

The sound of her voice calling from the house brought him back to his present assignment. He shook his head. He needed to focus on finding the man, not envying him.

After lunch, Mike stepped outside to smoke, and Josh joined him. Sitting in a rocker on the porch, he propped his feet on the railing. Mike leaned against one of the posts. He flicked his cigarette onto the sand. "I found car tracks on the other side of a gulch."

"What?"

"I walked over there before lunch. Another road circles around this town ending up at the mountain. There are fresh car tracks. I didn't want to say anything in front of the women."

Josh quickly got to his feet. "Show me!"

Hurrying to the edge of town, they crossed over the rocky gulch to the face of the mountain. Josh could see the entrances of many mines, and as Mike had said, another road led to this area. The base of the mountain, however, was too rocky to show footprints.

"Seems to me a mountain would be a great place to get rid of a body," Mike said.

Josh nodded as he looked up the mountain. Was the body of Charles Laughery in there? Sweat soaked the back of his shirt. He didn't know if it was the heat of the afternoon sun or the thought of climbing into one of those mines.

Mike started to say more, but Josh saw the women walking in their direction and shook his head.

"It's hot out here," Josh called out. "Let's go back to the house." He hurried to Caroline, took her arm, and together they retraced their steps across the gulch. Agile, she stepped from one rock to another, not really needing his help but not pulling away either. Once they reached the street, they walked silently through the town. It wasn't until they reached the front porch of the house that Caroline spoke.

"So, what were you two talking about over there?"

Josh knew he wasn't going to be able to keep this astute woman in the dark for long. "We found fresh car tracks, Caroline. You haven't been over that way, have you?"

Turning pale, she shook her head.

"Do you think they have anything to do with Charles?"

Josh just looked at her.

"You believe he could be in one of those old mines? My God! We have to do something." Caroline turned as though to run back toward the mountain, but Mike grabbed her arm.

"Do you know how deep those mines go?" he asked, "or how many entrances there are? You could search for years and never find anything. Not only that, the authorities are going to want more than just our suspicions before they commit any resources to a search."

"Forget the authorities," Caroline said. "His company will have people out here tomorrow." She headed toward the parlor door. "I'll be back in a minute."

Caroline's minute turned into twenty, and when she walked back onto the porch, she looked furious. "Charles's assistant wasn't there. I had to talk to his partners." She took a deep breath. "Those sons of bitches. I never did like them. Do you know what they said?" She paced back and forth.

"That I'm overreacting. Jenson, the youngest partner, kept assuring me that Charles could take care of himself." She looked at Josh.

"They said to tell you to send them a bill. You're off the case. They said the State Police would handle things from here on."

Josh was stunned. This made no sense. What was going on here?

Caroline sat on the porch steps. Mike stooped in front of her and, in a gentle voice, assured her that one way or the other, they would solve the mystery of her ex-husband's disappearance.

"Don't worry about it. Josh and I will go through every mine up there if that's what it takes."

Josh was surprised. This was a different side of Mike. Then his words sank in.

Shit. Mike had just committed them to going inside that damn mountain.

Charles awoke, reluctantly. Sleep was his only friend now, the only time he wasn't afraid or in pain.

How long had it been? Two, three days? Surely they were searching for him by now. Raising himself on one elbow, he turned on the flashlight and looked at his digital watch. 13.00. Early afternoon.

Why couldn't he remember anything after turning the keys over to Stephen in the parking lot at the Bellagio in Vegas? The cut on his head and symptoms he recognized as a concussion seemed to indicate that they had been in an accident but....

He concentrated. The attendant had brought them his Maserati. Dizzy...he'd felt a little nauseous and dizzy when he opened the driver's door. Stephen must have noticed as he offered to drive. Of course, the kid was dying to get his hands on the high-powered car. He remembered thinking, oh, what the hell. Let him have some fun.

He had handed Stephen the keys with the admonition that he had to stay within five miles of the speed limit once they started across the desert floor heading west. Had he obeyed? Charles had no idea. The next thing he remembered was opening his eyes and staring into total blackness.

He rubbed his throbbing head. Would he be here if he hadn't let Stephen drive? Would he be at the small house in Odessa with Caroline, enjoying the beauty of the mountain and desert?

Right now the sun would be high in the desert sky. He could almost feel its warmth on his face and smell the fresh, clean air.

When he got out of here, he would never again take all that for granted.

If you get out, the voice inside his head chided.

"I will, goddamn it. I will!" Charles immediately felt foolish. Who was he shouting at? Himself? Was he arguing with himself now?

Maybe that was the goal. Someone wanted him to go crazy before he died in this black hole. But who hated him that much?

He had made enemies in his sixty-one years. There were a few men he had ruined financially. But that was just business. It was understood in his world. But then so was revenge.

He was thirsty. Reaching for the water bottle, he wondered once more why his abductors had left him the knapsack. Maybe they were coming back for him.

Or maybe they want it to look like you died accidentally in a cave in.

"I should have thought of that."

You just did.

He laughed. It was amusing, this going crazy business.

Work, he needed to stop thinking and work on the wall of rock that blocked his way to freedom. He tried to stand but could only make it to his knees. He laid the flashlight on the ground, pointing the beam forward, then crawled across the shelf and began once again lifting rocks from the pile. A low rumble caused him to pause. Then....

Charles dove to the side as rocks rolled down around him, and the little progress he had made was erased.

The mountain was winning.

CHAPTER FOUR

Caroline sat with Kate on the porch, while inside the house, Mike and Josh studied the maps of the mines Caroline had found. "How are you feeling?" Kate asked.

"I'm all right I guess. I don't know what I would do without the three of you. One minute, I'm sure Charles will call and tell me he's fine, and the next, I have a feeling something terrible has happened to him."

"Why don't you rest? The men seem to know what they're doing. I'll check out the kitchen and see what I can find for supper tonight."

"Maybe I *should* lie down for a while," Caroline said.

Once inside the house, she decided a bath in the claw-footed bathtub sounded better. Thank goodness Charles had filled the water tank in back and installed a propane gas water heater.

Ten minutes later, she relaxed in the tepid water, letting it soak away the dust of the desert and thought about Jessica and her five children. How had she done it? Water had been a real luxury in those days. It had to be hauled up the mountain in kegs according to the history of the town that Charles had left for her.

Charles. Without warning, tears began to flow, falling into the bath water. She allowed herself the luxury of crying then washed her face and got out of the tub.

Drying off and putting on a robe, Caroline went directly to the bedroom and stretched out on the bed. She could hear the murmur of voices in the parlor. Closing her eyes, she envisioned Charles. He was a distinguished-looking man. An aura of authority made him intimidating at times, but she knew his softer side. He had always treated her lovingly. Well, except where his other women were concerned. It had always surprised her that he could be so blind and thoughtless in that one area. It was as though affairs were the natural prerogative of powerful men. Of course, Charles had expected her to be faithful.

She'd endured it for twelve years. If there had been a child, she might have overlooked it completely. Some of her friends did, and she couldn't quarrel with their decision. Other people might believe it was because of lifestyle and status, but the women she knew were simply in love with their husbands.

It finally became too painful for her, however, and she remembered Charles's amazement when she gave him an ultimatum. He, in turn, accused her of having an overactive imagination. Furious, she packed her bags and left, expecting him to come after her, apologize and commit to their marriage.

Instead, he went abroad for his company and returned with Brenda, who eventually became his second wife. Ironically, the tabloids were now suggesting that Charles was divorcing her for the same reasons Caroline had left him.

She was glad *their* divorce hadn't received the same attention. Every week, there was another picture of Brenda and her young lover in the tabloids.

Was Charles hiding out somewhere to escape the publicity?

No, Charles took control of situations. He didn't give in to his emotions. Caroline could picture him throwing Brenda out of his life and fighting her over money, but he wouldn't run away and hide.

Caroline sighed and got out of bed. She slipped into a sleeveless, blue cotton dress and was brushing her hair when a knock sounded on the French double doors. She opened them to find Josh, holding a glass of wine in one hand, a can of beer in the other.

"Kate found a bottle of Chardonnay in your pantry," he said. "Or would you like a beer? I have another one in the truck."

Caroline stepped out onto the porch, took the glass of wine and touched his can of beer.

"To this beautiful place," she said.

Josh returned the toast. "To one of the most beautiful women I've ever seen."

Startled, Caroline stared at him. There wasn't a trace of insincerity in his voice or face. She hadn't heard such a compliment in years. Yet, this man was looking at her the way he probably looked at sunsets, with respectful awe. She took a sip of wine.

"Have I embarrassed you?" he asked.

She lowered her eyes. "I just don't know exactly how to respond. I'm sure you mean it, but, well...."

"Trust me," he said, smiling, "I never say what I don't mean."

Caroline was touched and impressed. Josh must be a very self-assured man to be so honest and open. It would be interesting to get to know him, to.... No, she really wasn't seeking a romantic relationship. Well, maybe, with Charles again. And he must have considered the possibility, too, because the house was prepared thoughtfully, as though for a romantic rendezvous.

Caroline's mind cleared. Of course. Charles had planned all this with great care. He wasn't depressed over his divorce. He wasn't hiding out somewhere.

"No, of course not!"

The man in front of her stiffened. Realizing how it must have sounded, she said, "I'm sorry. I was thinking out loud about something else."

She explained and watched as Josh slowly shifted emotional gears.

"I agree with you," he said, "but if Charles planned to rekindle your relationship and made these elaborate preparations, I'm afraid that only something drastic would keep him away."

Long after the others had returned to the motel, Caroline tossed and turned, unable to go to sleep. Tomorrow Mike and Josh would begin exploring the mines. Was Charles lying inside that mountain? She couldn't bear the thought.

She propped herself up on pillows. The night outside was cold and still. Shivering, she pulled the covers up under her chin. In LA, she might paint for a few hours, but although Charles had encouraged her to bring her painting supplies, she hadn't set up her easel here yet, not finding the right place, the perfect light.

She decided to make some herbal tea.

In the kitchen, Caroline waited for the water to boil and thought about Jessica. There must have been many nights when she had to get up to feed babies or care for ill children.

Sitting at the table, she warmed her hands on the cup while the tea steeped.

Charles. Where are you? She closed her eyes.

The night wrapped itself around her, and she began to sense something in the silence, like a presence, a kind of energy.

She sat very still.

When she finally opened her eyes, she knew.

Somewhere, Charles was alive.

Caroline, he cried out, silently, help me!

It had become his mantra. He also caught himself praying to a god he didn't believe in.

Was he proving the adage about atheists? Did this hellhole qualify as a foxhole?

He shifted into a sitting position. He needed to stop feeling sorry for himself and concentrate on getting out of this mountain. When he did, the bastards who did this to him were going to pay! But who the hell were they? The list in his mind kept growing: old business enemies, Brenda, his partners, maybe even Adam. They had argued fiercely two weeks ago. He had almost fired him.

Or was it his rival, Barton? They had been competing for as long as he could remember. Members of the cartel, they both had been searching for the perfect place to.... Yes, that must be it. Barton had found what the cartel was looking for and just needed time to finalize the deal. That's why he had been left with supplies. Barton wasn't a murderer, but he wouldn't care if an old enemy suffered for a few days or weeks before being rescued. The son of a bitch! When I get out of here....

He took a deep breath. Anger made his head pound. He needed to calm down.

Caroline. He'd focus on Caroline. When he remembered his life with her, a life he had so casually thrown away, he was filled with regret, but it also brought him a sense of peace—and hope. Somehow Caroline would find him. Wishful thinking born out of desperation? Maybe, but it calmed his fears.

He smiled. Caroline was so different from Brenda. She had never really enjoyed his social status or political life, preferring her friends, her painting and supporting the causes she believed in. Charles had never understood Caroline's detachment nor had he paid much attention to her spiritual beliefs. He had a business to run, money to make, deals to broker. He believed in power, control and action. Only after his 61st birthday a few months ago had he begun to wonder about the future. Death wasn't something he could control.

He shook his head. He must focus on life, not death. On Caroline. He reviewed the last few weeks. He had planned everything so carefully, wanting her to arrive at the house first. He knew the impact his secret desert hideaway would have on her.

What she didn't know was that the house, land, and town were now hers. That had been his surprise. He'd transferred the deed a week ago, and because of their pre-nup, Brenda couldn't do a thing about it. He had bought the property before their marriage.

If he didn't make it back, Caroline would at least have this last gift from him. The rest of his assets, however, would go to that bitch of a wife. As long as he was alive, she could only hope for a portion of his empire as part of their divorce settlement. Dead, she would get it all.

He had to admit to himself that few people would care if he died. What a sad epitaph. No children. Parents and brother dead. No one to mourn, except perhaps Caroline.

He felt for the flashlight then hesitated. He needed to save the batteries as long as possible. Regardless of food or water, he would never survive long in total, unending darkness.

He had never allowed his emotions to rule him. Even when Caroline left, he'd distracted himself with travel, women and business. It had taken ten years and a second, disastrous marriage before he could finally admit to himself that he still loved and needed her.

When he realized he was burned out career-wise and that his wife had been unfaithful, he did what he did so well. He took action. He made plans to divorce Brenda, sell his business, move on to his new venture—and win Caroline back.

He had everything under control.

Right up to the moment he found himself trapped, alone in the dark, inside a mountain.

CHAPTER FIVE

In the motel room, Kate pulled the covers tighter over her shoulders. How could she be sweating yesterday and cold tonight, or rather this morning?

She found the desert to be a strange place. Maybe she should just get up and continue her journey westward. Nothing was holding her here except the irrational guilt about a man she'd never met. Yet the thought of leaving Caroline, Josh and Mike—even Malcolm—made her feel sad. What was this connection that she felt with them?

Through the motel window, she could see a lightening of the sky. Sunrise. She had never seen a sunrise in the desert. Kate found her robe and shoes, stepped outside and sat on the steps of the narrow porch. The sky over the craggy mountaintop changed from dark gray to light blue then white-gold as the sun tipped the horizon.

With the first rays, the long shadows of the mountain shortened and within minutes, morning arrived full-blown.

Kate clapped her hands. A chuckle startled her. Mike was leaning against a post a few doors down, smoking and watching her.

He's pretty cute when he smiles, she thought.

"Do you applaud every sunrise?" he asked.

"Do you know how bad smoking is for you?"

"Do I care?"

Cute but irritating. Standing with hands on her hips, Kate started to speak again, but Mike held up his hand. "Hold it. Let me worry about my health. You worry about combing your hair." She blushed, ran fingers through tousled curls and hurried back inside.

By the time Kate entered the dining room, Josh and Mike were already eating. There were several other customers and rather than bother Malcolm, she poured her own coffee from a pot on the counter and carried it to their table. Mike muttered, "Looking better." She ignored him.

Malcolm soon joined them, filling her cup again. The coffee was good, if strong, and she was wide-awake now. She listened as the men discussed plans to explore the mines.

"Thanks for letting me off work, Malcolm," Mike said.

"That's okay. Slow this time of year anyways. Just hope you and Josh find somethin'. You gettin' paid for this, aren't you?"

Mike reddened slightly. "Caroline insisted on it, but I would have done it for nothing. I want to help find her ex-husband." Kate was about to say that she had decided to stay, also, when Mike added, "If only Kate hadn't fainted that night. I hate to say it, but I doubt we find Laughery alive."

Kate felt weak as memories descended, blotting out her surroundings. The old familiar guilt pressed down on her. It was like a heaviness on her chest, a darkness that was always ready to envelop her. Now there was a growing new fear. Another man might be dead because of her.

I have to get out of here, she thought, as the panic attack gripped her. Jumping up, she fled through the door. Instead of going to her room, however, she went around the corner and out into the desert. She ran until, sliding down a sandy gorge, she fell backwards onto the sand, eyes closed, letting the desert sun warm her. Finally, she sat up and propped her arms and head on bent knees.

The sand shifted around her. A subdued Mike was standing over her.

"Are you okay?" he asked.

She didn't answer.

"I didn't mean it the way it sounded back there," he said. "I wasn't blaming you for anything. Josh and I were just brainstorming. The man you saw may not have anything to do with Charles Laughery." He stooped beside her.

"I'm sorry if I upset you."

Kate pushed herself awkwardly to her feet, brushed sand off her jeans and turned to struggle up the sandy incline. At the top, she looked at the flat, desert land and the road that continued west. Maybe she should leave. Forget what happened here and just drive as far as the road took her. But she'd driven across the whole country and so far hadn't outrun a single memory.

"Come on," Mike said, from behind her, "let's get some more of Malcolm's coffee. I'll buy." Kate glanced at him. He was trying to be nice.

On their way to the dining room, Kate stopped at her room to wash her face while Mike got their coffee. When she came back outside, he was waiting. They sat on the porch steps in silence. The quiet of the surrounding desert had its usual calming effect.

"You must think I'm crazy, running off like that," Kate said.

"No. I've done my share of running. Sometimes it helps, most times it doesn't."

"I don't know what to do. I've tried everything, but although it's been over seven months, I still...."

Kate sighed and leaned against the porch railing. Maybe it was time to tell Mike the whole story.

"I spent eighteen years in foster homes," she began, "and when I was twenty, I married a wonderful man. Two years later, I got pregnant and was thrilled that I finally would have a family of my own. We even bought a house. All my dreams were coming true.

"The night of the accident, my husband and I quarreled. Danny didn't want to go to a church fundraiser. It was raining hard. He wanted to stay home, but I was co-chairman of the committee with his mother and felt I had to be there. I couldn't let her down. She'd been so good to me. Anyway, I told him he didn't have to go, that I'd drive myself. Of course, he wouldn't let me. We didn't speak as we drove through the downpour."

Kate took a deep breath then continued. "The rain turned into sleet, and I began having second thoughts. I was about to tell Danny to turn around and go back when, without any warning, an eighteen-wheeler slid through a stop sign right in front of us. Danny tried to stop, but there was no way he could avoid it. In seconds, it was over. His air bag never released, and the steering wheel crushed his chest. All I could do was hold him and wait for help. Later that night, I lost the baby. My life, as I had dreamed and lived it for a short time, was over. And I had no one to blame but myself."

Kate clutched her coffee cup tightly.

"And now, if another man is dead because of me...." She choked on her tears. "Oh, dear, you must think I'm a nut case!"

"Well, it takes one to know one."

Mike stared off into the desert. "I've been half crazy for the past year, too. Like you, I've been trying to outrun memories—and my own anger. I swear if I'd stayed back home, I probably would have killed the only two people I ever loved. If running in the desert helped, I'd be out there every day.

"I was a long-haul truck driver and gone a lot. Laurie, my wife, didn't seem to mind though, and Pete, my best friend, lived close by and helped her out when I was gone. The three of us were buddies in high school." He paused again.

"To make a long story short, when Laurie found out she was pregnant, she told me the truth. The baby wasn't mine. At first, she wouldn't say who the father was, and when she did, well....

"So, today, my two best friends are married with a new baby, and I'm sitting here crying in my coffee. Pretty pathetic, huh?"

"No," Kate said, "just terribly sad." She paused then said, "I guess they must be pretty miserable, too, knowing how much they hurt you."

Mike stood, throwing the rest of the coffee onto the ground.

"Well, I sure as hell wouldn't want them to be unhappy!"

He stomped off and all Kate could do was stare after him.

The door of the dining room slammed behind Mike. Expecting startled stares, he was surprised to find the room empty. The diagrams of the mines at Odessa were spread out on a table. Josh walked into the room from the kitchen, carrying a knapsack.

"There you are. I've packed us some food. Did you find Katie? Is she all right?"

"She's okay," Mike said. "I guess we better get going if we plan to get any exploring done today."

"Well, I'm ready if you are."

"I'm raring to go, but I wish we had help. We could spend months inside that mountain. There's no way to guess which mine shaft to search first."

"I know," Josh said, "but until Search and Rescue agrees to help us or Laughery's company sends reinforcement, we're on our own."

When they arrived at Odessa, Mike saw Kate's blue Toyota parked at Caroline's house. Josh pulled in front of it.

"Need to let Caroline know what's going on," he said.

They could hear voices coming from the bedroom off the porch. Seeing Kate standing in the doorway, Mike felt ashamed. She'd been through a lot, and he shouldn't have lost his temper. He flashed a tentative smile, and she smiled back then turned to help Caroline with her suitcase.

"Going somewhere?" Josh asked.

Caroline sat on the bed.

"I have to do something, Josh. I can't just sit around waiting. Until the local authorities agree to search the mines, we need the resources of Charles's company. I want to confront his partners in person and maybe get help from Brenda. Also, I want to talk to Charles's assistant. He might be able to help me with the partners. Kate has offered to go with me."

"You're going back to LA? That's going to take a few hours. I wish I could fly you there."

"You have a plane?" Caroline asked.

"Yeah, about thirty miles from here. It was the closest landing strip. I flew there and then rented a truck."

"But that's perfect. I hated to think of the long drive to LA and back. Can I borrow it?"

CHAPTER SIX

Forty-five minutes later, Caroline and Kate arrived at the Apple Valley Airport where Josh's Cessna 172 was hangared. Caroline called the Riverside Flight Service Station to check the weather and file a flight plan to Van Nuys. Riverside recommended flying through the Cajon Pass and westward paralleling the foothills of the San Gabriel Mountains.

Once out of the hangar, Kate watched in admiration as Caroline proceeded with the preflight check of the plane and taxied to Runway 18. Kate had never flown in a small plane before and hung on for dear life as they lifted off and up into the sky. Once they were a few hundred feet in the air, however, she found it exhilarating to be soaring over the desert floor. The plane headed straight toward the mountains a few miles away.

How cool that Caroline is a pilot! She had explained on the drive to the airport that her father, a military pilot, had taught her to fly as a teenager.

In a short time, they were flying though the mountain pass and out the other side. A large valley spread out before them. The plane banked right and flew along the foothills toward Los Angeles. In a relatively short time, they landed at the Van Nuys

Airport where Caroline requested fueling and made arrangements to leave the plane in the transient parking area. Kate was sorry the trip was over so soon.

Renting a car, they drove to downtown Los Angeles, arriving at a tall building on Wilshire Boulevard. On the top floor, Caroline went in search of Charles's partners, while Kate waited in the reception area. The offices took up the entire floor, offering an impressive view of the city. She picked out a comfortable chair with ottoman, put her feet up and closed her eyes. A few days ago, she was driving across an empty desert and now here she was in downtown Los Angeles. It was exciting, but she did feel guilty to be enjoying herself when a man was missing. If Caroline could convince Charles's partners to help, however, maybe—

"Are you Kate?"

She opened her eyes and looked into the handsome face of an elegant, African-American man in a gray Armani suit.

He didn't wait for an answer.

"I'm Adam Hill. I know you must be Kate, because I was sent out here to find a pretty young lady with auburn hair."

Kate held out her hand. "Hi, yes, I'm Kate. Nice to meet you, Adam."

"Caroline asked that I bring you back to the private dining room. She said you two haven't had lunch yet. She'll join us there as soon as she can."

On the way to the dining room, Adam showed Kate around the offices, introducing her as Caroline's friend in from the desert for the day. No one seemed surprised at her rumpled attire even though they were immaculately dressed. Both the men and women reminded Kate of the lacquered covers on expensive magazines. However, they were friendly and interested in Kate's description of the plane trip from the high desert.

Adam led her through double doors and into a room filled with round tables covered by white linen cloths and fresh flowers. The floor-to-ceiling windows framed the mountain range that tomorrow would lead them back through the pass to the desert.

It was almost 2:00 p.m., past the usual lunch hour, and they were the only ones in the dining room. The waiter was taking their orders when Caroline walked in. She looked angry. "What's wrong with those men? No matter what I said, I couldn't get through!"

Giving the waiter her order, she took a deep breath and continued, "Okay, I need to calm down. Adam, how have you been? I was so sorry to hear about your parents last year."

Kate watched Adam struggle for words. "Yes, it was hard. First Dad, and then Mother six months later. I think she just didn't want to live any longer without my father. They married right out of high school, you know."

"I'm sure it was difficult for your brother, Jimmy, too. He's always been rather emotional, hasn't he? I remember when he was in our environmental group, he would get so upset about everything!"

Adam's eyes grew dark with anger. "Unfortunately, he cares more about the environment than his own family. He hates that I work for Charles, believing that men like him are responsible for global warming. My parents tried to understand his obsession, and he did call them fairly often, but he never visited during their last days. I can't forgive him for that. I haven't spoken to him since their deaths."

Caroline tactfully changed the subject to other people they both knew. Adam responded by entertaining them throughout lunch with stories about his recent trip to Europe. He was in the middle of an amusing anecdote when Caroline looked at her watch and interrupted.

"I'm sorry, Adam, I'm going to have to leave. But first I need to ask you something. What's going on in this company? Why am I the only one worried about Charles?"

Adam hesitated then leaned forward and spoke softly. "You have to understand that it might be in the partners' best interests if Charles never shows up. He intends to sell his controlling interest in the business but not to any of them, so of course, they're not happy campers. Actually, I'm not too pleased myself, but that's another story."

"Sell the business? I can't believe Charles would ever do that. It's his life."

"A life that he doesn't find satisfying anymore."

Caroline shook her head in disbelief. "But what about you? You've been his right-hand man for years."

Adam shrugged.

Caroline looked at her watch again. "I need to get going. There's one more card I want to play before we leave. Brenda is coming to the office for a meeting at 3:00 p.m., and I want to talk to her."

Adam raised an eyebrow. "Now that should be interesting. When was the last time you two met up?"

"I believe it was at a charity event two years ago. She wasn't thrilled that Charles spent so much time talking to me."

"I'm sure she wasn't. You've never been her favorite person, and now that Charles is divorcing her, she undoubtedly sees you as the enemy." He frowned. "Be careful, Caroline. Brenda has a wicked tongue, and she'll use whatever weapon she can to get what she wants in this divorce. Don't be too surprised if she isn't much help."

"Well, I'm going to lose the element of surprise if I don't get out of here and position myself in the right spot. If I know Brenda, she'll stop by the ladies room before the meeting, so I'll wait there."

"Do you want me to go with you?" Kate asked.

"No. This is something I have to do alone, because I doubt it's going to be pleasant. Adam, can you make sure Kate is okay for a while?"

He nodded, and Caroline hurried out of the room.

Kate felt embarrassed. This important-looking man must have better things to do than baby-sit her. "You don't have to worry about me," she assured him. "I'll be fine."

"I'd *like* to spend some time with you. Why don't you tell me how a nice young girl like yourself got mixed up in all this. Caroline mentioned you found Charles's wrecked car. Start from the beginning. I want to hear all the details."

Caroline sat in the lounge area of the Ladies Room, waiting. If Brenda didn't come in soon, she would have to come up with a different plan of action.

The door opened.

A petite woman with silver-blonde hair walked in. At first, she didn't see Caroline in the corner as she was absorbed in checking every detail of her appearance, adjusting the jacket and skirt of her wine-colored designer suit. The reflection in the mirror appeared to please her. She carefully smoothed the shining hair pulled tightly into a chignon. Exquisite ruby and diamond earrings glinted as she turned her perfect features one way then another. Finding no flaw, she was about to leave, when she noticed Caroline.

The cobalt blue eyes narrowed, and Brenda leaned lazily back against the vanity.

"What a nice surprise," she said, with a trace of a French accent. "Here to see Charles?"

"Have you any idea where he might be?"

"Why, my dear, I heard through the grapevine that he was joining you for a romantic rendezvous! Did he stand you up?"

Caroline sighed. This was not going to be easy. "Charles never stood me up in his entire life."

"Of course, you must not be counting the time he left you and married me."

"You know quite well that I left Charles."

"Only because you recognized that it was just a matter of time. We'd been having an affair for months. Didn't you wonder why he went to France so often?"

Caroline didn't answer.

"Maybe not. Poor Caroline. Charles always said you were naive." Brenda laughed and stared at Caroline's casual attire. "Mon Dieu, is this how you dress these days? I don't think Charles would approve."

Caroline ignored the comment. She needed to get through to the woman. "Listen to me!" she said. "Charles is missing, and no one seems to care."

Brenda turned away and began checking her lipstick in the mirror. When she answered, she addressed Caroline's image. "I'm sure there's no reason for concern," she said. "Charles often disappears for days at a time. Just because he changed his mind about meeting you doesn't mean he's in trouble."

Furious, Caroline moved to stand in front of Brenda. "You aren't hearing me! Charles's Maserati was found wrecked and abandoned on an isolated desert road. There were fresh car tracks leading to the mines at the ghost town that Charles owns. On top of all that, we both know that Charles would never keep me waiting without any word of explanation. If you don't know that much about him, you don't know him at all!"

"You're the one who doesn't know Charles. He deceived you for years with other women. Now he's pursuing you again and apparently you are interested. How pathetic is that?"

Caroline was shocked at the venom in her voice.

"I'm late for a meeting," Brenda said. "I don't have time for this!" She muttered something else in French, pushed past Caroline and left the room.

Caroline watched her leave. She couldn't believe it. Neither Brenda nor Charles's partners were going to help.

Kate listened as Caroline talked to Josh on her cell phone. They were driving toward the hills surrounding Los Angeles. Leaving the crowded city behind, the car climbed a winding road. Judging from Caroline's side of the conversation, Kate knew the news wasn't good.

She was feeling guilty. How could she have relaxed and had such a good time with Adam when a man might be dying somewhere?

Ending the call, Caroline gripped the steering wheel tightly with both hands. "Josh and Mike's day was as fruitless as our trip has been."

Ten minutes later, Caroline pulled into the driveway of a cottage set in a cluster of trees. Kate hadn't dreamed that such private, secluded places existed in Los Angeles.

As they walked through the small house, Caroline turned on lamps in each room. Kate breathed in the scent of apple-cinnamon potpourri and exclaimed over everything she saw, particularly Caroline's paintings on the walls.

In the kitchen, Caroline took a chicken and broccoli casserole from the refrigerator and warmed it in the microwave. She explained that Mattie, her housekeeper, had prepared the house for their overnight visit. Filling their plates with the casserole, rolls and a salad, the women carried their supper into the den.

Kate loved the Southwestern colors of this room and was fascinated by Caroline's paintings of dark-eyed Indian children.

After they ate, Caroline pushed back into the large recliner, laying her head on the soft, beige leather. "Oh, Lord, it's good to be home."

Kate studied the large painting of a desert mesa hanging on the far wall. The soft, muted pastels were soothing and peaceful.

"I hate that woman!" Caroline said.

Startled, Kate looked at Caroline.

"Sorry 'bout that," she said.

"Don't apologize. I can imagine how you must feel. Brenda sounds like a real piece of work!"

"You could say that. But you know what? I don't want to think about her or anything else tonight." Caroline yawned. "I'm really tired, and you must be, too. We both need to get a good night's rest."

In the guest bedroom, Kate was delighted to find a four-poster bed. The breeze through the open window brought in the mixed fragrance of flowering shrubs.

She entered the large bathroom that Caroline had readied for her. Lit candles of various shapes and sizes sat on a wide window ledge behind the tub. A small vase of porcelain roses and fragile, unique bottles stood beside the candles. There were no curtains on the windows, but Caroline had promised that her only audience would be deer and other wild life.

The scent of lavender rose from the hot bath water, and Kate luxuriated in the tub until the water cooled. Then, wrapped in a fluffy towel, she returned to the bedroom, put on her blue-striped pajamas, crawled into bed and fell into a deep, dreamless sleep.

The next morning, she opened her eyes to bright sunlight and the aromatic smell of coffee. Stretching lazily, she looked around the room, her eyes resting on an antique washstand with embroidered linen hand towels hanging on it. An old-fashioned washbowl and pitcher sat beside a large arrangement of silk flowers.

There was a light knock on the door, and a voice called out, "Good morning! May I come in?"

"Please do," Kate said, propping herself up in bed.

Caroline entered, carrying a tray with coffee, orange juice, warm muffins and fruit. Setting it beside Kate on the bed, she pulled up a chair and sipped coffee from one of the bone-china pedestal coffee cups.

"Did you sleep well?"

Her mouth already full of blueberry muffin, Kate could only nod. Washing it down with orange juice, she asked, "Did you bake these this morning?"

"Hardly, I just warmed them up. I'm afraid I'm spoiled rotten by Mattie. I knew she would have my favorite foods waiting for me."

"Would you consider adopting me?"

Caroline laughed.

After breakfast, they sat out on the patio. Fuchsia-colored bougainvillea spilled over the latticework above their heads. Potted plants lined the patio on both sides. A vegetable garden was on the right. Lemons hung on a tree in the corner and oranges on two other trees. A tall oak grew beside the stone wall at the edge of the gently sloping hill, which was lush with tiny yellow wildflowers, sumac and green undergrowth.

Kate noticed a building at the far left. Caroline followed her gaze. "Would you like to see my studio?" she asked.

"I'd love to!"

Entering the small wooden structure, Kate was surprised at the quality of light inside. Then she saw the skylight in the roof of the building. No trees obscured the blue sky.

A half-finished seascape sat on the easel. The only other painting hung on the far wall where it dominated the room. The eyes of the man sitting in a red leather chair were a cool steel gray. They reflected strength and self-confidence and a touch of arrogance.

Kate stared at the portrait. She had no doubt that it was Charles.

"He *is* an extraordinary-looking man, isn't he?" Caroline said. "I worked from an old photograph and memory, but I believe I did capture his essence."

"Does he like it?" Kate asked.

"He's never seen it."

He watched in horror as the lid of the coffin slowly lowered. No! Stop!! He struggled to sit, to get out before it was too late.

Charles opened his eyes, his heart racing. A dream. Only a dream. Or was it a premonition?

He began to take deep breaths and think about Caroline. It always calmed him. If only he could talk to her. Tell her how sorry he was about everything. How stupid he'd been to allow himself to be manipulated into marrying Brenda after their divorce.

I just want one more chance, he prayed, one more chance.

"Shit," he muttered. "I'm doing it again. Who the hell am I talking to?"

He sat up and fumbled in the dark for the knapsack. He should eat something. He chewed the beef jerky slowly, thinking about his dilemma. He'd been over and over it in his mind. Imagined every scenario that might result in his rescue. None seemed possible.

One more time, he began enumerating his enemies.

First on his list was Barton.

Then there was Brenda. He recalled their last angry encounter when she'd discovered that their prenup was airtight. Adding the morality clause had been a stroke of genius. Or had it buried him in this mountain?

Maybe she was in cahoots with his partners. They had a lot to lose if he sold his controlling shares to the wrong person.

And Adam. He'd been furious not to be included in the cartel's plans.

There were a number of business opponents who would be happy to see him disappear. Most of his wealth had come from successful corporate takeovers in the eighties, and his list of enemies had definitely grown during that time.

No. Barton. It had to be Barton!

So many enemies and no real friends.

No one but Caroline would care if he lived or died. But she didn't have access to information that might help find him. All she had were her beliefs. Charles remembered their discussions about extrasensory perception. He would tease her about it, but inevitably, she would call him just before he picked up the phone to call her or answer a question before he spoke.

What if she were right? Maybe she would hear him if he concentrated on her.

He collected his thoughts. What did he have to lose?

CHAPTER SEVEN

Josh stood at the edge of the mountain plateau staring toward the western horizon. The road through the desert disappeared in that direction with no vehicle in sight. Hopefully, the women were on their way back. He never loaned his plane out, but Caroline had assured him she had the necessary skill and experience.

After a day and a half exploring miles of underground mine shafts, his whole body ached. They had quit early today, as even Mike's young body was rebelling. Maybe Caroline would return with reinforcements, and he wouldn't have to go back in those damn mines tomorrow.

Mike joined him. "I thought they'd be here by now."

Josh turned to watch sagebrush blow across the hard-packed sandy street behind them. "I'm sure they're okay, but the desert winds can be tricky this time of day, and I don't know if Caroline has ever landed under these conditions." He sat on the nearest rock, unable to hide his exhaustion. Maybe he should just come clean with Mike.

"You know," he began, "I have to admit that I'm worn out from the past two days. I guess the old body just can't take the abuse it once could, and I'm afraid I'm holding you back. Maybe Caroline will bring someone younger to help you."

"No way. We're a good team! I know I can trust you. That counts for a lot when you're inside a mountain."

Josh hesitated and then decided to be honest.

"To tell you the truth, Mike, it scares the shit out of me to go into those damn holes. For some reason, I'm sure I'll never get back out. Makes me feel like a fool, but there it is."

Mike looked shocked. "No kidding? Hey, I know lots of people who feel that way. Don't worry about it. For that matter, you couldn't get me up in that small plane of yours for a million dollars."

Mike looked off into the distance. Following his gaze, Josh saw a vehicle moving across the desert floor until it turned onto the road leading up the mountain.

The four new friends ate supper in the tiny kitchen of the house. Shadows played on the walls from the kerosene lamp. Caroline looked around the table. "Okay, what should we do next? I'm out of ideas."

Josh wished he had an answer for her.

"I was so sure I could convince someone at Charles's company to offer assistance," she said, "but even Adam seems ambivalent. I just don't understand what's going on."

Josh tipped his chair back, leaning against the wall behind him. "Let me get this straight. Charles's partners think searching the mountain is a waste of time, and they want to leave the investigation of the abandoned car to the State Police and the local desert authorities."

Caroline nodded.

"Okay. No help from Charles's company and this soon-to-be ex-wife of his—what's her name?"

"Brenda."

"Brenda's not concerned either. But she makes a special trip to the office, probably meeting with the partners to find out where she stands if he never shows up. Interesting."

"And maybe this other guy, Adam," Mike interjected, "isn't offering much help, because he might not have a job if Laughery sells the company."

Josh noticed that both Kate and Caroline frowned at that possibility. "What did you think of the people you met in LA, Kate?" he asked.

"I'm not sure. I mean, well, they were all nice to me, especially Adam, but no one seemed to want to talk about Charles."

"So I guess we're on our own," Josh said. "Tomorrow we'll tackle another mine."

Mike shook his head. "No, we agreed you weren't going back in there. You know, uh, your old back injury. I'm going by myself."

Josh leaned forward. "I'm not going to let you go in there alone."

"He won't have to. I'll go with him."

Both men stared at Kate.

"Don't give me those looks. I spent my childhood exploring caves and caverns in Virginia, and I loved it! Josh can rest tomorrow and keep Caroline company while Mike and I have all the fun."

It wasn't until later that evening that Josh admitted to himself how relieved he was that Kate was replacing him. He felt guilty, but he'd never felt such irrational fear before. It was as though death, or worse, waited for him inside that mountain.

Mike and Kate prepared carefully for the day's expedition. Choosing a mine not too deep and easily accessible was Mike's priority, and he insisted that Kate be tethered to him—just in case.

"In case of what, for heavens sakes!" she said. "Was Josh tied to you? Don't bother to answer. Look, I'll let you lead, and I'll follow your instructions, but I will not be tethered to you, and that's final!"

At the base of the mountain, Caroline could still hear the young couple arguing as they climbed the path to the mine entrances.

"I think Mike has met his match in Katie," she said to Josh. He held out his hand to steady her as they headed back over the rocky gulch.

Halfway through the town, Caroline stopped to look at a partially demolished building. "I believe this was the General Store. Charles mapped out the town, building by building. He really did his research."

She watched as Josh sifted through the rubble. *I do love a man in jeans.* She sat on what had once been a step. The morning was warm with a slight breeze, the cloudless sky above a dome of translucent blue. Stretching, she closed her eyes and held her face to the sun. When she opened her eyes again, Josh was standing over her. He smiled and helped her up. Caroline laid one hand on his broad chest. It felt solid and warm under her fingers. They stood unmoving, bodies close together, until she gently pushed away. Neither spoke as they turned and walked down the street.

Inside the mines, Kate stumbled over loose rocks, almost falling. By the time she regained her balance, Mike was around the next corner. With only the light of one lantern, the walls seemed thicker and darker.

"Where the hell are you?" Mike yelled.

"I would be right behind you if you'd just wait a minute!"

Rounding the corner, Kate stopped short.

Mike's light shone into a large dugout space. To her surprise, it wasn't empty. What looked like an iron bed sat against the rock wall and broken pieces of pots were scattered around.

"What in the world?"

"Interesting, huh? Josh and I found places like this in the other shafts too. You know what it is, don't you?"

"No." Kate moved closer to peer into the man-made room.

"The men didn't come out of the mines every day," Mike explained. "They brought in food and water and lived down here for weeks at a time. They slept when they were exhausted, ate when they got hungry and just kept working."

Not to see the sun for weeks, Kate thought. What would that be like?

Mike crawled into the rocky alcove. A thought occurred to Kate. "Do you suppose that's what Charles is doing? Hiding out in a place like this?"

"It's possible, I suppose. In this day and age, you could equip it with all the comforts of home. But why would he want to?"

Kate offered a few theories, from a mental breakdown to hiding out from his enemies.

Mike shook his head. "Caroline's description of her ex-husband doesn't fit a man who runs away from anything." Remembering the portrait Caroline had painted, Kate had to agree.

"And there's something else," he said. "I get the idea that Laughery wanted to get back together with Caroline. He wouldn't upset her by not showing up. I wonder how Josh feels about that?"

"About what?"

"About Caroline and her ex-husband. You haven't noticed how Josh looks at her?"

"Well, sure, but men tend to look at women. It doesn't have to mean anything. Besides, they just met."

"You don't believe in love at first sight?"

Kate thought about her husband. She had loved him from their first date. "Was it that way with your wife?" she asked.

Mike got a faraway look in his eyes.

"No, we grew up together. Now that I look back on it, in a lot of ways, we were more like brother and sister. Maybe that was the problem."

Kate waited, hoping for more, but Mike climbed back out, and they continued down the tunnel.

Josh listened to the rising wind outside the house and watched Caroline make sandwiches for lunch. She moved easily around the kitchen, seemingly comfortable in the small space. Joining him at the table, she set a ham sandwich and a beer in front of him.

"Josh, I don't know what to do. It could take months to explore all those mine shafts. Malcolm says there are over thirty miles of tunnels. It's a pretty hopeless task and maybe we're off track here. When I'm feeling more rational, I can't believe that Charles was really kidnapped, let alone in that mountain."

"I know," he agreed. "It's occurred to me we may have misconstrued the facts. Maybe we should focus on solving the mystery of why he disappeared; then we might have a better chance of finding out where he is."

Caroline sighed. "That would be possible if the people at his company would cooperate. They must know about his recent projects, although I admit Charles could be pretty secretive. He may not have shared the information with anyone, except perhaps Adam."

"Who doesn't seem inclined to help either."

The sound of an approaching car motor brought both of them to their feet. They hurried outside. Caroline was amazed to see the subject of their conversation open the door of his Porsche. She rushed over to hug him then introduced the two men.

Adam shook Josh's outstretched hand. "I've always wondered what this place looked like. So this is where Charles comes to get away from it all."

"This is it," Caroline said. "He apparently came here often over the years."

"I'm glad I got here before the storm."

Caroline realized dark clouds were moving swiftly across the sky—from opposite directions.

The wind blew sand around them. Adam glanced at his car. "I don't suppose you have a garage up here?"

Caroline rolled her eyes.

"Never mind. I have a cover in the trunk."

He looked down the dirt street toward the mountain.

"I knew about this desert hideaway," he said, "but Charles never invited me to visit until last week when he asked me to hand deliver the deed up here. I wonder if he had some kind of premonition that something was going to happen to him." He paused. "I picked up the registered deed today. The place is officially yours now, and because of their pre-nup, Brenda can't do a damn thing about it."

Adam rolled up the sleeves of his Ralph Lauren sports shirt, oblivious to Caroline's astonishment until she said, "What do you mean? This town is mine? Charles turned the deed of this place over to me?" She sank down on the porch steps.

Josh knelt beside her, laying his hand on her arm. "I think she needs a few minutes to absorb the news," he said to Adam.

"Caroline, I'm sorry. I thought you knew." He shielded his eyes as sand began to swirl around them. "I'll be right back. I need to cover my car before this sandstorm gets any worse."

Caroline turned to Josh.

"Oh, dear God. This was his big surprise. He was going to tell me that this beautiful place is now mine. He knew how much I loved the desert. But give it to me? Why would he do that?"

It was no mystery to Josh. If you wanted a woman back, and you had the resources, you'd give her something extraordinary, something special that would mean a great deal to her. Charles Laughery was a very smart man.

"Do you think Adam's right?" Caroline asked. "Did Charles suspect something was going to happen to him?"

Josh shook his head. "I don't know. What I do know is we need to get inside, because it looks like we're in for a freak storm." He looked up. "When those two storm systems collide...." Thunder drowned out the rest of his words.

CHAPTER EIGHT

Kate walked faster through the tunnel. The sight of daylight ahead meant food and a long soak in Caroline's bathtub. Muscles she'd forgotten she had were beginning to ache intolerably.

Mike, on the other hand, seemed almost sad that their excursion was over. He hadn't spoken for the last mile or so and was lagging farther and farther behind. Kate picked up her pace.

Stepping out of the tunnel, she was shocked at the sight in front of her. The mine opened near the top of the mountain, and the desert vista stretched for miles in all directions. Instead of the usual expanse of blue sky, however, roiling dark clouds were converging on one another. Lightning streaked horizontally between the clouds, followed immediately by deafening thunder.

Below, Odessa had disappeared under a layer of dirty yellow dust.

"What the hell!" Mike's voice shouted from behind her.

A huge drop of rain hit Kate's face, then another and another, but she couldn't move. She stood transfixed by the sand storm below and the lightning show before her. Then the sky opened, and she was soaked by pounding rain.

Mike reached out and yanked her into the mine opening. Another streak of lightning blinded her for a moment, and thunder echoed in the tunnel behind them. She clung to Mike.

"It's okay," he said, wrapping his arms tightly around her. "We're safe in here."

She knew he was right but couldn't stop trembling. A world she couldn't control seemed to be exploding around her, bringing back the fiery memory of the accident that stole her husband and child.

She buried her head in Mike's shoulder. They stood together until the sound of thunder began to recede into the distance. As Kate calmed down, she became aware of Mike's warm body against hers. Another feeling, as elemental as the raging storm outside, began to grow in her.

Mike pulled away. Confused, she looked up into eyes that mirrored her feelings. Finally, he said, "The rain should stop soon. We'll just wait it out."

She nodded, and they sat near the opening, close but not touching.

On the porch, Josh and Adam talked about the freak storm that had just passed. Caroline stared into the rapidly changing sky. Behind trailing tendrils of dark clouds high above, patches of blue and pink-tinged white clouds appeared and below, melon-colored ones were forming. Across the street from the house, tall desert cacti were etched in black against the golden horizon.

The eerie calm reflected Caroline's feelings of disorientation. She still hadn't found a place in her mind for Charles's gift.

"Well, here come your two explorers," Adam said, waving at a surprised Kate. She started to jog toward him, ran up the wet porch steps, slipped and fell into his outstretched arms.

"Oops, sorry 'bout that!" Laughing, Adam held her at arm's length. "Good Lord, you're soaking wet."

Caroline handed Kate one of the towels she had brought out to dry the porch chairs. "I was getting worried about you two," she said.

Kate wiped off her muddy arms and face then threw the towel to Mike, who was standing beside the covered Porsche. She looked at Adam. "What in the world are you doing here? Do you have news about Charles?"

"No such luck, I'm afraid. I needed to bring some documents to Caroline." He stared at her in concern. "Are you sure you're okay? You look exhausted." Before she could answer, he said to Mike. "You took her into those old mines?"

Kate bristled. "No one 'takes' me anywhere. I wanted to explore the mines with Mike.

"But you're right about one thing. I need to get cleaned up." She turned to Caroline. "Do you mind if I use your bathtub? The motel only has a shower, and I need to soak for a while."

"Of course. Get out of those wet clothes. You'll find a robe on the back of the bathroom door."

Josh walked over to Mike and gestured with the beer cans he held in each hand. "I guess I should introduce you two. Adam, this is Mike. Mike, Adam." Neither man moved to shake hands. Both reached for the beer Josh offered.

Mike lifted one edge of the cover off the Porsche then looked at Adam. "Good thing you covered this beauty up."

"Yes. I guess it wasn't too smart to bring it up here. Sand storms wreak havoc on paint."

Mike smiled for the first time. "Yeah, not too smart." He tipped the beer can back, drank it down, then lit a cigarette and stared into the desert.

Caroline decided to break the silence.

"How did it go today, Mike?" she asked.

Crushing the can and catching another that Josh tossed him, Mike shook his head. "Nothing to report. We searched several tunnels, but it didn't look as though anyone had been in them lately." He turned to Josh. "We found another one of those dug out spaces. Kate was surprised to learn miners sometimes lived down there for weeks." He drained the beer can then asked, "You ready to head down the mountain, Josh? I need a shower and some of Malcolm's grub."

"Not quite yet, I'd like to talk to Caroline and Adam about a few things."

"You go on, Mike," Adam said. "I'll run Kate and Josh down later. I'm going to spend the night at the motel and head back in the morning."

Mike gave a quick nod and walked toward the truck without a backward glance.

"Friendly sort of guy," Adam said.

"He's okay," Josh said. "Probably just worn out. I sure as hell was when we searched those tunnels."

"You can't really believe that Charles is…?" Adam glanced at Caroline.

"We hope not," Josh said. "But if you could fill us in on Charles's latest business deals, it would certainly help."

Adam looked down. "I've been debating whether or not to say this." He hesitated then said, "The truth is, I think Charles is jerking us around."

Caroline felt too stunned to reply, but Josh said, "And how the hell did you arrive at that conclusion? What about the abandoned car? And his not contacting Caroline?"

"I'm sorry, but I've worked with Charles on projects for years, and when he's focused on accomplishing something, he's not the most thoughtful guy in the world. What better way to throw his business competitors off the track than to make it look like he might be dead?"

"I can't believe you're even suggesting such a thing!" Caroline said.

Adam quickly changed the subject. He talked about several of Charles's projects until Kate reappeared on the porch in a robe, her hair wet.

"Oh, Lordy, that was wonderful! I hate to get back into my dirty clothes."

"If you bunked here tonight," Josh said, "Mike and I could bring some clothes up for you tomorrow morning. How does that sound?"

"Great, if Caroline doesn't mind."

"To tell you the truth, I'd appreciate the company."

"Good," Josh said. "Okay, Adam. Let's see how your fancy car does on mountain roads. I'll drive." Adam raised one eyebrow and climbed into the driver's seat.

"Guess not," Josh said, laughing, as he hurried down the porch steps.

After the men left, the women ate their light supper and discussed Caroline's surprise gift from Charles. Instead of having dessert at the kitchen table, they carried tea and cookies to the parlor and opened the front door to let in the rain-fresh evening breeze.

"This is nice and cozy," Kate said, looking around.

The kerosene lamp smoked slightly as Caroline adjusted the wick then sat on the mauve velvet settee, putting her feet on a matching hassock.

"You know, I've been thinking," she said, "I hate to admit it, but maybe Adam's right. Maybe Charles's abandoned car was a way to throw his business competitors off guard. He's incredibly clever. I'd rather believe he's being thoughtless than.... Maybe this deed transfer is his convoluted way of making it up to me." She stopped, wiping away a tear. "I'm sorry. This is all just so...."

"I understand," Kate said. "Too many emotions in a short period of time can be overwhelming. I felt the same way only a few months ago."

Kate had told her about the accident.

"It must have been a terrible time for you."

"I was still grieving," she said, "when the trucker's insurance company offered this huge amount for settlement. Then the life insurance arrived, and the house sold, all within weeks. It was really disorienting. I finally just got into my car and started driving."

Caroline listened without interruption as Kate continued to talk until the night chill entered the room.

Early the following morning, the men dropped off Kate's clothes, and Adam left for Los Angeles, promising to call if he discovered anything. Soon afterwards, Mike and Kate went into the mines, and Josh and Caroline found themselves alone again.

"I really appreciate Malcolm letting Mike off to work for me," she said.

"It was good of you to offer to pay him for his time. He wouldn't be able to afford it, otherwise."

"Kate insists she doesn't need compensation, and I do believe it's helping her to focus on something other than her own grief. But I wish you would let me...."

Josh held up his hand. "No way. I don't need the money either, and I want to solve this case. It's become personal to me."

Caroline glanced at him—then away.

"So what do you think we should do now?" she said. "I'm full of nervous energy. I can't stand this waiting around."

"Unfortunately, unless Search and Rescue helps us, that's about all we can do at this point. You've made your calls. I've made mine. The State Police are working the case. We have to wait for that one phone call that will head us in the right direction." He pushed his chair back.

"Why don't we walk off some of this energy? I'd like to see that old schoolhouse at the other end of town."

The school sat by itself on a high, sandy knoll. Walking past it to a large rock ledge, Caroline looked down the mountain to the road below. "This couldn't have been a safe place for little kids to play."

"I guess they had to get used to danger if they were going to become miners."

"The boys you mean."

"Right. They didn't have much choice. Unless, of course, their fathers were store keepers or maybe owned a saloon."

"You enjoy imagining life back in those days, don't you?" Caroline said, sitting on the weathered steps of the old school.

"It fascinates me. Which reminds me, have you any idea what you might want to do with this place? I mean—after we find Charles."

Caroline stared out across the desert. She'd had a disturbing dream last night. Charles was part of it.

When she didn't answer, Josh said, "It would make an interesting tourist attraction. I know I'd visit an authentic ghost town if I were on vacation. Of course, renovating it could get expensive."

Caroline tried to concentrate on Josh's words, but the dream kept coming back. In it, Charles was lost and afraid. In a dark cave or....

"Caroline?"

"Josh, when do you think Search and Rescue will agree to help us?"

"The captain's supposed to call me. He's waiting for final approval from higher up."

Caroline shivered in the heat of the desert sun. "We need their help, Josh. I feel like time is running out."

He was still alive. The mountain hadn't killed him yet. He checked his watch—morning. How he yearned to see the blue-white morning sky again.

He slid his hand forward in the dark, fingering the items he had emptied from his pockets. His abductors hadn't even taken his wallet. Every few hours, he would look at Caroline's picture and remember their life together.

Was she searching for him? Had Adam told her that the town belonged to her now? Thank God, Brenda signed that prenuptial agreement. Property he owned before his marriage was exclusively his. She wouldn't be able to fight Caroline on this.

Caroline. He could almost see her standing in front of him, feel her in his arms. They fit perfectly together. He remembered every soft curve, how it felt to encircle her waist, pull her close and....

Charles pounded the dirt floor of his prison in frustration. How could he have been so stupid? Leaving a woman like Caroline, marrying Brenda and agreeing to the complex cartel scheme. Would he be in this mess if his decisions had been different?

His chest began to feel tight and uncomfortable. The tightness turned into pain. What now? Was he having a heart attack? Was he really going to die in this black hole? Disappear into nothingness? No longer exist? He couldn't wrap his mind around nonexistence.

Relax, he told himself. Relax and breathe. The pain began to subside.

Caroline. Think about Caroline, he told himself. What would she tell me to do?

He grimaced, knowing she would tell him to pray. To the god he didn't believe in? Oh, what the hell, who else did he have to talk to?

"All right," he called out, "anybody listening?"

He didn't wait for an answer.

"I have a deal for you. Get me out of here, and I'll give you ten percent of my share of the cartel's profit. Ten percent. Paid to the charity of your choice!"

One of Caroline's watercolors slowly filled his mind, vivid in every detail. An angel, partially hidden in the misty background, looked amused.

CHAPTER NINE

When Caroline heard Mattie's voice, she expected a routine question regarding the house. Instead she heard, "I don't know if this is urgent, but I found an envelope with Mr. Laughery's office address on it stuck in your door today."

"Read it to me, Mattie!"

Caroline waited impatiently.

"Well, it's typed and says, 'Check out Judson, Nevada.'"

"That's all? No signature?"

"No, it's not signed." There was a pause, then Mattie asked the question Caroline had heard often from her maternal housekeeper. "Is everything all right, Miss Caroline?"

She quickly reassured Mattie and ran outside to tell Josh. After hearing the message, he immediately said, "I think we should take a plane ride."

In the motel room in Judson, Caroline dressed in beige pants and matching t-shirt. The excitement of yesterday was still with her. Even though they hadn't found Charles, this was the same motel where he had stayed last week. Today, they would track his movements throughout the town. Someone should be able to tell them why he came here and maybe even know where he was now.

Pulling back her long hair, she studied her face. Why did Josh seem so pleased with what he saw? She might have understood it ten years ago but in her mid-fifties, well…. She understood her ex-husband's attraction. In his mind's eye, she was still the woman he married years ago, and in truth, she still felt like that woman. She glanced at her watch. Josh was probably waiting for her.

When Caroline entered the motel dining room, she saw several people eating breakfast but no Josh. She ordered a cup of coffee and began reading the local paper that she'd picked up in the lobby. Engrossed in the front page, she heard, "Good morning," and looked up to see Josh standing beside her. Staring at his ornate belt buckle, she leaned forward to see the design— the head of a wolf—then realized Josh was smiling broadly at her, and she felt herself blush.

After they ordered breakfast, he told her about his conversation with the manager. "Charles stayed here often over the past two years, although this last time, it was just for one night. But the manager overheard Charles talking on his cell phone to someone in the real estate office in town. So that will be our first visit today."

The waitress brought their orders of scrambled eggs, bacon and biscuits for Josh and cereal for Caroline. She sipped her coffee, feeling hopeful for the first time since Charles's disappearance. Maybe today, they would find him alive and well.

She glanced at Josh behind the wheel of the truck. He had slid down, tipping his Stetson forward and resting his head on the back of the seat as he watched the real estate office. From behind several trees, where the truck was parked, both the front and back entrances were visible.

Caroline tucked one leg under her, attempting to get comfortable. She wasn't sure why Josh was so interested in the woman in the office who had denied knowing a Charles Laughery. He had picked up on something, however, and was determined to talk to Linda Jamison outside the office. In the meantime, they had spent the day checking out businesses in the small town with no luck and now were back, waiting for the woman to leave for the day.

"Is this what they call a stake-out?" Caroline asked.

Without taking his eyes off the building, Josh said, "You could call it that."

"You really think the woman in there knows something?"

Josh raised one eyebrow. "Definitely. I want to get her alone for more questioning. Trust me, we're on the right track here." He sat upright.

The front door of the real estate office had opened, and a woman hurried out to a black Bronco. Josh waited until she drove off, then started the truck's engine and followed. On the flat desert road they could stay far behind and still keep the Bronco in sight.

After a few miles, it turned off the main road and headed south toward a small housing development. Josh closed the gap between them as she turned onto side streets. She drove into the driveway of a small, adobe-style house, and they pulled in behind her. Stepping out into the carport, she turned toward them with a look of panic on her face. Trying to look friendly, Caroline walked up with her hand out.

"Hi, we met briefly at your office today."

Linda Jamison stared, unmoving. Josh took over.

"We need to talk to you, Miss Jamison. May we come inside?"

His words seemed to frighten the woman even more. She looked toward the house.

"It's Mrs. Jamison," she said. "And I don't want my husband to know anything about this. If you'll wait for me at the end of

the street, I'll tell him I'm going to the store and join you there."
Josh nodded. "Okay, but if you don't show up, we come to the
door and ring the bell."

Josh and Caroline drove to the end of the block and waited
outside their truck. Fifteen minutes later, the Bronco pulled up
beside them. Josh spoke through the rolled-down window.

"I'm going to just cut to the chase, Mrs. Jamison. We know
you're working with Charles Laughery. Where is he?"

After a moment's hesitation, she said, "Listen, I don't know
where Charles is. I really don't. He said he would contact me in
a few days but never did." She stared at Caroline. "You're his ex-
wife, aren't you? I saw your picture in his wallet one time. Don't
you know where he is?"

Caroline was too surprised to do anything but shake her head.
What was this woman to Charles? Why would she have access to
his wallet?

Josh began asking questions about Charles's real estate
purchases.

"He's a big land owner around here," Linda said. "I'm his real
estate agent, but that's all I'm at liberty to say. When you locate
him, please have him call me right away. I need his signature
on some contracts I'm finalizing for him." Glancing nervously
around, she added, "I'm sorry, but I have to go now."

Josh handed her his business card. "If you hear from Charles,
call me immediately."

She nodded, rolled up the window and drove away.

"I don't believe this!" Caroline said. "Why would Charles buy
land out here? There's nothing but desert and dry lakebeds. And
why be so secretive? You'd think that woman had sworn a blood
oath or something. She apparently doesn't even want her husband
to know she works for Charles."

Josh looked thoughtful. "What I find interesting is that she's
finalizing contracts for Charles. Maybe someone doesn't want
that to happen and would like to have him out of the way, either

for a short period of time, or permanently and...." He stopped. "I'm sorry."

"That's all right. I guess that's one possibility. But then again, maybe Adam's right. If Charles is involved in something complex, he may want others to think he isn't able to finalize things." She sighed. "This just keeps getting more confusing. What should we do now?"

"Linda Jamison needs to be under surveillance. I know someone who can come out and keep an eye on her. I don't expect her to contact us if Charles calls. Something bigger than a simple land deal is going down here, and she's involved. Come on; let's go back to the motel. I have a few calls to make."

Caroline nodded. "And I should call Kate and Mike. Can I borrow your phone?"

"I'm starved," Mike said.

Kate rummaged around in the refrigerator. She was hungry, too. It had been a long day in the mines, and her phone conversation with Caroline had taken awhile.

"It sounds as though Caroline and Josh have come up with something," Mike said. "I don't know what it means, but I bet Josh is going to find out." He stretched and groaned. "I'm glad, because I don't know how many more miles of mine this poor old body can take."

"You think we're wasting our time, don't you?"

"I'm afraid so, but I guess it's better than sitting around doing nothing."

"Why don't you go soak your poor old body in the tub while I make us supper."

Mike was in the bathroom when the phone rang again.

"Caroline?"

Kate recognized the voice.

"Hi, Adam, she's not here. We have her cell phone." Kate told him about Mattie's message. "So Caroline and Josh are in Nevada," she concluded. "Do you have any news?"

The silence went on for so long that Kate started to ask if he were still there. Finally Adam said, "Actually I have something that should be checked out right away. If Caroline and Josh aren't available, maybe you and Mike can come and handle it. I have to take off for Europe this week or I'd do it myself."

After listening to Adam's information, Kate agreed that she and Mike would leave for LA in the morning.

Better than going back into that mountain again, she thought, hanging up.

Adam looked at the two young people seated across from his desk. He was probably only ten years older, but they seemed like such kids to him. He doubted either of them had ever found themselves in a situation quite like this before, but for that matter, neither had he.

"Have you heard any more from Caroline?"

Kate shook her head. "Not since last evening. I called her back after talking to you, and she said to come here and do whatever you suggest."

Mike stared out the window as Kate talked. Adam knew the young man didn't trust him. "So," Kate said, "don't you think we should contact these people right away? I mean isn't it possible that a phone call could explain this whole mystery?"

Adam smiled. "Katie, my sweet, if Charles is in the middle of secret negotiations with people in high places, we could spend the next month on the phone and not get answers. I only came across this information accidentally. I never know what Charles is up to until the last phase of a deal. He keeps his own counsel, and no one is let into that mind of his until he's ready to put his cards on the table."

Mike leaned forward, frowning. "You want us to check out this lead without alerting anyone involved? That's going to get a little tricky, isn't it? And it's also going to take some money. I don't know about Kate, but I don't have much cash on me."

Adam reached for the intercom. "Lily, get me $1000 from petty cash."

Mike stared at him coolly, while Kate's eyes widened in admiration. Adam felt a twinge of guilt. Eventually, they would realize this was a wild goose chase, but in the meantime, it would keep Katie out of harm's way.

CHAPTER TEN

Mike stood on the cliff, mesmerized by the sight of so much water. *I'm standing on the edge of a continent.*

Kate was beside him, staring out over the Pacific Ocean, lost in her own thoughts. Waves crashed on the rocks below, and he watched her carefully, making sure she didn't step too close to the edge.

As though reading his thoughts, she moved closer to him, and he put his arm around her shoulders.

"Be careful. It's a long way down."

She glanced down then back at the horizon.

"It's so wild and beautiful!"

Typical of Kate, he thought, to see only the beauty and not the danger. The sun sank lower in the sky, and the air turned cooler.

"Want to watch the sunset?" he asked. She nodded. "I'd better get our jackets then." Kate sat down, arms encircling her knees.

As Mike walked back to the truck parked on Pacific Coast Highway, he thought about their trip so far. Everyone they visited said the same thing. Yes, Charles Laughery had been there, but it had been at least three months ago. He'd concluded his business with them, and there was no reason to believe he would be contacting them again any time soon.

The business conducted had been straight forward. Nothing that anyone would find particularly interesting or suspicious. Why had Adam felt it so important to check into these particular activities?

Driving up the coast had been great, but with a man missing, Mike felt guilty about enjoying himself. He knew Kate did, too.

He rejoined her, draping a jacket over her shoulders.

The wind picked up and whitecaps dotted the ocean. The water turned a darker blue. In moments, a spectacular ball of fire sank below the horizon.

Mike leaned closer to Kate and whispered, "You clap at sunrises. What about sunsets?"

She fell straight back, staring up into the sky overhead.

"I tend to faint at sunsets."

Mike stared down at her. In the lingering iridescent colors of twilight, everything about Kate seemed to shine. Her auburn hair, her bright green eyes, her soft skin, her lips…. He leaned over and covered them with his own.

For a few seconds, Kate didn't move, then she pushed against his chest so hard that he fell backwards. Before he could move, she was on her feet, running along the cliff. Terrified that she would get too close to the edge, Mike took off after her. By the time he caught up, she *was* too close, and he threw himself forward, tackling her. They rolled to the ground. Mike held on with all his strength until Kate lay quiet beneath him.

Afraid to let go, he said soothingly in her ear, "It's all right, Katie. It's okay. Everything's okay." Finally, he moved away and gently lifted her to a sitting position. She put her face in her hands.

"Kate, I'm sorry. I'm really sorry. I promise you it will never happen again. I don't know what came over me. I…."

She put up her hand then looked up at him, her face a crimson red.

"Please, Mike, don't apologize. It's not you. It's me."

"Listen, it's okay. I understand."

He jumped up and reached out his hand to help her up. "Come on. You need some food and a good night's sleep."

They walked silently back to the truck.

At the motel restaurant, Mike chose a table near the large window. Although it was too dark now to see the water, they could hear the waves breaking on the shore.

Mike kept sneaking peeks at Kate as she ate. He began to relax as she seemed to have regained her composure and was enjoying her food. For dessert, she ordered a hot fudge sundae. He watched as she enjoyed each spoonful, finally licking off the remains of hot fudge and whipped cream from her lips.

What had he been thinking? She was just a kid who had lost her husband and baby less than a year ago.

"I'm a jerk," he muttered to himself.

"What?" Kate asked.

Mike continued eating his apple pie. A small hand touched his arm, and he looked up to see a tender smile on Kate's face. "You're not a jerk, Mike. Maybe a little grouchy sometimes but definitely not a jerk."

The waiter brought the bill.

Mike dropped $100 in the tray and told him to keep the change. Surprised, the young man thanked him profusely. Kate stared at Mike.

"I'm very generous with other people's money," he said, "especially if it's Adam's."

Kate laughed but then asked, "Why don't you like him?"

He wasn't sure how to answer.

"Are you prejudiced? I mean I know you were raised in the South."

"Hell, no. You were raised in the South, too. Are you prejudiced?"

"No. You're right, of course. It doesn't automatically go with the territory. I just don't understand why you're so antagonistic toward Adam."

"Maybe because he's so damn arrogant. He wears $2000 suits, $300 ties and shows off by handing us $1000 without batting an eye. Give me a break."

Kate listened quietly.

"I know that sounds like I'm jealous or something, but I'm not. I wouldn't want to live his life. I like things a lot simpler. He just irritates the hell out of me, especially the way he acts with you."

The words were no sooner out of his mouth then Mike regretted them. Kate was staring at him with a confused expression on her face.

"With me?"

"Forget I said that. You two get along, and that's none of my business. But you're right; the guy gets under my skin. And I'm telling you—he's hiding something. I don't know what it is, but he's not being up front with us."

Before Kate could argue, Mike continued, "Not one of the people we talked to had seen Laughery for months. And my gut instinct tells me they're telling the truth about their business with him. Nothing unusual about it. I think the only suspicious character in this whole scene is Adam. I'd sure like to know what he's doing in Europe right now, if that's where he really is."

"I agree," Kate said.

"You do?"

"Yep. I think we should get up tomorrow morning and head straight to LA and Adam's office. I have a feeling we'll find him there. I also want to talk to Caroline and Josh and find out what's going on with their investigation."

Josh made reservations for dinner at the restaurant next to the motel in Judson. After showering and shaving, he went to the lobby to wait for Caroline. In a few minutes, she walked in, wearing a white Mexican style pleated blouse and skirt. Delicate silver earrings and necklace accented the silver streaks in the long, dark hair that lay loose on her shoulders.

It was a short walk to the restaurant. Once inside, Josh asked if they could be seated near the dance floor. When they sat down, Caroline carefully spread a napkin on her lap, toyed with her knife and fork, glanced up then away.

"I've been thinking," Josh said. "For this one evening, let's not talk about Charles. Let's assume we're going to find him, alive and well."

"You're right. We need a night off."

He began telling her about his ranch outside of Durango, Colorado.

"You're a rancher?"

"Most of the year. Fortunately, I have an able manager who runs the place for me when I'm not there. After my wife died eight years ago, I got pretty lonely, especially during the Colorado winters. A few rancher friends needed an investigator they could trust. It started out as a kind of hobby and ended up as a part-time job."

Caroline seemed fascinated. "So it's a real ranch? With horses and cows?"

Josh laughed. "And cowboys." He hesitated then added, "Maybe you'd like to visit sometime."

Caroline smiled but didn't answer.

At the end of the meal, she waved off the offer of dessert, and Josh signaled the waiter for the bill. After it was paid, they sat quietly, watching the band assemble.

Josh was about to ask Caroline if she would like to dance when she had a question of her own. "Do you think Mike might be interested in Kate?"

"Where in the world did that come from?"

"I don't know. I was thinking about how protective he was when they argued about going into the mines and have you noticed the way he looks at her?"

"Is it similar to the way I look at you?"

A soft rose color spread across Caroline's cheeks.

The band began to play a ballad, and Josh stood, holding out his hand. "I think we should be the first ones on the dance floor."

When they reached the center of the floor, Caroline turned to face him. Pulling her close, he breathed in the clean scent of her hair, feeling the softness of her breasts against his chest. There was grace in her movements, no tension, no strain. When the music stopped, neither moved away until Caroline leaned back slightly to look up at him. He couldn't decipher the look in her eyes.

She smiled. "It's getting late. Maybe we should call it a night."

He nodded and guided her through the room and out onto the porch of the restaurant. The moon was bright, and Josh could see the dark ridge of a distant mountain. A soft voice mirrored his feelings as Caroline moved closer to him and took his hand.

"I love the desert at night."

Josh lifted her hand to his lips. He kissed her palm, the inside of her wrist, then leaned down and touched her lips lightly with his, once, twice, and then more firmly. Caroline wrapped her arms around his neck.

When she moved away, she stumbled. Josh caught her. "I'm sorry," he said. "I didn't mean to...."

"No, it's all right. Really. It's just that.... I mean if Charles weren't missing...."

"Shhh. I understand." He took her hand, and they walked back to the motel. At the door of her room, she reached up to touch his cheek lightly, then said goodnight and went inside.

The next morning, Caroline stood in the hot shower, washing her hair. She was aware of her body in a way she hadn't been in a long time. Toweling herself dry, she slowly spread on lilac scented lotion, thinking about Josh.

She wished that she could be more open to whatever was happening between the two of them, because she hadn't felt like this in years. Yet, only a short while ago, she'd fantasized about a possible reconciliation with Charles.

A knock on the door interrupted her reveries. She grabbed a robe and hurried through the room to open it.

Josh walked through the doorway, filling the room with his presence. "We need to talk," he said.

Caroline followed and propped herself against the backboard of the bed. He pulled up a chair, sat down and leaned forward, elbows on his knees. She was apprehensive about discussing last night, but his first words surprised her. "We've got to decide what to do next, then have breakfast and get on with it."

Relieved, she adjusted her thoughts. He was right. They needed to get back to the business at hand.

An idea had occurred to her during the night while she tossed and turned.

"Josh, I think our next step is to go to Los Angeles and get Adam to help us check on this land deal in Judson. Maybe we can even get into Charles's computer. And I want to pressure the partners again to help us, because I've thought of another card to play. If they don't cooperate, I'll threaten to take Charles's disappearance to the press. That will scare the hell out of them! The media would have a field day with this."

Josh beamed. "Good thinking! In the meantime, my buddy will come out here to watch the Jamison woman." He stood. "You get dressed, and we'll get going."

Caroline reached for the phone beside the bed. "First, I want to call Mike and Kate and see if they found out anything in northern California."

What the hell is going on? Adam wondered, as he looked up to see Caroline, Josh, Mike and Kate walk into his office. He put on his best, noncommittal face and walked around the desk to welcome his unexpected visitors.

"What a surprise. Come in, come in!"

"Hello, Adam." Caroline gave him a hug. "Sorry for barging in. Your secretary wasn't at her desk."

Mike eyed him, suspiciously. "Thought you were on your way to Europe, Adam."

"Change of plans," he said, closing the door and going around to the other side of his desk. "Please, sit down. What's happening?" The women sat on the couch, and the men pulled up chairs across from him.

"I didn't expect you two for another few days," he said to Kate and Mike. Kate explained they had decided it was a waste of time. "Every business transaction involving Charles the past few months didn't seem to have anything to do with his disappearance. Why did you think your information was so important that we had to rush up the coast?" Adam rambled on about the importance of checking out every possible lead until Caroline interrupted.

"You're absolutely right," she said. "We must investigate everything. That's why we're here." She told him what they had discovered in Nevada. "We need to get into Charles's files and computer and find out about this land deal in Judson. Can you help us?"

Adam could feel perspiration begin to bead his forehead.

"I can try. The paper files won't be a problem, but his computer is a different story." He paused. "You have to understand what you're asking of me. If Charles walks in that door and finds out I broke into his computer, he won't hesitate to fire me."

Caroline looked shocked. "You can't mean that, Adam. Surely he will understand that whatever you do is out of concern for his well-being."

Adam resisted the temptation to take the silk handkerchief out of his breast pocket and wipe his brow.

"Caroline," he said, "there's a lot you don't know. Charles has connections with some pretty powerful people. He wouldn't want anyone to know their names or find out about his dealings with them. Don't get me wrong, I'm not saying it's illegal or anything, but...." He stopped, waiting for Caroline to take in his words.

"Okay...I get the picture," she finally said. "Just check to see if there's a paper trail. While you're doing that, I plan to pressure Charles's partners to help us. Maybe they'll be willing to get into his computer. This time I'm going to put the fear of God into them by threatening to go to the media about his disappearance."

Adam nodded and began to breathe easier. Everything was still under control.

It was after midnight by the time Josh and Caroline pulled up in front of the house in Odessa. Kate and Mike had driven on to the motel. They sat in the desert silence, and Caroline stared at the mountain in front of them.

"What are you thinking?" Josh asked.

"I've had Charles on my mind ever since we left LA, and now that we're back...I don't know...it's as though he's close by."

She sighed. "I'm just tired." She reached for her bag, opened the door and stepped out of the truck. "See you tomorrow."

Caroline watched as he drove away then, placing her bag on the ground, she sat on the porch steps and thought about the day's events. Charles's partners had finally promised to send help. Her threat to go public had worked its magic.

She leaned back and gazed into the star filled sky. A streak of light brought back childhood memories. What would she wish for if she still believed in falling stars? That was easy—to have Charles home, safe and sound, beside her right now.

She was confused at the intensity of her desire. Josh had filled her mind and heart the past two days, but now that she was back here, all she could think about was Charles. His face was clear in her mind, except it wasn't the face she remembered. It was drawn and fearful. Caroline shivered. She had never seen Charles afraid. She turned to look up the side of the mountain to the stars shining between the jagged tops.

Help us, Charles! she silently called out. Help us to find you!

Charles stared into the blackness. He had programmed his mind not to expect light when he awoke and felt proud of that accomplishment.

He flicked on the flashlight and checked the time—01.23. If he were home, he'd be checking the international markets.

That seemed like a lifetime ago. Now all that mattered was staying alive, seeing Caroline again and beginning a new life with her.

First, however, he had to get out of this godforsaken place. He directed the beam of the flashlight to the rocks barricading the tunnel. Was it dimmer? He quickly switched it off.

In the darkness, he listened to the silence.

The voice inside his head had finally stopped chiding him. At the peak of his fear, he'd wondered if it might be the ghost in that haunted mine Malcolm talked so much about.

Good old Malcolm. He loved the myths of the high desert.

But then maybe this *was* Malcolm's haunted mine. A thought began to take shape at the edge of his mind. How would strangers know the perfect place to hide someone? Unless they somehow knew about an old cave in that had been opened over a century ago and could easily be resealed. And that it was marked on the maps in the house in Odessa.

He needed to think about this. Only a few people knew about Odessa. Who had he told about the haunted mine and the maps? Who had used his own mountain to bury him?

CHAPTER ELEVEN

The roar of engines and the sound of men's voices outside the house awakened Caroline. What in the world? Then she knew. Her threats had brought help even faster than she had anticipated.

Hastily putting on her robe, she pushed open the French doors. At least a dozen men stood around trucks. Adam was talking to them, gesturing toward the mountain. When he saw her, he walked over to the porch.

"Sorry if we woke you!"

"I can't believe you're here this early!"

"I was instructed to be here at the crack of dawn to oversee this crazy search for Charles. I know you wanted me to check the files, but it's going to have to wait until I get these guys going."

Caroline realized she was half-dressed. "Adam, give me a minute to get myself together. I'll be right out."

Before she could turn to go inside, Josh pulled up with Mike and Kate. She waved and hurried back into the bedroom. By the time she threw on jeans and a blue, short-sleeve shirt, everyone had assembled in front of the house. Josh and Mike were spreading maps out on the porch floor, marking the mines already explored. Caroline walked over to Kate, who was talking to Adam.

"Can you believe this? First I couldn't get anyone to help, and now we have half of California here."

"I think it's great!" Kate said. "Mike and I could have spent the rest of our lives exploring those miles of tunnels." She reached into her knapsack and took out Caroline's cell phone. "I forgot to give this to you yesterday. Adam called to let you know they were almost here but got me instead."

"Caroline!" Josh called out. "We're going across the gulch to the mines!"

Caroline watched the group of men walk down the middle of the sandy street, talking and looking around the town. It could have been a scene from the town's past, men heading to the mines to extract silver from the mountain. When her eyes followed Josh, however, she caught her breath. Fear for him filled her. She wanted to call him back.

Now what was that all about? Caroline wondered. The feeling had lasted only a few seconds but left her shaken.

"I hope you have some coffee," Kate said, yawning. "Malcolm's was still brewing when we left this morning."

Caroline glanced toward the retreating men once more then said, "Actually, I just rolled out of bed. Come on, I'll make us a pot."

At the kitchen table, Kate said, "I'm glad I don't have to go back in that mountain. I wish Mike wouldn't either. A lot of the shafts end up in closed off tunnels because of cave ins. It really isn't safe."

Caroline frowned. "You never mentioned that when you and Mike were exploring. I didn't realize you were in danger."

"I didn't want to worry you. After all, I was the one who insisted on doing it."

Josh and Adam appeared at the kitchen door. Caroline got up to get two more coffee cups." So you two didn't go with the men?" she said.

Adam laughed. "You've got to be kidding. It will be a cold day in hell before you get me inside a mountain."

Caroline handed Josh his coffee.

"Well, I guess if Adam can 'fess up," he said, "I should come clean, too. Mike covered for me the other day. The truth is, every time I go near that damn mountain, it scares the shit out of me. It's the damnedest thing." He leaned back in his chair. No one spoke.

Finally, Caroline turned to Kate. "Can you keep Adam company for a few minutes? I have something I want to show Josh."

He followed her out of the house.

In the street, Caroline said, "I just wanted a few minutes alone to talk to you about something."

As they walked through the town, she told him about her quick vision and fear for him. He listened then said, "From the first minute in those mines, I was overwhelmed with fear but too embarrassed to admit it to Mike." He shook his head. "I never knew I was claustrophobic. Maybe it's something that shows up when you get older."

When they reached the old schoolhouse, Caroline sat on the steps as Josh stared across the wide flat ledge to the desert below. "Josh," she said, "I want you to promise me something. Don't go into the mines again. I've learned to pay attention to feelings like these."

Josh smiled. "You have, have you?"

Caroline sighed. "You sound just like Charles. He never gave credence to any kind of psychic phenomena. Seriously though, humor me and let the other men search the mountain."

Josh stooped down, picking up sand and letting it run through his fingers. Caroline continued, "I've had happy feelings about this place, too. When I'm alone in Jessica's house, I feel her presence. It's the most loving feeling—as though she wants me to know how happy she was here." She paused. "I know this doesn't make much sense if you've never experienced anything similar."

She didn't see the amusement in Josh's eyes she had expected. Instead, he said, "I've had a few strange experiences in my life. Not exactly like yours, but I know what you mean when you talk about things others wouldn't understand."

When he didn't elaborate, Caroline said, "There are also things I feel I know about this place that weren't in the town's history. Like this school. I don't believe it originally sat close to the edge of that ledge. In my mind, I see an earthquake and half the ledge dropping down the mountain."

"Well, that could have happened. Earthquakes do shake this area periodically. You might be picking up on it."

He does understand, Caroline thought.

"So," she said, "there must be a reason for your fear, because I felt it, too."

Josh stood and held out his hand. "We'd better be getting back."

When they reached the house, Adam and Kate were on the porch.

"Hey, you two," Kate called out. "We were about to come look for you. Adam's got an idea."

"Really?" Caroline pulled up a chair. "What's that, Adam?"

"I don't think we're going to find anything about the Nevada land deal in the office files. Charles is too careful for that. But I had another thought."

"Go on."

"Charles has taken a few trips this past year to Switzerland, probably to stash some cash in bank accounts that Brenda doesn't know about. His itinerary also included several other countries, and if we can find out exactly who he visited, we may come up with some answers. I think someone should go over there and—"

"Hold it right there," Josh said. "Caroline and I aren't traipsing around Europe. For us to try and track down Charles's business affairs abroad would be as useless as exploring that mountain by ourselves."

"No, no," Adam said, "I don't mean that you should go over there. I'm offering to follow up on the lead. If Caroline uses her influence to convince Jenson and the rest to ante-up expenses, I can be on my way tomorrow."

Josh looked at Caroline and gave a subtle shake of his head. She knew he didn't trust Adam any more than Mike did, and she was beginning to have doubts, herself.

"Adam, I think we need you in LA to keep on top of things at the office. If it eventually looks like someone should go, I'll see what I can do, but for now we should stick to searching Charles's files.

"I'll go back with you today and work with your computer staff to get into Charles's computer. I'll take full responsibility, so you won't get into trouble. Josh, can you handle things here?"

Caroline watched Adam's reaction. The handsome face momentarily betrayed dismay then became a smooth mask of compliance. That quick moment, however, told her what she needed to know.

Josh was worried. Caroline hadn't called. Should he try her cell phone? No, she might be at the office with Adam, and he didn't want to interrupt.

Malcolm's dining room was filled with members of the rescue crew, who were eating a supper of steak, mashed potatoes, gravy, homemade rolls and cherry pie. Kate had already eaten and gone back to her room.

Malcolm poured more coffee while Mike talked about the day's search. Josh only half-listened, thinking about Caroline and their discussion earlier. "So how was your day?" Mike asked.

Josh hesitated for a minute. "To tell you the truth, I spent the day trying to figure out why I have this fear of going into that mountain. It obviously doesn't bother any of the men here or you or even Kate, but I had the craziest thoughts when we were exploring those mines."

Malcolm cleared his throat and said, "Maybe it's because you...uh... heard some moanin' down there."

Josh and Mike stared at him.

"Well, did ya?"

"Good Lord, no, Malcolm," Josh said. "If I'd heard anything, we would have investigated. Why in the world would you ask such a thing?"

Malcolm looked around the room. The din of male voices seemed to reassure him that they wouldn't be overheard. "Well, I just wondered if maybe it was the old spook in the haunted mine that scared you."

"Haunted mine?" Mike started to laugh.

Anger lit up Malcolm's pale eyes. "You young people don't know nothin' about nothin'. Watch too much TV, that's your problem." He started to walk away.

Josh quickly spoke up. "Wait. Forget Mike. I want to know more about this haunted mine."

Malcolm scowled at Mike but sat down. When he started talking again, he spoke directly to Josh. "There's a legend 'round these parts that I first heard when I was a small boy. Back when Odessa was in its heyday, a young fella named Murphy was a dump car shover. He was sacked out in one of them livin' spaces—like the ones you saw—when there was a cave in. It took days to dig through the ton of rock in the tunnel, and when they got to him, he was dead as a door nail."

Malcolm leaned forward. "No one could figure out why the kid died. He weren't hurt so you'd notice, had plenty of supplies and should have had enough air. Maybe it was bein' alone for days, thinkin' about how he was buried alive." Malcolm stared off into space for a few seconds. "From that day on, the miners would hear a groanin' and a callin' out whenever they went into that tunnel. Finally, they started leavin' that mine alone. I know, by god, I would."

Josh felt a tightening of his chest, a stifled feeling growing in him, of being trapped in the dark. Was it like that for Charles? He felt the blood drain from his face.

"Hey, you okay?" Mike asked. "You're white as a sheet. What's wrong?"

Josh held onto the table and pushed himself up. Mike reached out to help, but he waved him away. "I'm okay. Just felt sick there for a minute. Think I'll get some fresh air and then go on to bed. I'll see you in the morning."

With a worried look, Mike backed away, and Josh made his way through the crowded room. He walked into the parking area, bent over, hands on his thighs, breathing deeply. Finally he straightened up.

The Odessa Mountain was a looming dark shape against the night sky.

CHAPTER TWELVE

It was six o'clock, and Caroline was tired and hungry, but she was not going to leave Adam and Larry, the computer technician, alone. They had gotten into Charles's computer but so far had found no reports of any land negotiations in Nevada.

"Caroline," Adam said, "you need to get something to eat. I'll stick around here."

"I was just thinking that maybe you could go out and get us something—Chinese? Would you mind? I'll make coffee to keep everyone going in the meantime." Giving him no chance to argue, she turned and crossed the room to the credenza that held the coffee supplies.

After Adam left, she joined the young man at the keyboard.

"Check the deleted files," she said.

Ten minutes later, Larry shouted, "Got it! This might be what you've been looking for."

"When were the files deleted?"

"A few days ago."

Caroline felt the hair on her arms raise. Who else but Adam could have done this? Trying to sound nonchalant, she said, "Good work. Just retrieve the files and save them on a CD for me."

Within twenty minutes, Caroline had the CDs tucked safely into her pocketbook. Larry had only been gone a few minutes when Adam returned.

"I'm sorry for taking so long. You can't imagine how many people...." He stopped, realizing they were alone in the room. "Where's Larry?"

"Oh, I told him to knock off for the night. You were right. We're all too tired. Here, let me help you with those bags. I'm going to take mine home. I want to eat, take a long, hot bath and go to bed."

Caroline chatted nervously, as they divided the food up and left the building. She then drove to her house, grateful she had rented a car and didn't have to depend on Adam for a ride.

Back home, Caroline locked the door behind her and called Josh's cell number.

"I was beginning to get worried," he said.

"Well, I've got some news. While Adam was getting take-out for us, the technician was able to retrieve some deleted files regarding Judson, Nevada. Now here's the interesting part, the files were deleted a few days ago."

"O...kay," Josh said. "Sounds like Adam's been a busy boy. Wait a minute. Where is he now?"

Caroline explained that Adam had gone home. "But I do need to get out of here before he gets to work tomorrow. Larry will undoubtedly tell him that I have copies of the deleted files." She paused. "Can you fly here in the morning and get me?"

"I'll come tonight!"

"No, that's not necessary. I rented a car so I'm going to leave here and spend the night at a motel near the airport. Adam won't know where I am."

There was a moment of silence. Finally, Josh said, "All right, but call me as soon as you get to the motel. I need to know you're safe tonight. In the morning, meet me at the airport. The rental agency can pick up your car there, so we can head back here right away. I can't wait to see what those files have on them."

"Me either. I'm going to pull some of them up tonight on my laptop."

"Get going to the motel first!"

"I'm out the door as soon as I hang up."

By the time Josh was in the air, the sun was well over the horizon. Damn it, he thought. This business of driving thirty miles every time I want to use the plane is getting old. Maybe Mike can help me clear a short landing strip near the motel.

At the bottom of the Cajon pass, a cloudbank hid the valley. Josh flew above it until, finding a hole, he spiraled down, spotting the Van Nuys airport in the distance.

Caroline was waiting as Josh climbed out of the plane. She walked into his arms. He held her tightly.

"It's all right now," Josh said. "Good job."

She stepped back. "Thanks. I'm so glad to see you. I can't wait to get back and print some of the files I checked out last night."

"Find anything interesting?"

"I'm not sure. They're basically reports on earthquake faults and underground water levels in the state of Nevada. The truth is I don't have the expertise to interpret the files. Maybe you do."

During the trip back, Josh talked about his plan to clear a landing strip behind the motel. "We can follow up on leads faster that way."

"Which reminds me," Caroline said. "I convinced Jenson to put you back on the payroll."

"I wasn't concerned about that. Like I told you, this has become personal for me. I don't intend to quit until we find your ex-husband!"

Josh waited for the last pages to print out. He and Caroline had been in his motel room all afternoon. The more they found, the more confused he felt. What the hell was Charles into?

Caroline sat at the desk reading and highlighting. He walked over and stood behind her, massaging her shoulders.

"Are you ready to take a break?"

Leaning back against him, she said, "That feels good. Yes, let's have an early supper. I don't think I can look at another file. Charles must have had every piece of land in Nevada surveyed all the way to the Colorado River."

"What did you just say?"

Caroline looked up at him. "I said—"

Josh grabbed the map of Nevada and spread it out on the bed. "That's it. I bet if we check off every piece of land on these files, they will back up against one another until the last one reaches the Colorado River. Charles bought right-of-ways from the river to Judson."

Caroline stood beside him, staring down at the map.

"So this is about water?"

Josh sat down on the bed. "That can't be all of it. A number of the files have to do with underground caverns. Those surveys dot the whole of the state of Nevada. He was obviously looking for something. But why would he be interested in caverns? And why the files on earthquake faults in the state?" He grabbed his Stetson. "Okay, no more. Let's see if Malcolm will feed us before the crew stampedes the dining room."

The room was empty, tables set and ready for the evening meal. Josh could hear Malcolm giving orders in the kitchen. He had imported help from the next desert town to help feed the hungry search party. Besides breakfast and supper, he packed large lunches.

Malcolm came through the kitchen door carrying a heavy tray of condiments, and Josh jumped up to help him.

"Don't need no help," he insisted, almost dropping the tray on the nearest table. "You two ready to eat?"

"Whenever you have time, Malcolm," Caroline said. "I know you're busy preparing for tonight's meal. We can wait."

"I'll be right back," he said, heading again to the kitchen.

Josh poured two cups of coffee from the pot always brewing on a table in the corner and handed one to Caroline. He poured a third cup when he saw Kate walk through the door.

Her face was flushed from the day's heat, and she had on a flowered cotton dress that made her look ten years old. Josh thought about all the years he and his wife had tried to have children. Why hadn't they adopted? They might have had a daughter like Kate. Or a son like Mike.

Malcolm pushed the kitchen door open again, carrying another tray, and Kate rushed over. He accepted her help. Josh smiled. She had won the old codger's heart.

"Hi," Kate said, sitting beside Caroline. "Please tell me there's something I can do. Mike won't let me in the mines. Malcolm won't let me in the kitchen. There's no cable or satellite. I'm going stir crazy."

"Imagine what it must be like for that poor fella' in the mountain up there," Malcolm muttered, as he set condiments on each table.

Josh ignored the comment. He couldn't bring himself to think about Charles, or anyone, trapped, alone in the dark in a mountain. Sweat broke out on his forehead.

"Josh, what's wrong?" Caroline asked.

Malcolm said, "You feeling peaked again, like the other night?" Josh shook his head at him, but it was too late. Both women said in unison, "The other night?"

"We was talking about the spook in that old mine, and Josh took sick and had to leave. Not that I blame him none. Makes me queasy, too."

"I swear to God," Josh said, "for someone who never says two words, you just can't shut up about that damn mine." Indignant, Malcolm stomped off. From the looks on the women's faces, Josh knew he was in for it, so he quickly told them the story of the haunted mine then changed the subject.

"I think we should catch Kate up on our research," he said to Caroline. At the sound of men's voices outside, he added, "But let's wait for Mike to join us." Mike walked in and sat down.

For the next hour, the four ate and discussed Charles's computer files. Everyone had at least one possible theory, but no one could come up with a plausible explanation.

Later that evening, Josh took Caroline home.

"Thanks for the ride," she said. "I'll see you in the morning." She quickly turned to open the truck door.

Josh watched her walk away. It happened whenever they were in Odessa—the distancing. As though Charles was watching them.

She was in his arms. He felt her mouth against his, so soft and full and....

The dream ended. Awake now, he tried to recapture it and succeeded for a few minutes but then it faded away. More and more, Caroline was a part of his sleeping world. Sometimes she was only smiling at him, other times she seemed to be looking for him. Over here, he'd shout, I'm over here, but she wouldn't hear him and turn away.

He reached for the flashlight to check the time but held it in his hand, without turning it on. What difference did it make? Day, night, they were all the same. And he'd run out of time. An hour ago, he had eaten the last piece of beef jerky, washing it down with the last drop of water.

The past twenty-four hours he had focused on Caroline, sending the message that he believed would save him. I'm here, he had called out in his mind. I'm in the haunted mine.

For some reason, he was sure this was true, but if someone didn't find him soon, it wouldn't matter. Like that man a hundred years ago, it would be too late. He gripped the flashlight tightly.

Had his life really come to this? Was he going to die alone here in the dark?

Not alone.

He lay unmoving, listening.

This was a different voice. Not a hateful whisper, undermining his determination to survive. Something else. "Okay," he said, forcing out the words. "So I'm not alone. If I'm not alone, who are you?"

He waited.

There was no answer, but he felt strangely peaceful. He closed his eyes and drifted off to sleep.

A few hours later, he awoke, still holding the flashlight. He flicked the switch.

Nothing.

He shook it hard and tried again.

No more light.

She sat straight up in bed. The voice had awakened her from a deep sleep. It had come from outside the house, and yet she knew no one was there. This had happened before, and it was always just one word—Caroline!

She lay back down and listened, but there was only the moaning of the wind.

"Dear God," she prayed. "Please, please help us find Charles."

She tossed and turned, unable to sleep. She kept visualizing the poor young man trapped in the same mountain years ago, dying from fright. How terrible. No wonder his ghost haunted the mine. Haunted. The word kept repeating in her mind.

CHAPTER THIRTEEN

"What do you mean, Adam?" Caroline shouted into the phone. "They can't do this! I won't let them!"

"Nothing you say is going to change their minds. They had another board meeting, looked at the cost and decided it was a foolish expenditure. They don't believe Charles is in that mountain. And frankly, neither do I." His voice was cold. She knew he hadn't bought the story about her sudden departure.

Hanging up, Caroline watched as one by one the trucks pulled away. Josh stood across the street talking on his phone. Ending his conversation, he walked over to her. "Well, that's that. I just contacted the local authorities and Search and Rescue. They insist we don't have enough evidence to warrant their help, either."

Mike and Kate came out of the house, and everyone stood on the front porch, watching the last truck disappear.

"I bet this is Adam's doing!" Mike said.

"Why do you always blame Adam?" Kate protested. "It's not his fault no one will listen to us." The two young people glared at one another.

Josh intervened. "Okay, kids, let's not start fighting among ourselves. Actually, Mike may have a point. Adam's not happy with us at the moment."

Caroline sank down on the nearest chair. She hadn't slept well last night.

Josh reached out to touch her shoulder. "You okay?"

"For some reason, I keep thinking about the awful story of the man dying in that mine and his ghost haunting it." She shook her head. "Haunted, I hate that word. It was in my mind all night."

Kate pulled up a chair beside her. "Maybe it means something. Maybe someone is trying to tell you something."

Caroline stared at Kate then asked, "Where are the maps of the mines?"

Kate jumped up and went into the house, returning to spread them out on the porch.

"Most of the mines seem to have names, but what are these numbers?" Caroline asked.

"The numbers are known cave ins that block those particular tunnels," Josh explained.

Caroline ran her finger over the myriad of names and numbers then stopped. "I wonder why this number is circled."

"I understand how you feel, Caroline," Josh said, "but I'm not sure this is a good idea."

She finished lacing up her hiking boots. "I know it doesn't make any sense, but I need someone to check out that circled mine! And I'm going, too."

"Oh, no," Mike said, "I'm not taking anyone into a tunnel that has caved in. It's too dangerous."

Caroline grabbed the lantern on the table. "Fine. Then I'll go by myself."

"Not without me you won't," Kate said, following her out of the house. The men looked at each other then hurried to catch up with the women.

Josh walked beside Caroline. "Let's talk about this. If it's that important to you, Mike and I will check out the mine."

"I don't want you to go into the mountain again, Josh."

"You don't think for a minute that I'd let you go in there without me."

Caroline stopped walking and smiled up into the face of the man she had come to trust. "Thank you, Josh."

He shook his head and smiled back. "You are one stubborn woman."

It wasn't until they were far inside the tunnel that Caroline began having second thoughts. Never had she been so deep underground before, surrounded by rock on all sides. The light from the lanterns played off the walls, creating an eerie, surreal effect.

Her uneasiness grew. Had she endangered her friends for nothing? Should Josh have come back inside this mountain?

"Here's where the tunnels divide," Mike called out. Ahead the tunnel branched left and right. It was Josh's expression when he looked right that told Caroline where they needed to go.

"Well, no moaning or groaning yet," Kate said. Everyone laughed except Josh.

"Follow me," he said, walking around Mike.

The deeper they went, the more small rocks cluttered the dirt floor until straight ahead a wall of large fallen rocks closed off the tunnel.

"Wow," Kate whispered, "this is awesome. Just think, no one has been here for over a hundred years."

Mike leaned over, holding his lantern close to the ground. "I'll be damned," he muttered. Everyone gathered around him.

Half-crushed under a rock was a fountain pen.

Dying wasn't so hard. Nothing really hurt anymore. Even the hard dirt floor felt softer beneath him. He was no longer afraid, just a little impatient and curious to find out what came next, if anything.

The ghost in his mind hadn't returned. Only when he let fear darken his thoughts did he hear a whisper. So he chose to dream of Caroline and stay in the light of her memory. It was a peaceful place.

He began to drift off again to a dreaming place where there were people talking.... Charles! Someone was calling. Of course, it was all in his mind. He understood that.

"Charles!"

He opened his eyes.

"Charles!"

Caroline. Caroline's voice?

Then he heard another sound—rocks scraping against rocks.

A male voice shouted. "If you can hear us, hang in there, man!"

Trembling in shock and disbelief, he struggled to pull himself up.

A flicker of light broke the darkness. He watched, holding his breath, afraid to move, afraid to believe this was real. Another flicker. And another. The voices were closer. They were real. They'd found him.

Tears began to roll down his face. He wasn't going to die. He was going to live. Caroline had heard him. A circle of light appeared on the far wall. It grew larger, brighter.

"Be careful, Mike, not so fast," an older man's voice admonished. "Stay back, Caroline, we have to be careful, or we'll all end up trapped down here."

"Charles!" Caroline shouted. "Can you hear me? Are you in there?"

He cleared his throat. "I'm here," he said, his voice barely more than a hoarse whisper. He tried again. "I'm here."

"He's alive! We're coming, Charles, we're coming!"

As more light filled the area, he saw several small boulders moving. They'd made it. They'd gotten through! Suddenly there was a low rumble and a man's voice shouting, "Get back, get out of the way!"

The dust was so thick, Caroline could hardly breathe. Josh had pushed her backwards, knocking both Kate and her to the floor of the tunnel. They lay there, coughing. The silence was ominous.

Kate started screaming, "Mike, where's Mike?"

Mike was nowhere in sight. They were again faced with a wall of fallen rocks.

"God almighty!" Josh said, shaking his head in disbelief.

"Oh, no," Caroline cried out. Kate's hand covered her mouth in horror. Josh quickly helped both women to their feet.

"Listen to me!" he said. "Go for help! It was stupid of us to think we could dig through this by ourselves." He looked at Caroline. "Call Search and Rescue. Tell them we've got two men trapped down here who need medical attention." When neither woman moved, he shouted, "Go—now!"

Kate tugged on his sleeve. "What about Mike?"

Josh grasped her arms. "Let me worry about Mike! I'll find him, but I'll need help getting him and Charles to the surface. You have to hurry!"

Kate nodded and turned to run back through the tunnel.

"Wait," Caroline said, "wait for me."

She glanced back at Josh. His face was grim.

Charles coughed the dust out of his throat and rubbed his eyes. Expecting darkness, he was surprised to see the light of a lantern. When his vision cleared, he gasped. A man's hand seemed to be reaching for an overturned lantern.

The arm protruded out of the rocks. Charles crawled across the dirt floor and reached for the wrist of the buried man. There was a pulse. "Thank God," he whispered.

With strength he didn't know he had left, he grabbed the nearest rock and carefully removed it. The rocks were not large, and he was able to work his way carefully up the man's arm. In a few minutes, he knew he was looking at a miracle. Instead of the crushed skull he expected to find, there was a pocket of space created by a larger boulder, where a man's head lay in an expanding pool of blood.

Charles didn't dare touch the boulder, afraid that the rest of the rocks would tumble down. But he had to stop the bleeding. Clutching the sleeve of his shirt, he tugged until it tore loose. Charles held it to the man's head. Applying pressure on the makeshift bandage, he lay down beside his would-be rescuer. "A little longer," he prayed aloud. "Give us both a little longer until they can get us out."

Josh slowly removed one rock after another. Mike had disappeared only a few feet from him. Pulling away a fairly large boulder, Josh saw what he'd been dreading to find. A boot and leg. *Shit*. He felt a tremor in the rock pile and stopped, afraid to go farther. It was going to take more than one man to get Mike safely out. He had to wait for the rescue team. And God only knew how long that would take. Josh wiped sweat, grime and tears out of his eyes. Laying his hand on the motionless leg, he said, "Hang on, son, hang on."

He looked behind him where his light illuminated the tunnel. He should go back there to wait. It would be safer. Another cave in would bury him, too.

The fear that he had been trying to ignore returned full force. He knew others might think it crazy, but he felt as though he'd been in this situation before. He'd died under a mountain of rock, just like the young man in this haunted mine. Just like Mike?

The feeling of being trapped, buried alive, was so strong that Josh instinctively shifted toward the tunnel, to escape, to breathe fresh air. To live.

But he stopped himself. He had to stay. He couldn't leave Mike. Or Charles. No, by God, no one else was going to die in this damn mountain!

"Why are they taking so long?" Kate asked, standing across from the house, looking down the mountain. "Wait, what's that sound?" A whirring noise grew louder. Kate and Caroline watched as a helicopter appeared over the top of the mountain.

It circled several times before heading to the old schoolhouse. The women started running toward the area. "I hope that bluff is stable enough to hold the copter," Caroline shouted. She watched it touch down, perilously close to the edge.

Two men jumped out while the rotor blades were still spinning and immediately the helicopter lifted off. Confused, Caroline ran up to the nearest man and asked, "Where is he going?"

A man, with a rope, ax and shovel strapped to him, explained the pilot was trying to find a safer landing spot.

"Don't worry, lady, he'll find a place, and then we'll transport the injured to the closest hospital. I'm Skip, and this is Joe."

"I'm Caroline Laughery. Please, come with us."

"Ms. Laughery," Joe said, "one of you has to wait for the rest of the crew to get here in the trucks."

Kate yelled, "Follow me!" and was off running.

Oh, Lord, Caroline thought, watching her race with the men across the gulch and up the mountain to the mine opening. Kate shouldn't go in there if Mike is....

The helicopter landed on the other side of the town. Caroline walked back to the house and sat on the porch steps. She wanted more than anything to be in the mine with the others. Gazing out over the desert floor, she wondered which direction the rescue crew was coming from. The distant sound of motors answered her question; they were already on the mountain road.

She jumped up and stood, waiting. When the first of the two trucks pulled up, she waved the driver down. In moments, the men had gathered their gear and were following her across the gulch and up the mountain to the entrance of the mine. Caroline led them as quickly as possible through the tunnel to the cave in. The sight that greeted them was exactly what she had feared.

Kate was looking desolate as she watched Josh, Skip and Joe working to shore up the area and remove rocks off poor Mike's body. The tunnel was too narrow for more than a few people to get through, so Caroline reached for Kate's hand and drew her back behind the men. Josh joined them. The three stood together, holding on to one another, not speaking.

The rescue team worked carefully and methodically. Caroline held her breath. A flicker of light appeared as they carefully removed the last of the rocks. She looked at Josh. "Mike's lantern," he said. Finally there was a shout. "We're through. They're both here." There was a long pause. "And alive."

CHAPTER FOURTEEN

Kate sat in the dimly lit hospital room, fighting to keep her eyes open. It was 1:30 a.m., but she couldn't bring herself to leave. Mike's lean body lay motionless, his head bandaged and his left arm in a plaster cast. He had several broken ribs. The doctors planned additional tests in the morning when he stabilized. Their serious faces had not reassured her.

She had only known an energetic, often angry, Mike. Seeing him still and helpless touched something in her, as though a part of herself was hurt.

He's young and strong, she tried to reassure herself. But then, Danny had been, too.

Her husband had been in a coma for several hours before he died, and she hadn't been able to be with him because of the baby. She'd lost their child anyway, and Danny had died before she could get to his bedside.

She closed her eyes and fervently prayed, "Please God, don't let him die." Taking a deep breath, she added, "I promise I won't fight with him anymore. I'll be more patient. Please, please let him live."

Kate heard a soft moan. She leaned forward and held the bruised right hand gently in her own hands. "Mike," she said softly. "It's okay, it's going to be all right." A frown appeared. "I'm here, Mike. I'm right here."

"Laurie."

Caroline stared down at the man who had once shared her life. She still couldn't believe they'd found him.

Charles looked younger than the last time she'd seen him. Perhaps it was the weight he'd lost. Or maybe it was because she'd never seen him so vulnerable.

His eyelids moved; his eyes opened. "You heard me, didn't you?" His eyes closed.

Caroline gently smoothed back hair from his forehead, tucked the covers around him and turned to leave. Josh stood in the doorway.

"How's he doing?"

Caroline put a finger to her lips, walking across the room and into the hall.

"The doctors say he's going to be all right. What about Mike?"

Josh shook his head and sat on the nearest chair. "He's not in great shape. The doctors are noncommittal, which isn't a good sign."

Caroline sat beside him and put her arm around his shoulders. "You two have gotten close, haven't you?"

Josh stared straight ahead. In a low voice, he said, "If he doesn't make it, I'll never forgive myself."

"Josh! It wasn't your fault!"

He stood. "Come on, you and Kate need to get some rest."

In Mike's room, Kate was curled up asleep in a large, upholstered chair. Caroline touched the auburn curls. "Katie," she whispered, "Wake up, honey."

Kate sat straight up. "Is it Mike? Is he all right?"

Josh stooped beside the chair. "He will be, sweetie. He will be. Now, you have to go back to the motel and sleep. Mike's going to need you in the morning."

"No, I can't leave. I promised myself I wouldn't leave. What if he wakes up again?"

"He woke up?" Josh asked.

"Only for a few seconds. He called out his ex-wife's name." Tears filled her eyes.

"Come with me, honey," Caroline said, "you're worn out."

"I'm staying here," Josh said. "Mike won't be alone."

Kate wiped her eyes. "You won't leave him? You promise? I'm just so afraid…I mean…." She turned to Caroline, "He's not going to die, is he?"

With as much conviction as she could muster, Caroline said, "No, of course not, he's strong, Katie. And stubborn!"

Kate's face lit up. "Yes, he is, isn't he? He's really stubborn, and that will help get him through this, won't it?"

Caroline nodded. "That's right. And you need to be rested so you can be here for him tomorrow. Okay?"

Josh gently helped Kate to her feet.

"You go on with Caroline. I promise you I won't leave this room. If Mike wakes up, I'll be right here."

Caroline led Kate out of the room, thanking Josh with her eyes.

Josh sat on the large chair and propped his feet up on a smaller one. He intended to keep his promise to Kate. It was very important to be here when Mike opened his eyes. The boy needed to know he wasn't alone—not anymore.

Josh laid his head back. He was tired, but his mind wouldn't turn off. They'd found Charles, but now they had to worry about keeping him safe. Those who masterminded the kidnapping were still out there, and if they wanted him dead, well….

He yawned. Tomorrow. I'll deal with everything tomorrow. He glanced over at Mike. If the kid makes it, I can handle the rest.

When Caroline opened the door to Mike's room in the morning, she found both men sleeping. Josh was stretched out awkwardly on two chairs that he'd made into a makeshift bed. She slipped quietly in and walked over to Mike. He looked so young and defenseless, the bravado and tough image gone. His mother, Caroline thought—this boy must have a family somewhere. We need to get in touch with them.

"Caroline." She looked over at Josh then walked around the bed. He stood, and they held each other for a moment. Josh searched her face. "How are you doing?"

"I slept pretty good. How about you?"

Josh stretched, hands on his lower back. "I've slept in worse places." He looked down at Mike.

"I talked to the night nurse," Caroline said. "His vital signs have stabilized. They'll know more after the tests today. Charles had a good night, too. Listen, why don't you go to the motel, clean up and get some breakfast? I'll stay with Mike until Kate gets here. She was still sleeping when I left."

Josh tucked his shirt into his jeans and ran his hand through his hair. "I think I'll do just that. But don't leave him alone."

She patted his arm. "Don't worry, I won't, but I hope you or Kate are here when he wakes up. It will reassure him to see one of you. He's come to trust you both."

Josh nodded. "And that's a miracle in itself."

It was late afternoon, and Caroline sat in the corner of Charles's room. Kate and Josh were with Mike.

The doctor wrote on Charles's chart then spoke to Caroline. "Your friend here must have been in very good shape before this happened."

"So, the prognosis is good?" Caroline asked.

"Excellent. But it's going to take awhile for him to get his strength back." He turned to Charles. "You should be able to go home in a few days."

"Tomorrow," Charles stated, emphatically. "I'll be leaving tomorrow as soon as I make some arrangements." He reached for the phone beside the bed. The doctor looked at Caroline then left the room.

"That's right," Charles said into the phone, "I want everything set up by tomorrow. And not a word of this to anyone. No, not even Adam. The more time I can buy the better. I've already talked to the hospital administrator. No reporters have shown up, which gives me hope I can sneak away undetected." He paused, listening. "I know it's a long shot. Just do what I tell you! I'll call again in a few hours!"

Caroline frowned as Charles hung up the phone. "What are you talking about? We have to let Adam and your partners know—and Brenda, of course."

"No one will know I'm alive until I'm ready for them to know!" Charles's eyes were blazing. "The bastards who did this to me are going to regret it!"

Caroline saw sweat break out on Charles's forehead. He was far weaker than he wanted to admit, but she knew how determined he could be. He would leave the hospital, with or without his doctor's blessing.

She went to the sink, wet a cloth and started to lay it on his forehead, but he took it from her hand.

"Caroline," he said, pushing himself upright. "It's important that we keep my rescue under wraps for as long as possible. It will give me the advantage I need if I'm going to find out who's behind this." He swiped his forehead with the washcloth, tossed it aside then continued. "I need a place to hide, so I want to go to Odessa tomorrow. I've arranged for a bed to be set up in the parlor.

"Since I'll need help getting around, as well as protection, I've hired your friend, Josh Logan, to work for me. He can be my legs until I'm up and around."

As Charles outlined his plans, Caroline felt as though she'd stepped back in time. How often had she seen Charles take charge and let nothing get in his way? When he stopped talking, she began listing her concerns, knowing he would have an answer for each of them.

"Josh is already working for your company. He can't work for you and keep the fact that you're alive a secret."

"Logan and I talked while you were sitting with Mike, and we worked out a plan. He's going to fax them a letter of resignation today."

Caroline's eyes widened in surprise.

"I see he didn't tell you. Good. That tells me he's a man I can trust. Now, all I need to know is—are you willing to be a nursemaid for a while? If you want to go back to LA until this is resolved, I understand. It's completely up to you."

Caroline thought for a moment. "I'm willing to help, of course, but how can I leave Kate alone here with Mike? He's still on the critical list. If both Josh and I leave, she...."

Charles held up his hand. "I've taken care of that. Logan told me he has a plane. He suggested we clear a short runway next to the motel. The hospital is less than a half-hour away by air. You and he can visit every day if necessary.

"If the boy makes it, we'll bring him and Kate to Odessa, where he can recuperate. A construction crew is on its way to fix up the old saloon building and build the runway. They have no idea why, of course, and will be gone before we get there."

Caroline could only stare in amazement at the man who had been close to death only twenty-four hours ago.

Charles waited while Stephen's father, Leonard, got on the phone. He had to find out about the young man who had been with him.

He wasn't sure what he was going to say to Leonard, however. When Stephen had asked him for a ride in Vegas, he'd promised not to tell his father about his losses at the casino.

"Charles! You son of a gun. We thought for sure you'd bought it."

Charles laughed. "I wasn't about to leave you guys in a lurch. Listen, I'm only calling members of the cartel that I can trust. I need for you to keep quiet about this for a while."

For the next twenty minutes, the two men talked strategy. Finally, Stephen's father presented Charles with an opening. "While we're talking, Charles, I want to run something by you.

"When things get back to normal, I wonder if you might have an entry-level position for my son in your company. He graduated last year from UCLA and has been living high on the hog ever since—my hog. He needs to buckle down and get a job."

"He's living in LA?"

"Yes. I talked to him a few days ago, and he's finally ready to get serious about job hunting—if I get him a new car. And of course, he wants only the most expensive one. Honest to god, kids these days!"

Charles listened in amazement. Apparently the boy was all right. Where had he been all this time? There definitely had been an accident. Maybe he went for help and came back to find no one in the car. So why hadn't he gone to the police? Of course, the kidnapping had been kept out of the media, so he wouldn't have known anything about it.

Had he feared his father's wrath for wrecking the car? Probably so, if Leonard was still supporting him. It was times like these that he was glad he'd never had children.

Promising Leonard he would look into a possible position for his son, Charles ended the conversation. Hanging up, he felt relieved. Stephen was all right and in LA. One less person to worry about.

In the hallway, Kate and Josh stood outside of Mike's room with his doctors. Has something happened? Caroline wondered. The younger of the two doctors was talking when she joined them.

"We have to relieve the pressure on his brain, but we need written permission. Are either of you family?"

Caroline saw panic in Kate's eyes. "He doesn't have any family," she said. "His mother died when he was young, and his father just took off. An aunt raised him, but she died two years ago. There must be other aunts and uncles, but Mike never told me the name of his hometown. Oh, dear, what are we going to do?"

Josh spoke up. "I'll take responsibility. Caroline, take Kate to the cafeteria. I'll join you there in a few minutes."

A half-hour later, Josh walked into the cafeteria, looking tired and worried.

"I'm so sorry," Caroline said.

"For what?" Josh asked.

"For everything. Mike wouldn't be fighting for his life if it weren't for me. He was right about the danger, but I insisted on going in anyway."

Josh shook his head. "No, if anyone is at fault, it's me. You were right about checking out the haunted mine. Charles wouldn't be alive today if you hadn't insisted. But I should have been in the lead, not Mike. I let him go ahead of me, and consequently—"

Kate rolled her eyes. "I can't believe you two! The only bad guys here are the ones who kidnapped Charles and buried him in a mountain! It's *their* fault!"

Kate sat by Mike's bed, reading.

By the time I finish this book, she thought, Mike will be up and around and his old, ornery self.

She glanced up. Of course, he had to open his eyes first.

She missed Josh and Caroline. They'd stayed until after Mike's operation then left for Odessa with Charles, promising to return as soon as they got him settled.

Charles Laughery was an enigma to her. For one thing, he had lied. When they asked him about the other man in the car, he'd insisted he was alone, yet Josh said Charles had left Vegas with someone. And Kate knew she hadn't imagined the man under that tree in the desert.

Out of the corner of her eye, Kate saw something move. Mike was lifting his right hand as though to touch his head. She dropped her book and leaned over him.

"Mike?" she said. "It's Kate. Can you hear me?"

His eyes opened, closed and opened again. He didn't seem to recognize her. "It's me, Mike—it's Kate!"

"Katie?" The word was almost inaudible. Then he whispered, "Where the hell am I?"

Kate laughed. Mike was back.

CHAPTER FIFTEEN

Caroline ran into the parlor, holding her cell phone in the air. "He's okay! Katie just called. Mike's awake, and he's going to make it!"

Charles had forgotten how Caroline glowed when she was excited or happy. What a pleasure it would be to make her look like this every day. That was one of his new goals—after he'd found the sons of bitches who did this to him.

Caroline sat on the settee near the bed in the middle of the parlor. Charles wasn't happy that he had to spend so much time in bed. Apparently, lying on the cold floor of the mine had done some damage to his right hip. But it wasn't broken, and the doctor had assured him that he'd be up and around soon. In the meantime, he had Caroline to take care of him, which fit into his agenda perfectly.

He smiled at her. "You care about those two kids, don't you?"

"I really do. They've both been through so much this past year. Now maybe they can find some happiness again."

"With each other?"

"I'm not sure where their relationship is heading. They basically just met and certainly not under the best of circumstances. But

I believe people come into our lives when we need them, and maybe they can help one another heal. That's possible now, because Mike is going to be okay!"

She stood. "I need to go down to the landing strip and let Josh know. Will you be all right?"

"Sure, you go on. Leroy's right outside if I need help. For that matter, why don't you and Josh fly to see Mike today? You need a break, and I have my cell phone if anything comes up."

Caroline looked out the door at the sullen man sitting on the porch. "I don't really know Leroy as you hired him after our divorce. I never understood why you needed a bodyguard then but thank goodness he's here now. He *is* a little strange though."

"Maybe a little," Charles said, "but I can trust him."

Caroline's phone rang. Checking the I.D., she sat back down. "It's Adam," she said. "I've got to take this or he's going to get suspicious. I've been avoiding his calls."

Charles knew how hard it was for Caroline to lie.

"Be careful," he warned her.

She took a deep breath. "Hello? Oh, yes, Adam. I was going to call you today." She listened then said, "No, I'm not upset anymore about the rescue crew being withdrawn. I'm beginning to believe you're right. He can't be in that mountain." She looked at Charles, who nodded. "Oh, yes, Josh told me he'd sent in his resignation. It's too bad but don't worry, Mike, Kate and I will follow up on any leads we get." For the next few minutes, Caroline let Adam talk then said, "Well, if you really think you should go to Switzerland, I'll call Jensen and…oh, he's already agreed? Okay. Call me if you find out anything. Thanks so much, Adam. Bye now."

Caroline turned off the phone with a sigh of relief. "I am so bad at subterfuge. But now at least, Adam won't be calling again for a while. We've bought a little more time."

"You did well, Caroline. I'm proud of you." He frowned. "I wonder what Adam thinks he's going to find in Switzerland. No people in the world are more discreet than the Swiss. He must have an ulterior motive. Some financial transactions of his own."

"I just can't believe we can't trust Adam anymore. What in the world happened between the two of you?"

"We had an argument just before I left. He stumbled onto some confidential information, and I lost my temper and threatened to fire him."

"Fire him? That must have been important information. Oh, that reminds me. You aren't going to be happy about this, but I insisted that Adam help me break into your computer. We retrieved some deleted files. Now wipe that look off your face. We were trying to find something that would lead us to you."

Charles tried to keep his voice calm as he casually asked what files they had retrieved.

She was about to answer when the sound of a truck interrupted her. "Oh, that must be Josh. He'll be so relieved to hear about Mike. I'll be right back." With those words, she was out the door.

He started to call her back then stopped. It didn't really matter. No one would ever guess the significance of the files regarding Judson.

Adam stared at the speakerphone he had just turned off. There was something in Caroline's voice, something unsaid that bothered him. Did she know more than she was willing to share with him? The scenario regarding the deleted files still worried him. Was Caroline aware of when the files were deleted?

He pushed back from his desk and walked over to the floor-to-ceiling windows of his office. The San Gabriel Mountains were free of smog today. He had a sudden impulse to drive to the high desert. The thought of seeing Kate made him smile.

He turned to the stack of papers on his desk. No, he needed to stay focused and tend to the business at hand. Damn it, if only Charles had included him in his plans, things could have been different. He'd been loyal to him for years, but in the end, it hadn't mattered. When he'd confronted Charles, he had been told, "You're out of your league, Adam." And that had been that.

Well, Charles may not have seen fit to include him in the cartel's scheme, but he now had information that could ruin all their plans if he leaked it.

Maybe a little blackmail could buy him a piece of the pie. He looked at his Rolex watch. His meeting with the partners in twenty minutes would help him come to a decision. A good promotion from them, and he could afford to be altruistic, release the information to the public and let the chips fall where they may. Otherwise, he was off to Switzerland and then on to meetings with Charles's international partners. He might as well share in the windfall that would result if the cartel's plans succeeded.

Happy to be able to give Josh good news, Caroline threw herself into his arms.

"Well, hello! Missed me, did you?"

"I was just on my way to find you! Kate called. Mike woke up, and the prognosis is good. Our prayers have been answered!"

Josh leaned back to look into her eyes then gently pulled her into an embrace again. Finally, he moved away and said, "Thank God. Do you want to fly up there today?"

"Absolutely! Let me throw some clothes into a bag in case we decide to spend the night."

When she reentered the house, Charles was again on his cell phone. She stood in the doorway. Only by listening to his many calls had she gleaned any information. Both Josh and she had tried to get him to open up, but his answers to all their questions had been evasive.

Charles saw her and waved her into the room. He hung up the phone without saying good-bye, a habit Caroline had always found disconcerting.

"So," he said, "you gave Josh the good news. Are you two going to the hospital today?"

"Yes, if you're sure that you will be okay."

"I'll be fine. You need a break, and I know you'll feel better if you talk to the doctors yourself."

"Don't you think it would be wise to get more men here for protection? I know Leroy's a good bodyguard, but with Josh gone, he's just one man."

"I'm not really worried about my safety yet. I'm more concerned that I haven't been able to figure out who's behind all this. We could use your ESP abilities."

Caroline pursed her lips and raised one eyebrow. "You mean that after all the years you made fun of me, you now admit there just might be something to the idea?"

"Well, deductive reasoning certainly didn't come to my rescue. The only way I could get the necessary information to you was to trust your ESP. And by god, you did pick up on the haunted mine." He paused then said, "I'll take whatever help I can get to find out which one of my enemies out there is behind this."

"You have more than one?"

Caroline waited while Charles adjusted his pillows allowing for a higher sitting position, wincing slightly from his injured hip. Except for looking pale, he was the same self-confident man she remembered. She wished, however, he would talk more about his experience in the mountain.

Finally, Charles answered her question. "Every successful businessman has more than one enemy. But we compete with each other. We don't kill one another, for Pete's sake! I admit to a few ruthless financial moves in the past, particularly in the eighties. I had some unpleasant confrontations. I remember one young man harassed me for months after I took over his father's company. What was that kid's name? John Harrison's son. A few others made threats, too, but that was over twenty years ago. Most of the men affected by those takeovers went on to build new companies."

"So you don't have any idea who could be behind this?" Caroline asked.

Again he hesitated. She walked over to the bed. "Charles, if you want me to stay here and help you, you're going to have to trust me. I'm not going to risk my life or the lives of my friends if you're going to keep us in the dark."

He frowned. "I wouldn't know where to start."

"Start with the computer files. Explain the surveys and diagrams of the land you purchased in Nevada."

Apparently seeing the determination in her eyes, he said, "Come over here."

She sat beside him on the bed.

He reached out and took one of her hands, raising her fingers to his lips. She felt herself blush, and she moved away. Instead of appearing hurt, he seemed amused. She moved back to the settee. Charles began talking as though nothing had passed between them.

"First, forget about the computer files. They're unimportant. I'm just buying some land in Judson, Nevada for business purposes. In fact, you and Josh can do me a favor and fly there on your way back to pick up some contracts. But in regard to my suspect list, let's start with my charming wife, Brenda. I know she's perfectly capable of working with my partners to take advantage of my possible demise. After all, she'd inherit my shares and would be happy to sell them to Jenson and the others, if the price were right. On the other hand, although she's greedy and selfish, I don't believe she or my partners have the necessary contacts or balls to pull off something like this. And they don't know about Odessa. No one in the company knows." He paused. "Except for Adam." Caroline didn't respond. She refused to believe that Adam was capable of murder.

"I know how you feel about Adam," he said, "and I admit he's been invaluable to me over the years, but he crossed the line. I had to put him in his place, and he didn't appreciate it. However, that was only a month or so ago, and you can't put together a scheme like this on the spur of a moment. It takes careful planning. Of course, that doesn't mean he didn't provide information to the culprits, either innocently or deliberately."

Caroline remembered that Brenda knew Charles had planned to get together with her. When she said as much, he nodded. "I'm sure Adam told her. He probably aligned himself with her after our fight."

"You keep referring to this argument. What did Adam find out that upset you so much?"

"He wanted in on something way over his head. When I pointed that out, he pushed. I pushed back, and things got a bit heated."

"Maybe he expected some reward for all his hard work."

"He pulls down a good salary and has plenty of perks by working for me. Besides, this wasn't personal. It was business."

"And people always come second to business with you, don't they?" Caroline said.

"Not where you're concerned." Charles's eyes were so loving that she had to look away, but she wasn't going to be distracted.

"Okay, let me get this straight. You doubt that Brenda, your partners or Adam were the masterminds behind your abduction, except perhaps to provide information. So who does that leave?"

"I have a few other suspects, but we'll talk more about that later. You get packed and go see Mike. I know you want to see for yourself that he's going to be okay."

Caroline knew Charles had deliberately changed the subject. She also knew he was not being truthful about the computer files. It was clear that if they wanted more information, she and Josh were going to have to find out for themselves.

CHAPTER SIXTEEN

Josh circled the field once then landed at the Judson airport. He's such a good pilot, Caroline thought, watching him at the controls. Yesterday's trip to the hospital had been reassuring. The doctors were optimistic that Mike would make a full recovery. They had spent last evening and most of this morning with Mike and Kate. It was hard to leave them, but Caroline knew Mike was getting the care he needed. Charles was still recuperating in Odessa, and she needed to get back to help him. Hopefully, this Judson stopover wouldn't take long.

The plane taxied toward a black Bronco beside the airstrip. Linda Jamison walked across the runway to meet them as they climbed out of the plane. She barely resembled the frightened woman they'd met weeks ago. Her first words told Caroline more than she wanted to know about her relationship with Charles.

"He's really all right? I couldn't believe it when he called to tell me you were coming. He was in some kind of accident? Where is he now?"

Josh ignored the last question and assured her that Charles was fine. The look on her face brought back unhappy memories to

Caroline of other women who had been infatuated with Charles when he was her husband.

"I assume Charles explained why we're here, Mrs. Jamison," Josh said.

"Please, call me Linda. Yes. Here's the paperwork." She handed him a folder. "It just needs Charles's signature. He said he'd have it notarized and returned immediately." She paused then asked, "When do you think he'll be able to travel?"

"You mean come to Nevada to see you?" Caroline asked. Hearing the coolness in her own voice and seeing the color rise in the other woman's face, Caroline felt ashamed. She had no right to take a proprietary stance where Charles was concerned. She softened her tone. "I mean, do you need anything else from him? He may not be able to come here for a few weeks."

Josh had been quietly listening to their conversation. "Is that a problem, Linda?"

"No, not really, I just thought he might need my help when...." She stopped. "Oh, never mind, just tell him to call me."

As she walked away, Caroline looked at Josh.

"Don't worry, I'm having her watched," he assured her.

"Does Charles know that?"

"No. And I think we'll keep it that way for the time being. However, if we come up with anything, we'll take it to him."

Caroline stared after Linda Jamison. Linda knew more than she was telling them, but her loyalty obviously was to Charles.

Linda drove the Bronco slowly through the streets of Judson, not ready to return to her boring job, mundane life and a husband who kept bugging her about having children. Now that Charles's ex-wife was back in the picture, she knew her affair with him was over. In her heart, she had always known that once the land deal was finalized, and Charles didn't need her anymore, he'd be gone. She didn't know what she would miss more—Charles, or the excitement and intrigue he brought into her world.

She turned into the driveway leading to the real estate office. Behind her, she saw the same old Ford pick-up she'd seen earlier in the week. Someone must be visiting friends. No tourists ever came here. It was too far out of the way.

She smiled to herself. But that's soon going to change—big time!

When Linda drove around to the back parking lot, she saw two men walking toward a red Corvette. She pulled into her parking space on the far side of the lot. Peering through the side mirror, she watched as a young man opened the driver's door, and an older man with a goatee climbed in the passenger side.

For some reason, she had the feeling that the men were looking for her.

I need to finish this business with Charles, she thought. I'm getting paranoid.

Caroline was glad to be back in Odessa. Their trip had reassured her about Mike, and now she could concentrate on getting Charles back to health.

She sat on the porch, drinking her morning coffee and watching Josh's face as he listened on his cell phone to his contact in Judson.

"Okay, stick close by her. I'll get back to you."

"What's going on?" Caroline asked.

"I'm not sure. But I've changed my mind about telling Charles we're having Linda watched. Come on. Let's go talk to him."

Entering the parlor, they found Charles surrounded by papers on his bed. He was angrily complaining that the battery of his laptop had just died.

"Leroy, take these damn batteries down to the motel and charge them again." He tossed him his cell phone. "Charge my cell phone, too, while you're at it."

As soon as Leroy left the room, Charles's face brightened. Caroline had often seen this transformation. He was his most charming after an outburst, leaving everyone around him wary and uneasy.

"I'm glad to see you two. I have the papers ready for Linda."

"Really? Notarized, too?" Josh asked, looking surprised. Caroline wasn't. She had assumed Leroy was a notary public. Charles's employees always wore more than one hat.

"Everything's ready to go," Charles said, "and I need for you to get back to Judson right away. But before you leave, go get the wheelchair from the storage shed. I want to look around, and it's a bit farther than I can probably handle just yet. Caroline can push me around."

Turning to her, he asked, "Have you read the history of the town?" She nodded. "Well, I've learned even more over the years from Malcolm and a few of the other desert residents on this mountain."

"I thought we were alone up here," Caroline said.

"Not completely. On the other side of the mountain, there's a scattering of cabins."

Josh interrupted. "Charles, this is all very interesting, but we came to talk to you about something urgent that's come up." He talked about the surveillance he'd ordered.

"Let me get this straight," Charles said, in a hard, cold voice. "You're working for me, but you put a tail on Linda without my knowledge?"

Josh glared back at him. "No. Before I took on this job with you, I arranged to have Linda watched. We were doing whatever it took to find you."

"Well, I'm found, so stop the surveillance. As of today!"

"Have you been listening to me? My man says someone besides him is interested in Linda. Two strangers are in town asking questions about her. Now, assuming she's a key player in this land deal that you refuse to discuss, it seems to me you'd want someone looking out for her."

Caroline watched for Charles's reaction. So few people stood up to him. He didn't like having his orders questioned, even if the argument made sense.

He finally said, "Okay, you have a point. I'll call Linda and let her know what's going on. Tell your contact to introduce himself and stay by her side until we find out who these men are. In fact, when you go to Judson, stick around until you're sure things are under control. Leroy and I will handle things here."

"What a gorgeous day!" Charles exclaimed, as Caroline pushed his wheelchair down the hard packed sandy street.

"See that building over there. Know what it was?" Caroline wheeled him closer. "I believe," she said, "that it was marked bathhouse on your layout of the town. The miners had to come here to get a bath or haircut, right?"

"Right. But they didn't come often. A keg of water cost $5.00, and miners only made $2.00 a week. Actually, bathing was considered unhealthy, so no one complained. Some of the more affluent families in town did have tubs, but the whole family washed in the same water."

"I can't imagine Jessica having to deal with that."

"Who?"

"Jessica, the woman who lived in the house."

"Oh, yes, of course. Well, it was common practice in those days."

He gestured with a broad sweep of his arm to the next building down the road.

"Let's go over there. I want to show you something."

When they reached a tall, weathered building, Charles pointed to an iron grill in the top of the door. "Look inside."

Caroline peered in. Large half-barrels sat in the middle of the building, along with bellows, an anvil and a long-handled sledgehammer.

"The barrels you see," Charles explained, "were for cooling the hot metal quickly. The blacksmith was one of the most important men in town. He repaired tools, made horse and mule shoes, nails, hinges and sharpened the miner's drill bits."

"In other words," Caroline added, "He was indispensable."

"Yes, especially when it came to the rims for wagon wheels."

He looked toward the side of the building. "Pretty clear what that wagon over there was used for, isn't it?" At first, she thought he was referring to a two-seated buggy with large wheels, but following his gaze, she saw a long, crudely built, decaying wooden box on a flat wagon bed.

Charles smiled, grimly. "The other busiest man in town built coffins. Most miners didn't live to a ripe old age. The mountain killed them, one way or the other."

He stared down the street toward the mines. Sweat broke out on his forehead.

Caroline understood now what this tour was all about. Charles could relate to the men who had once lived in this town. Men who had braved the darkness of the mines to support their families. Charles was trying to tell her about his terrible experience, without talking about it.

She reached out and touched his shoulder. He shrugged away her hand.

"Let's head back," he said.

It was cold. And dark. Black dark.

He couldn't move. He was trapped...trapped in the darkness that weighed down on his body, a monstrous pressure that was going to crush him unless....

Charles told himself that he was dreaming—to wake up. And he did.

Feeling cold, he began tugging at the sheets twisted around his legs, searching in the dark for the rest of his covers. He reached down and yanked hard. The jumble of covers came loose, and he pulled one of the blankets over his shoulders. He breathed in and out, reminding himself that he wasn't trapped anymore. He never had to go into that damn mountain again.

The dreams came every other night or so. Before the kidnapping, he seldom remembered his dreams. Most nights he worked late, slept a few hours and was back to work early the next morning. Now, his days were long. He had time to think, time to worry.

What had he gotten himself and the others into? If Barton was behind this, Charles knew he had brought all this on himself and the others. But it wasn't supposed to turn out this way. Played right, the success of the cartel's plans would make them heroes, at least on the west coast. But now, he was in hiding and had to worry about Caroline's safety, as well as Linda and the others.

Through the bedroom wall, he heard the squeak of bedsprings. Maybe he should send Caroline home. She was right. Leroy was only one man. Josh would be gone a good deal chasing leads. Maybe.... The glow of a kerosene lamp filled the room, and a voice whispered from the back doorway, "Charles? Are you awake?"

"Come on in." Before she reached his bed, Leroy was at the front door. Peering through the screen, he asked, "Everything okay, Boss?"

"Go back to sleep, Leroy. I'm fine."

Caroline set the lamp on one of the marble-topped small tables and started adjusting his covers.

"Did I wake you?" he asked.

She shook her head. "No, I just had a feeling I should check on you. The nights have gotten cold." She tucked the blanket around him. "There. Do you need anything else?"

He held out his hand. "Come sit here with me." She sat on the bed, pulling her robe tightly around her. Charles cleared his throat. "I've... well, I've been having these dreams every night or so, and it's hard to get back to sleep."

"What kind of dreams?"

He didn't answer.

"About the mountain?"

He nodded, unable to get the words out.

She took his hand in hers. "Talk to me, Charles. I know how horrible it must have been for you. I can't bear to even think about you trapped inside that mountain, and you had to actually live through it!"

Charles felt tears well up. He coughed and turned away, mortified that he couldn't control them.

Caroline's hand touched his face. "I know, it's all right," she said.

He took her hand and pulled her down beside him. Neither spoke again before they fell asleep.

CHAPTER SEVENTEEN

From the kitchen, Caroline heard her cell phone ring. She dried her hands and hurried to the bedroom.

"Hello?"

"Good morning!" Josh's voice brought feelings of guilt, which was ridiculous since she'd only fallen asleep beside Charles.

"How are things in Judson?" she asked.

Josh assured her Linda was okay and that he'd be returning in a few hours. She was glad but nervous. The thought of having both men in such close proximity was unsettling.

"Caroline! More coffee!" Charles's voice ended the conversation. She went back to the kitchen, grabbed the coffee pot off the wood burning stove and carried it with her to the parlor. Pouring Charles another cup of coffee, she sat on the settee and told him about Josh's call. He was relieved to hear all was well in Nevada. Caroline started to ask again why he was buying land in such a remote area, but before she could speak, he said, "As soon as the papers are filed, we can relax. If this whole scheme was to keep me from finalizing the land deal, then we win and they lose!"

"Whoever 'they' are."

Charles sipped his coffee. Caroline knew he was about to change the subject as he always did when she pressed him for answers.

"I've been thinking about something," he said. "I remember joking once about a haunted mine I owned. Now if I could just remember where the hell I was at the time.

"Anyway, the contracts are signed, and so hopefully the danger is over. Now I don't have to worry about you, and you can stay in Odessa with me. Which makes me very happy, especially after last night. I loved waking up with you in my arms."

Caroline wasn't surprised that he was putting his own spin on what had happened.

It was her turn to change the subject. "You know I'm worried about Leroy. Is he warm enough sleeping out there on the porch at night?"

Charles laughed. "Warmer than we are. He's in a down sleeping bag. Trust me. He loves being outside. His favorite vacation is hunting in Alaska, sleeping in a tent. You don't have to worry about Leroy."

"I guess you're right. He hasn't complained." She stood. "I think I'll go over to the saloon and make sure everything is ready for Kate and Mike's arrival."

Charles was on his cell phone before she reached the door.

Outside, Leroy sat on a chair with his feet on the porch railing. He jumped up. "The boss want me?"

"No, but I could use your help. Since Josh is on his way back, and Kate and Mike are arriving this afternoon, I think we should celebrate with a barbecue tonight." Leroy grinned, surprising her. He seldom smiled.

"And I'd like for you to dig a fire pit on the ledge over there. There's lots of dry wood around. It would make a great bonfire."

"Yes ma'am, that sounds like a good idea. If the boss doesn't need me, I'll get right to it."

"Charles is glued to his phone again. When he's off, I'll let him know what you're doing."

Leroy sauntered away, wearing his gun openly in a shoulder holster. Caroline suspected he was enjoying this adventure more than the rest of them.

"This is great!" Kate said, looking around the main room of the old saloon in Odessa. Mike's bed was set up where the bar had once been. Doors led to two other rooms that had been converted into bedrooms for Josh and her.

"I want to sit outside and have a cigarette," Mike said.

"No way, no smoking. Doctor's orders. And he said you were to get in bed the minute we got here. You can get up after you rest for a while." She turned away before he could say more, calling out, "I'll be right back. I want to run over to the house and get us something to drink."

"Make mine a beer."

"Ha!"

Caroline and Josh were outside the house talking. When Kate reached them, she raised her arms over her head and twirled in the street.

"I love this place!" They both laughed.

"I came over to grab some drinks for Mike and me."

"Now that sounds like a good idea," Josh said. "Grab a Coke for me."

"There's an assortment of sodas in the ice chest on the porch," Caroline said. She felt strangely content, as though her family were home. Leroy had helped prepare the impromptu barbecue and was placing chairs around the fire pit.

"Here you go—catch!" Kate tossed a can of Coke to Josh and ran back to the saloon.

The fire leapt higher as Leroy added more wood. The smoke drifted into a night sky ablaze with stars.

The yipping of coyotes broke the silence.

"Oh, Lordy," Kate said. "I hope they aren't too close by."

"You're not scared of a few scrawny coyotes, are you?" Mike said, reaching over to take her hand, apparently trusting the dark to hide the gesture.

Kate relaxed, lulled by the warmth of the fire and the beauty of the desert night. Looking around the campfire circle, she studied the faces of the others.

Charles was an impressive figure, but it irritated her that everyone kowtowed to him, even Josh. Except when it came to Caroline. Then Josh seemed to ignore the fact that Charles was his boss. He looked at Caroline the same way he always had, much to Charles's obvious displeasure.

Leroy sat off to himself, almost hidden in the shadows. A strange man, totally devoted to Charles.

I wonder if he has a family of his own, Kate thought. Probably not. He's such a loner.

Caroline was between Charles and Josh, staring into the fire, seemingly unaware of the frequent glances of both men. The glow of the fire gave her a youthful look tonight.

She's such an elegant woman, yet down to earth, too, Kate thought. No wonder the men are smitten. She even has Mike under her spell. He's less tense, more thoughtful around her.

She turned to look at him. He squeezed her hand. She looked away but didn't let go of his hand.

Mike smiled at Kate's shyness. The firelight lit the auburn curls that framed her sweet face. The small hand in his felt fragile, but he knew how fiercely brave she could be.

Why did he give her such a hard time? Was he afraid she would capture his heart and then leave him like...? But maybe Kate didn't feel the same way he did. Why would a girl like her be interested in someone like him? Still, something in his gut told him she was, and she probably didn't understand the attraction any more than he did.

Out of the corner of her eye, Caroline saw Mike and Kate holding hands. It made her happy. She believed they needed one another.

Caroline glanced at Josh. Did she need someone like him to balance the reappearance of Charles in her life? Might she otherwise make a mistake?

She could feel Charles's presence on her other side. The space around and above them must seem like heaven to him after his weeks of entrapment. Coming to Odessa to hide out had been a wise decision. Maybe by facing the mountain, he would find a place in his mind for the horrific memories of his ordeal. And perhaps in this peaceful old ghost town, they could sort out their feelings for one another.

Charles stared up into the canopy of stars. He had visualized this scene so many times in the mountain. He was grateful to be here, but although he wasn't trapped anymore, he wouldn't feel truly free until he was completely in control of his world again. Or was that only an illusion? Maybe he'd never really been in control.

A murmur of voices interrupted his train of thought. Josh was talking to Caroline. She started to laugh.

Now here was something he could control. He could send Josh on another trip.

Josh loved to hear Caroline laugh. It had been a long time since he'd enjoyed anyone's company so much. Hopefully, the worst of this strange crisis was over, and they could spend more time together.

Of course, he knew that would not make his new boss happy. Well, too damn bad. The only reason he'd taken the job was to protect Caroline, Kate and Mike. As soon as they solved the mystery of Charles's kidnapping, he could focus his complete attention on this extraordinary woman.

Maybe he could convince her to visit his ranch. He'd invite her to Colorado and Charles be damned!

He leaned over and threw another piece of wood on the fire. As it blazed up, he noticed Leroy in the shadows staring at him.

Leroy scowled at Josh through narrowed eyes. Who the hell did the son of a bitch think he was? He was either stupid or braver than most men. Not that the boss would let him get away with it. He knew how to protect his own interests.

Of course, Caroline shouldn't be flirting with the man.

But then—what goes 'round, does come 'round. He'd heard stories about their marriage, although he hadn't been with Charles back then. He'd started working for him after he married Brenda. God, what a bitch. But she'd be gone soon, and Caroline would be back.

The boss always got what he wanted.

CHAPTER EIGHTEEN

The ringing of his cell phone woke Josh from a deep sleep. For a moment, he couldn't separate the sound from the confusion of his dream. Then he couldn't find the phone. By the time he said, "Hello," he was wide awake.

"I was afraid you weren't going to pick up."

"I was sound asleep, Thompson. What time is it anyway?"

"Four-thirty. I'm sorry, but I couldn't wait any longer. I've been up all night traveling, only to find out she isn't here. I think I've been had."

Josh tried to make sense of what he was hearing. Thompson had been ordered to stick close to Linda until he was told otherwise.

"Where the hell are you? More importantly, where's Linda?"

There was a brief pause, and Josh knew he wasn't going to like what he was about to hear.

"I blew it. After Laughery called and told Linda he wanted someone to keep an eye on her, she was very cooperative. Since she didn't want her husband to know anything, I tried to keep out of sight. I've been seeing her home safely then going back to the motel restaurant to eat supper before camping out in her neighborhood during the night. It never occurred to me that she'd skip off while I was gone."

"Damn," Josh muttered.

"When I got back to the house last night, her Bronco was gone. She was supposed to call me if she left the house. She didn't answer her cell, so I went to the door and asked her husband where she was, pretending I wanted some real estate information. He said she was delivering paperwork to another desert town and planned to spend the night there. But when I get to this godforsaken place, I find out she hasn't checked into the only motel in town. I've been driving around all night looking for her Bronco with no luck. I don't have a good feeling about this."

"Well, maybe she drove back to Judson last night."

"You don't get the picture, Josh. There's one road out here. One. I couldn't have missed her. But I'll call her husband. Of course, he's getting suspicious, so we probably should clue him in on what's going on."

"Just tell him you're working for someone important who needs to get in contact with her. I'll fly to Judson and take it from there. I assume you're in your own car. Where's the old pick-up you bought for surveillance?"

"It's parked at the airport. But I have the keys."

"That's no problem. I can hotwire it. Listen, get some rest, and I'll call you after I've talked to Charles this morning."

Josh washed up and got dressed. He walked quietly past Kate's bedroom and through the saloon. Mike was snoring. The morning sky was lightening outside, and as he walked through the swinging doors, he ran into Leroy. "What the...? You scared the shit out of me."

"Thought I heard something over here. Just checking it out."

Josh nodded, catching his breath. "Sure. Good job."

He hurried over to the small house. When he opened the door to the parlor, Charles awoke and sat up in bed. "What's going on?"

Josh told him.

"What kind of men do you hire?! I should have taken care of this myself."

"Thompson's always done a good job for me. Although I admit, in this case, he didn't use good judgment. Anyway, I'm going to fly to Judson and check out things myself."

"When you get there, go straight to the courthouse and find out if Linda registered the deeds. Hopefully, by the time you arrive, she will have contacted me." He reached for his phone, pushed a programmed number, waited then said, "Linda, this is Charles. Call me the goddamn minute you get this message!"

"What in the world is happening?" Caroline stood in the back of the room.

Josh started to answer, but Charles said, "Get going! I want to know about the deeds immediately."

"Before you find out about Linda?" Josh asked, his tone cool.

Charles frowned.

"I'm sure Linda is okay but of course, call me the minute you find her."

Josh stood at the front door of the adobe house. This had always been his least favorite part as a private investigator. Although he never took on cases where he had to spy on spouses, he often had to ask embarrassing questions. This poor guy hadn't a clue what his wife was up to.

Josh looked at his watch—7:45 a.m. A vintage 1964 Pontiac GTO sat in the driveway but no Bronco. Josh rang the doorbell.

The man who opened the door looked bewildered. "Mr. Logan?" he said. "Your friend, Mr. Thompson, called and told me that you'd be coming by. Didn't expect you so soon though. I've been trying to call Linda on her cell phone. I guess he told you she's not at the motel. I'm Gus. Come on in."

Josh held out his hand. "Hi, Gus. The name's Josh. Sorry to drop by so early."

He stepped into the small house that was attractively decorated in Southwestern colors. Josh was surprised the Jamisons could afford such expensive furniture, wall hangings and pictures.

"Would you like a cup of coffee?"

"That would be great. Make it black."

Josh took advantage of the few minutes alone to walk over to a desk in the corner that was covered with papers. Most appeared to be real estate listings. Before he could look closer, however, Linda's husband reappeared.

Gus placed two mugs of coffee on the custom-made coffee table, a large glass covering a piece of seasoned driftwood. The table separated two small couches. Josh sat on one of them, drank his coffee and studied Linda's husband as he rambled on.

"Mr. Thompson said you'd explain the situation. But I don't think there's anything to worry about. Linda probably changed her plans without letting me know. She's done that a few times lately. I mean I'm sure everything's fine...." He stopped.

Josh was perplexed. Two strangers appear in your life looking for your wife who isn't answering her phone and can't be found. And you're sure everything is fine?

He set his coffee cup down.

"Gus, I think we need to go over a few things. What do you know about Linda's latest transactions?"

Gus began talking about several houses Linda had recently sold. None fit the description of Charles's land purchases.

While he talked, Josh studied the oil painting over the fireplace, recognizing the style of one of his favorite artists, Diego Rivera.

"Is that an original?"

Gus shrugged. "I guess. That's Linda's thing, not mine."

Josh leaned forward. "Let's cut to the chase, Gus. Linda's been working for a very powerful man from out of state. She's acquired a lot of property for him. I work for the same man.

"Linda should have filed some important papers yesterday. I'm going to check that out as soon as the courthouse opens. If she did, then you may be right, there's just been a mix-up, and she'll be home soon. However, if she didn't, it puts a whole different slant on things, and we'll need to talk again."

The look of fear that Josh had expected to see earlier appeared. "I can't really tell you much more," Gus said. "Linda's been meeting with some man for almost two years now. It was confidential, so she couldn't talk about it. He paid good for her time, and when everything's settled, her commission is supposed to be…well, a lot.

"Then this guy just disappears. For weeks, she can't get hold of him. Finally, he calls her. He's been sick or something and wants her to finish up on everything as fast as possible. That's it. That's all I know."

Josh stood. "Thanks, Gus. I'd like for you to stick around today. Take off work, if you can. Linda might call, and I'm going to need your help later if I find the deeds weren't registered. Can you do that?"

"Yeah. Okay."

Poor guy, Josh thought. I just opened up Pandora's Box for him, and he's not going to like what he finds.

"You're sure?!" Charles shouted over the phone. Josh held it away from his ear then said, "I'm sure. Nothing has been registered in your name. I'm on my way to the real estate office now. If the paperwork isn't there, I'll get Gus's permission to search their house. But Charles, common sense tells me we're not going to find anything."

Josh waited for the expletives to stop before he continued. "I think the next step is to involve the police, both local and state. Treat it like a missing person case. In the meantime, Thompson and I will do our own search."

"Okay. Be sure to call me right away after you check the office and house. I don't want you back here until you come up with something. I don't care how long it takes!"

"Charles, there's one more thing. I'm worried about Caroline, Mike and Kate. I don't think they're safe in Odessa."

After a few seconds of silence, Charles said, "Let's not jump to conclusions, Josh. Linda could call any minute. Even if she doesn't, it doesn't mean anything happened to her. If someone made her an offer she couldn't refuse...."

"But you've trusted her up to now," Josh said.

"Things change. Our relationship is basically over, and you know what they say about a woman scorned. If someone offered her enough to get out of town and away from the life she finds stifling—who knows? But I promise you, if I decide anyone here is in danger, I'll get them out."

Turning off the phone, Josh sat in his car thinking about the sudden turn of events.

They needed to find Linda Jamison.

She counted the money again. Never had she seen so much cash before. Six months. That wasn't a long time. Then she could go back. Get her paintings and some furniture, divorce Gus and live wherever she wanted. Forget Charles. She'd have an exciting life of her own.

I'll call Gus tonight and tell him some story, she thought. He believes anything. He'll cover for me.

The knock on the door startled her.

Room service already? Well, that was quick.

CHAPTER NINETEEN

Charles sat on the front porch of the house in Odessa. The gun Leroy had given him was on a bench next to his chair. Caroline had taken Mike and Kate to Malcolm's for lunch; it would be Mike's first outing. He'd sent Leroy with them, because Josh was right—if his abductors knew he was still alive, everyone was in danger.

He welcomed the time alone to figure out his next move. With Linda gone, he had no one he could depend on to get the job done. If the signed contracts were lost, it was going to get complicated, although another set could be drawn up fairly quickly.

His cell phone had been ringing non-stop. The cartel members wanted to know what he was going to do about the latest developments. He was point man on the project, and up until now, everything had gone according to plan. Deregulation in California had resulted in exactly what they'd hoped for. Nevada and federal officials were now on board behind the scenes. The scientific team was ready and waiting to build on the selected site. Once public fears were addressed and quieted, everyone would benefit—a win-win situation. Granted, the cartel would reap the real financial windfall, but after years of hard work, they deserved it.

"*I* deserve it," Charles said out loud.

When Charles had asked about Barton, he'd heard surprising news. His old enemy had been out of the picture for several months, apparently getting treatment for prostate cancer. His illness had been kept quiet, not unusual in the world of high finance, where no one wanted to appear weak, even from illness.

Was he up to masterminding my kidnapping? And if it wasn't him....

The sound of a car engine broke into his thoughts. Charles reached for the gun beside him and laid it in his lap.

He immediately recognized the Porsche that pulled up. The engine turned off, but no one got out of the car. Charles couldn't see through the tinted glass windows, but he could imagine the stunned look on Adam's face. Finally, the door opened.

Adam's look of astonishment and relief reassured Charles, and he put the gun back on the bench.

"My god, Charles!"

In a few strides, Adam was on the porch with his hand outstretched. Charles ignored it.

"I had almost given up on you! What happened? Where have you been?"

Every word and gesture seemed sincere.

Charles waited a few seconds before responding.

"I was wondering when you'd get back from Europe, Adam. My buddies in the cartel tell me you've been harassing the hell out of them. Have you got a death wish, old buddy?"

Anger filled Adam's eyes. "They knew you were alive and didn't tell me? I can't believe it! What's with those men?"

"Those men would like to keep me alive, and, you, my friend—they don't trust."

Adam lowered his eyes then looked up. "I can see how my recent actions might look suspicious. But I really thought you were dead. I decided the cartel could use my expertise with you gone."

"In other words, you planned to blackmail them. Adam, you're such a fool. You're lucky to be standing here. These men don't take well to extortion. Okay, you played your one card, and you lost. Now tell me what you've done since I disappeared and don't leave out a single detail."

Charles listened until Adam ended his monologue with, "When I found out that Caroline had retrieved the files that I deleted from your computer, I knew I had to move fast. And I—"

"Exactly which files did she and Josh see?"

"The land surveys and diagrams of earthquake faults and water levels. But they'll never be able to figure out anything from just those files."

As soon as they pulled up behind Adam's car, Caroline jumped from the SUV and hurried toward the porch. Leroy and Kate helped Mike out and followed.

When she reached Adam, Caroline said, "I'm sorry. I couldn't tell you."

He shrugged. "I understand...I guess."

She stooped beside Charles. "Are you okay?"

He waved away the question. "I need to talk to you."

Following Charles into the house, she looked back to see Kate hugging Adam, while Mike stood beside them, frowning.

Without coaxing, Charles stretched out on the bed. Seeing Adam had apparently shaken him.

"Adam and I were discussing the files you retrieved," he said. "Tell me exactly what you think you found."

Feeling uncomfortable under the steely gaze, Caroline said, "All we could conclude was that you're interested in the land between Judson and the Colorado River. I assume you need water from the river, but I don't know why."

Charles fingered the cover on the bed. Caroline waited.

"When I was trapped in that mountain," he said, "I went over and over in my mind who would care enough to try and find me.

I could think of no one but you. I knew you wouldn't stop until you found me, dead or alive. In other words, I trusted you with my life."

Caroline moved over to sit beside him on the bed.

"So, you trust me with your life," she said, "yet you refuse to divulge any details that would explain why someone would go to such lengths to get you out of the way. Even when you ask me to stay here with you and possibly risk my own life, you refuse to confide in me."

He sighed and closed his eyes.

"Maybe we should talk about this later," she said, "I'm going to go talk to Adam."

She started to get up but Charles said, "Wait." He reached out and held onto her arm. At first, she resisted but then relaxed into an embrace. Memories of his strong body came rushing back, and she held her face up to his. His lips were firm yet tender, and for a moment, the past and present were one, the kiss between them both familiar and new. It made her feel loved and safe, and she didn't want it to end. When it did, she stayed in his arms, until he cupped her face again in his hand. Their second kiss grew in passion and intensity until Caroline could feel herself losing control. She pulled away, and before Charles could say anything, she backed off the bed and walked out of the room.

On the porch, she was greeted by several pairs of curious eyes. She hoped she didn't look as flushed and disoriented as she felt. Leroy was standing off by himself, smoking a cigarette. Mike and Kate sat on the porch steps. She chose a chair next to Adam.

"Have Kate and Mike brought you up to date?" she asked him.

"Have they ever! What a story!"

Needing to talk to Adam alone, Caroline said, "Kate, honey, why don't you and Leroy help Mike over to the saloon. He really should rest."

"I've been trying to get him there! Come on, Mike, stop being so stubborn. Caroline's right." She took his arm and with Leroy's help, they walked away.

Adam followed them with his eyes.

"Kate and Mike have gotten close, haven't they?" he said.

"People tend to bond during a crisis. Now, I want you to tell me everything you found out in Europe." Adam glanced toward the front door of the house. She grabbed his arm.

"For heavens sake, come with me!" Adam followed her back into the house.

Once inside, she said, "Charles, Adam obviously needs your permission to open his mouth! Give it to him!"

Charles motioned for them to sit down. "I think it's time we take you into our confidence."

Caroline saw Adam's face. She felt the same sense of amazement. Was Charles really ready to confide in her?

"Okay," Charles began, "Adam wanted in on a very big project. "He'd pieced together confidential information and found out the names of members of the international cartel that originated the project. I'm not at liberty to give you details, but let's just say that it's been a long and arduous journey to get to where we are now.

"After my disappearance, my partners in Los Angeles didn't offer Adam enough incentive to stay on with them if I never came back. So he took it upon himself to seek out the cartel members in Europe and attempted to blackmail them into cutting him into a piece of the action—a very dumb move."

Adam sat in the corner, staring at the floor.

"When these men generously let him return to the States with his head still attached to his body, they called and forewarned me about my trusted assistant. Of course, Adam had no idea that I'd be his welcoming committee when he came to Odessa to see you. Is that about right, Adam?"

He looked up. "That's right. But if you'd treated me with a little respect, I might have been able to help you. Instead, you threatened to ruin me if I disclosed what I discovered."

Before Charles could respond, he continued, "Regardless, I'd like to help now. I can go back and cover for you in LA. Or stay here, unless you don't want me around."

"On the contrary," Charles said, his smile not reaching his eyes. "You know what they say about keeping your enemies close.

"Now, I need to make a few phone calls, and then I'll tell you what I want you to do. Caroline, why don't you and Adam take a walk."

As they left the house and headed down the sandy road toward the mountain, Adam said, "Well, that was fun. What do you think? Am I back in his good graces?"

"I think you're on probation, and for goodness sakes, Adam, don't blow it. You may not want to work for Charles again after this is over, but you don't want to shoot yourself in the other foot."

Kate was sitting in front of the saloon.

"Want to take a walk with us?" Adam called out.

"Sure. Mike and Leroy are in the middle of a serious poker game. They won't miss me."

Kate chattered away as they continued down the street. When they reached the mountain, Adam stared upwards.

"I can't believe Charles actually spent time alone in there. How could he survive something like that emotionally unscathed?"

"I don't think he did," Caroline said.

"He seems the same to me," Adam grumbled.

Knowing Charles would not want her to discuss his nightmares or the flickers of fear she sometimes saw in his eyes, Caroline changed the subject.

"Adam, I have a few questions that Charles didn't address. Why were you so anxious to mislead the four of us when we first came to you for help? Like when you sent Mike and Kate on that bogus trip to northern California. Why didn't you want to help us find Charles? Had he really made you that angry?"

Adam glanced at Kate, who was listening, wide-eyed, then walked over to sit on the foundation of a torn-down building.

"At first," he said, "I didn't believe Charles was really missing. He had pulled so many disappearing acts over the years. And I knew that this master plan of the cartel's was about to be finalized, so part of me was covering for him.

"But as time went by, and he didn't get in touch with me, I began to believe he really might be dead. There was the wrecked car, and I knew that if he had fallen out of favor with the cartel, well.... Then I began to worry about everyone's safety, particularly you and Katie. Since you didn't know who or what you were dealing with, I was afraid you might stumble into something dangerous. Sending Mike and Kate on that trip was my feeble attempt to keep Kate safe."

"But if you believed these men to be dangerous," Caroline asked, "why did you seek them out and try to blackmail them?"

"Because, by that time, I felt I didn't have much to lose, and a lot to gain. I thought they'd need someone to help them finish their business, but Charles is right. It was stupid of me." He paused then admitted, "Actually, I was confused about what to do. For instance, I didn't want the information about Judson to come from me, because if Charles turned up, he wouldn't appreciate my talking about those land deals and his project with the cartel. But I thought someone should check it out, just in case Charles was there. So I left that anonymous note on your door in LA."

Kate frowned. "What exactly is a cartel and what is this big, secret project?"

Adam jumped up.

"I could tell you, Sweetie, but then I'd have to kill you! I'd rather race you up that ridge over there. I bet the view's terrific."

He began to jog up a small hill. Caroline watched as Kate ran after him. How different he is around her, she thought. Relaxed and easy-going. He needed someone like Kate in his life. But did she need him? Not only was he much older but far more complex than Caroline had realized. Greed had driven him to some very foolish actions. Could that happen again? And was he as innocent as he claimed to be?

CHAPTER TWENTY

The long make-shift table in front of the saloon was laden with food brought up the mountain by Malcolm—fried chicken, green beans, potato salad, deviled eggs, coleslaw and biscuits. When he pulled out two warm apple pies, Caroline patted him on the shoulder. "Malcolm, you are a true chef!"

"Cookin' always come natural to me. I'm glad you asked me up here. Haven't been to Odessa in a long time."

"You're welcome any time, Malcolm. If it hadn't been for you, we would never have found Charles. Your ghost story was the key to everything!" Malcolm looked pleased.

Kate and Adam carried a cooler with ice from Malcolm's truck and placed it beside the table. Caroline nestled bottles of beer and soft drinks into the ice and set several bottles of white and red wine on the table.

"Now that's what I call a good spread," Charles said, as he made his way to the table. "Good job, Malcolm, old friend."

Mike was already sitting at one end of the table. He hadn't taken his eyes off Kate and Adam, causing Caroline to feel a little nervous. Mike's fuse was always short, and she doubted he'd bought into Adam's story.

Malcolm began piling food on paper plates and passing them around. There was little conversation as everyone ate hungrily. They were eating their apple pie when Charles's cell phone rang.

"Laughery here. Hi, Josh, what's the news?"

Charles listened for several minutes then said, "Let me think about that. See you tomorrow." He turned to the others.

"There's no sign of Linda or the contracts. She either skipped town, or.... Josh doesn't think this place is safe anymore, and I tend to agree with him." He paused. "We'll decide what to do when he gets back here tomorrow morning."

A more subdued group finished their dessert and talked for an hour or so before heading to their respective beds. Caroline joined Charles in the parlor. She set a glass of water on the table by his bed so he could reach it during the night and tucked covers around him, knowing he was watching her every move. She was careful to stay out of his reach. There wasn't going to be a repeat of last night. Considering their contact over the years had been infrequent and only friendly, his sudden decision to reenter her life romantically was disconcerting.

"Caroline," he said, "we need to talk."

She sat on the settee.

"Josh is right," he said. "It's become too dangerous for the rest of you to stay in Odessa, especially now that Adam is here." He held up his hand. "I realize you think he just made a foolish mistake, but we don't know that for sure. What we do know is that it's only a matter of time before the rest of the world finds out I'm alive.

"We need a place where all of you will be safe until this is over. Josh suggested that he fly you to his ranch in Colorado. He has a spread there, and the location is relatively isolated. You would be safe and comfortable, and I wouldn't have to worry about you."

Caroline was stunned. She'd envisioned leaving as soon as Charles was up and around. But Colorado?

"Charles! You can't just ship us off to another state. For heaven's sake, I agreed to stay here and help you, not go for a vacation on some ranch." She immediately saw the change in Charles's face. He wasn't going to take no for an answer.

"This isn't up for negotiation. Josh is afraid that harm has come to Linda. I prefer to believe she's just skipped out, but until we have proof of that, I can't risk your lives. I got you into this mess, and now it's my responsibility to protect you until I can get you out. So like it or not, Josh is taking you to Colorado tomorrow, and that's final!"

Caroline knew it was futile to argue. In the end, Charles would prevail. And undoubtedly Josh would back him up.

"All right, we'll go," she said, "but this is definitely going to be temporary."

Charles smiled and reached out his hand, but she ignored it.

"I'm serious, Charles. I don't enjoy danger and intrigue the way you do. And I hate it that Mike and Katie are caught up in all this craziness. You need to get your life straightened out so the rest of us can get on with ours!"

Early the next morning, Caroline waited on the landing strip behind the motel searching the eastern sky for a sign of Josh's plane.

A dot appeared over the far mountains. It got bigger and soon the engine of the plane could be heard. She watched as it came closer and closer until Josh circled the motel then set the Cessna down. He taxied to where she was standing.

On the trip back up the mountain Caroline told him everything that had happened since he'd left. "Charles wasn't as upset over the computer files as I expected him to be," she said. The kiss between them flashed in her mind. "He, uh, he didn't even demand the copies back."

"He's got more to worry about than those files," Josh said. "Whatever this project is all about, people's lives are at stake. I don't know if Charles told you, but I tracked Linda to Vegas. She checked into Caesar's Palace, paid cash for her room up front. She didn't check out but no one has seen her since. Thompson is on the case, and I hope he finds her, but we're going to have to assume the worst and protect the rest of you."

They had reached Odessa, and Caroline pulled up beside Adam's Porsche.

"And now, this guy shows up again," Josh said. "Coincidence? Maybe. But I intend to keep a close eye on him."

Caroline sighed. Charles and Josh were obviously on the same page.

Kate packed as Mike complained behind her. She wasn't feeling too happy about this move either. A part of her just wanted to get in her car and go back east. Maybe come back when all this was over. But how could she leave Mike? He was still healing, and they had gotten close over the past few weeks. He really had helped her work through her feelings, almost convincing her that she wasn't responsible for—

"Kate!"

"Sorry, I was thinking about this trip. What did you say?"

"I said that I agree that you women should go, but why can't I stay? I'm okay now."

She looked at his left arm that was still in a sling and was tempted to point out the obvious. Instead, she said, "Well, maybe they want you to protect Caroline and me. Have you thought about that?"

She saw Mike's face change. Honestly, men were so easy.

"At least they aren't letting Adam come with us," he said.

Kate ignored the comment. She zipped up the last bag.

"I hope Josh can fit all this into his plane. I wonder how long it will take us to fly to Colorado. I just love flying, don't you?"

One glance at Mike, and she knew it was the wrong question.

"I've never been in a small plane before," Mike said.

Kate rolled the bags into the middle of the room. "I'm going over to the house and see if Josh and Caroline are ready. I'll be right back."

She hurried out of the saloon and was pleased to see Adam standing in front of the house. She had hoped to talk to him before they left. No one trusted him anymore, and she understood why, yet he was so sweet to her. And there were those sexy, dark eyes of his.

"Hi, there," he said, smiling down at her. "Are you ready to become a ranch hand? Listen, promise you'll call and let me know exactly where Josh's ranch is. Maybe I can join you there later, and we can go riding together. Here's my cell phone number." He handed her a business card.

Kate hesitated. "Josh didn't tell you?" she asked.

"No, apparently it's top secret for the moment."

They sat on the porch steps, the morning sun warm on their faces. Adam said, "I'm going to miss you, Katie. Except for Caroline, you're the only friendly face around here."

Kate studied Adam's handsome face. No one ever saw this vulnerable side of him. "You're very much alone, aren't you? Like Mike and me, you don't have family either, oh, except for your brother."

Adam frowned. "Jimmy doesn't consider me family anymore, but then we never did have much in common. I'm sure he's off somewhere saving the environment right now." He reached over and took her hand. "The truth is I don't miss him. You, now, I'm going to miss. When this is over, I want you to come to Los Angeles. I'll show you places you've only seen on TV. The nightlife is unbelievable, and during the day, we have the beach. And the mountains and the desert are within easy driving distance. Have you ever been to Palm Springs?"

She shook her head.

"It's beautiful. There's this canyon right outside of town—great for hiking. I have a friend there who lets me use his guesthouse whenever I want. What do you think? Doesn't that sound like fun?"

When she didn't reply, he added, "Just think about it. Don't let your buddy, Mike, talk you into staying on some ranch. You need to see something of life before you settle down."

Josh walked out onto the porch. "Ready to go, Kate?" he asked as he walked past.

Adam whispered, "Think about it, Katie. And call me when you can."

In the front of the small plane, Josh and Caroline shouted back and forth over the noise of the engine. Behind them, Kate glanced over at Mike, who was staring straight ahead, his hands gripping both sides of his seat as the plane lurched. She suppressed a smile and turned to look at the ground far below. This was a much longer and rougher ride than her first plane trip to LA, but she found it exhilarating.

She was wondering how much longer it would be when the plane began to descend into what appeared to be a large valley. Mountains rose steeply on both sides.

The late afternoon sun glinted off a large lake, and the plane seemed to be headed toward it. As they got closer, Kate could make out buildings just beyond the lake. One appeared to be a large two-story house, with several smaller houses and barns close by. She caught her breath. What a beautiful place!

The plane flew lower and lower, circling the buildings. Kate could see people now. Men waved hats. Cowboys, she thought, real cowboys!

The fire in the massive stone fireplace in the great room of the ranch house was blazing. Caroline pulled the velour cover over her legs. It must be hard to heat a room this size, she thought, looking up at the open beams overhead. She and Josh were on a black leather couch, Kate and Mike on two large chairs. In front of the couch, a tufted, leather hassock sat on a hand-woven rug. More Indian rugs hung on the walls, along with pictures of wolves, deer and horses. Thank heavens, she thought—no stuffed animals.

The planks of the pine floor were tongue and grooved. Directly behind them, on the other side of the room, a large desk fronted a wall of bookcases. In the opposite corner, there was a small organ. Beside it, Josh's two dogs, Shadow and Cody, were curled up on their padded beds, warily watching the strangers in the room.

Josh's cook, Lottie, had prepared a feast for their supper, and Caroline could barely keep her eyes open. Kate and Mike were quizzing Josh about the ranch.

"How many acres do you own?" Mike asked.

"A few thousand. About half of that I've placed under conservation easements. At least that land will never be developed and hopefully, whoever ends up with the ranch will keep the rest safe from developers. My wife and I felt strongly about that.

"There are some good ski runs around Durango, but fortunately the rich haven't invaded this area as they have Aspen and other places in Colorado."

"It's like Odessa," Caroline said. "There's so much open space and clean air and nothing as far as the eye can see. It's heaven, Josh!"

He laughed. "Well, it *is* beautiful. No doubt about that. But you haven't been through a winter here. Even I have to get back to civilization during those months. Thank God, I have a good manager. He keeps things going during the worst of the winter months and when I'm following up on leads. I couldn't do any of it without him."

Mike spoke up. "I'd love it here in the winter! Couldn't snow enough to satisfy me. When does it start?"

"There's already been some light snow, and it won't be long until we get the first big one, by Thanksgiving for sure. So you guys take advantage of the good weather now. Tomorrow I'll show you around. We'll check out your riding skills and find the right horse for each of you."

Mike and Kate looked worried.

"Don't worry, kids. We have some gentle horses. They'll take good care of you. Although Mike probably shouldn't ride quite yet."

Mike glowered, obviously ready to don a cowboy hat and boots and explore this new world.

Seeing his disappointment, Josh said, "You shouldn't have any trouble driving, however. I'll give you my jeep, and you can use it to check everything out. How's that sound?"

Mike's face brightened. "How early can I get started?"

Caroline leaned forward from the saddle to rub the sleek, long, neck of the beautiful roan Josh had picked out for her. Her name was Peaches. She was sweet and gentle, unlike Josh's stallion, Max, who needed a firm hand.

"How can you bring yourself to ever leave here, Josh?" she asked, looking down from the outcropping on the side of the mountain. Tall pines and aspen trees surrounded them.

Far below, Caroline could see the two-story ranch house. The original log house sat next to it.

The ranch hands and their families lived in small houses on the other side of the two barns. Caroline glanced at Josh, who was surveying his small kingdom with binoculars. He seemed far away. Was he thinking about the years here with his wife? How terribly lonely he must have been in this isolated spot when she died.

He turned in his saddle. "Hannah loved this view," he finally said. "She'd come up here a couple times a month when the weather permitted. Said it gave her perspective on life. Helped her see the whole picture and not just the part we were living at the moment."

"I'm sure I would have liked your wife," Caroline said.

"She would have liked you, too." He raised the binoculars again, laughed and held them out to her. "What do you want to bet that's Mike. Hope Katie's hanging on tight."

Caroline saw a jeep with two people in it tearing down the road toward the lake. "Kate's not having much luck keeping Mike reined in," she said.

"Reined in? Talking our language already?"

Caroline smiled at the man who had so generously invited her into his world. He kept surprising her. When she met him in the desert, she'd accepted his persona of private investigator without question. In LA, he had appeared comfortable in the corporate world. But now that she saw him on his home territory, she knew this was where he belonged.

"Ready to go back?" he asked. She nodded, and he started down the mountain trail. Before following, she sat for one more minute, enjoying the view. Next time I ride up here, I'll bring my sketchpad, she thought. This would make a wonderful painting. It would have to be large in scale to capture the grandeur. Just the challenge I need!

A shout came from Josh, and she hurried to catch up with him. By the time they reached the barn thirty minutes later, Mike and Kate were back, too. Ranch hands came up to take their horses.

"Goodbye for now, Peaches, my beauty," Caroline whispered. She handed the reins to the young man in front of her, then she and Josh walked over to the jeep.

Kate jumped out. "I'm driving next time! We could have been killed!"

Mike ignored her and addressed Josh.

"This place is unbelievable. Have you lived here your whole life?"

"Come on in the house. We'll sit around the fireplace, and I'll tell you my life story."

CHAPTER TWENTY-ONE

Josh prepared drinks at the bar in the corner of the great room while Mike and Kate settled in around the fireplace. Standing in front of a wall of books, Caroline was amazed at the diversity of reading material: *Tales,* Volume II, Edgar Allan Poe; *Romances,* Volume I, Voltaire; *The Fountain,* Eugene O'Neill.

Moving to another section of the floor-to-ceiling bookshelves, she found some of her favorites: *Wuthering Heights,* Emily Bronte; *Anna Karenina,* Leo Tolstoy; *Lost Horizon,* James Hilton; the journals of Anaïs Nin.

She was so engrossed that Josh's hand on her shoulder startled her.

"See anything interesting?" he asked, handing her a glass of Merlot.

"Very funny! This is incredible. Every book I've ever read or wanted to read seems to be here."

Josh reached up and pulled out *The Road to Rome* by Robert E. Sherwood. "I usually pick a book at random to read in the evening. Most of these books were acquired by my father and grandfather although over the years Hannah and I added to the library. One of her last projects was to catalog each book. She had

ost finished when she was diagnosed with cancer. She spent
er last months completing the project. She cataloged the last
book a few weeks before she died."

Caroline touched his arm. "You had a really good marriage,
didn't you?"

He nodded then looked toward the fireplace.

"Let's join the kids," he said. "I promised Mike the story of my
life. Feel free to sleep through it."

Caroline followed Josh across the room to the couch. Mike was
sitting on one of the leather chairs, his feet propped up on the
large hassock. Kate was curled up in the chair on the other side.

"Shouldn't we be helping in the kitchen?" Caroline asked.

"Lord, no," Josh said. "You're guests, and Lottie is in seventh
heaven. She's thrilled to cook for people who appreciate something
other than meat and potatoes."

Caroline stretched out on one end of the long couch, and after
Josh poked at the logs in the fireplace, he joined her on the other
end.

"So, what would you guys like to know?"

"Everything!" Mike and Kate said, at the same time.

"Okay, I'll start with my grandfather. He came to Colorado to
prospect for gold and was one of the lucky ones. He wisely spent
his new fortune on land.

"This ranch was his life. Except for buying and selling
excursions, he seldom left it. He built the original log cabin
where my manager now lives. Years later, he built this house.
Around twenty years ago, my wife and I renovated it and added
the second floor.

"He and my grandmother lived into their late eighties. Their
three daughters married and moved away, and my dad went off to
college and got his doctorate in biochemistry. To my grandfather's
credit, he supported my father's decision. My grandparents lived
here alone, until...." He paused.

"My mother and father died in a car accident while touring Europe, and as teenagers, my brother, Rod, and I came here to live."

"So where is your brother now?" Kate asked.

Caroline saw pain flicker in Josh's eyes before he briefly explained that his brother had died of a heart attack six years ago.

"Rod taught at the University of Denver, but we talked at least once a week, and he spent a lot of time here. He was my best friend."

"So your brother and your wife died within two years of one another," Caroline said. "How sad for you."

"And no children to comfort you," Kate, said.

The fire crackled and snapped.

"Well, it's true that Hannah and I were never able to have children, but I've been fortunate to have a close, extended family. My father's sisters and their children keep in touch, and Rod's wife and kids. Hannah's sisters and brothers have always treated me like one of their own." He sipped his drink. "I admit that life got lonely around here for me after Rod and Hannah died. That's why I got into private investigating and traveling. So there, now you know all my secrets."

Caroline knew Josh wasn't used to revealing so much about himself.

"Oh, don't stop," Kate said. "Tell us about—"

A woman's voice called out, "Supper's ready!"

"Saved by the supper bell!" Josh got to his feet and reached down to help Caroline up. He led everyone through the large archway into the dining room where the long oak table was laden with food. Lottie stood at the kitchen door, beaming at them.

The warm hospitality of the house wrapped itself around Caroline, and for the first time in weeks, she felt relaxed.

❦

Only a few lamps were on around the great room. The log walls and beams above them gave the room a cozy feeling in spite of its large size. The fire had died down but still warmed the room.

"Kate and Mike asleep already?" Josh asked.

"Kate plans to read for a while, but I hope Mike is asleep. He looked really tired after supper."

"I know. I worry about him. He's so interested in seeing everything that it's hard to keep him from overdoing."

Shadow joined them beside the couch. Caroline reached out and rubbed behind his ears. "You have an admirer," Josh said. "He misses having a woman around."

"He's such a sweetheart."

"Don't let him become a nuisance. That's how he got his name. From the time he was a puppy, he had to be near Hannah. Cody would run with Max and me around the ranch, but Shadow stayed right by Hannah's side. When she was sick, he never left her. I'd have to coax him outside to relieve himself. I finally brought his food up to her room. After she was gone, I thought he was going to grieve himself to death."

Caroline stroked the dog's head and was touched by the look of gratitude in his eyes. "Lay down, Shadow," Josh said. The old dog settled at Caroline's feet, heaving a sigh of contentment.

"Now Cody back there in the corner is happier not being bothered. Funny how dogs have temperaments and personalities a lot like people."

"I'm a little like both dogs," Caroline said. "I like being with people but need my private time, too." She stared into the fire for a few minutes then said, "Thank you, Josh for bringing us to this wonderful place."

"I'm glad you like it. Since I've always been more or less a loner, it suits me, but I imagine you would miss the social life and amenities of civilization."

"You'd be surprised. The hardest part of my marriage to Charles was the busy social life. Since our divorce, I've kept pretty much to myself. I love my little house in LA. It's not far from the theater and museums, but I don't go out that often. Like I said, I need time to myself and this peaceful solitude fits me better than you might think. In fact, I can't wait to set up my easel and begin painting. Thanks for squeezing my art supplies into your plane.

"Which reminds me, I need a large canvas for a scene I'd like to paint. I can sketch here, but I hate to wait until I get back home to paint it."

"No problem. You and I can fly to Durango. They have a good art supplies store there. We'll get whatever you need before I go back to Odessa."

"And when will that be?"

Josh got up and laid another log on the fire then sat on the hassock.

"My orders are to make sure you are safe and comfortable and then hightail it back. I have some work to do here tomorrow, and the following day we'll visit Durango, but then I have to go. Charles needs Adam to check things out at the LA office and wants me to go along and keep an eye on him. And Thompson hasn't found Linda, so Charles wants me to follow up on that, also.

"I'd rather stay here with you, but I did agree to work for Charles, and I can't back out now. Besides, until we resolve things, none of you will be safe. Charles could hire someone else to handle the investigation, but I want to know firsthand what's going on. In fact, that's going to be the deal breaker for helping your ex-husband—information. If he's not going to trust me with more details, I'm walking. And since I don't think he wants me back here alone with you, I believe I've got the leverage I need to convince him to tell me about this project of his in Nevada."

The morning air was cold and brisk. Kate and Mike walked hurriedly toward the barn. Kate moaned. "I didn't know I had so many muscles in my thighs and butt!"

Mike didn't want to admit that he was feeling just as bad. Yesterday, he'd convinced Josh that he was well enough to ride a few miles. It seemed impossible to get lost in such wide open spaces, but somehow he and Katie had managed it, and he was feeling the result of the extended ride.

Inside the barn, ranch hands were cleaning out stalls and working on a variety of tasks. Mike was fascinated. This was a real working ranch, and it seemed everyone was busy from morning to night. Josh had explained that a normal day's work included everything from herding cattle to repairing fences and working on streams and ponds. Some of the ranch hands actually lived in cabins in the mountains close-by. Now that would be great! Mike thought.

"I just love this barn, even the smell!" Kate said, sidestepping a pile of manure.

Tom, Josh's manager, was talking to several men a few stalls away. When he saw them coming, he called out, "So how's it going, you two? Want to go riding again today?"

Kate shook her head and put her hand on her butt. The men laughed.

"I understand," Tom said. "But don't wait too long to get back in the saddle. How 'bout you, Mike. Feel okay?"

Mike assured him he was just fine. Kate hit him on the arm. "Liar!" she said. "Trust me, Tom, he's as sore as I am. He just won't admit it."

Honest to god, she can be irritating. He changed the subject. "What can I do to help, Tom? I want to earn my keep around here." Seeing Kate open her mouth, he hurriedly added, "I know Josh told you I'm recuperating, but there must be something I can do."

"Follow me," Tom said.

Kate trailed behind the men, stopping to rub the nose of Brandy, the horse she'd ridden the day before. In the past few days, Mike hadn't gotten mad even once. Maybe this was the place where he could heal his anger.

Would it be the same for her? she wondered. Since coming here, she hadn't thought about Danny and the baby in that awful, painful way. In fact, she felt as though Danny was close by. Was that possible? Was he watching over her? The thought comforted her.

"Kate," Mike shouted, jarring her from her reveries.

She hurried to join the men. Mike said, "I'm going to ride in the truck with Tom to check things out. Want to come?"

She hesitated. She really wanted to be alone for a while and think about everything. About Danny and how she felt about Mike—and Adam. Maybe she would call and tell him about this great place. Maybe he could join them.

"You guys go ahead," she said. "I want to look through Josh's library and read until he and Caroline get back from Durango.

"I'm so glad you brought me here," Caroline said. "I've missed my café mocha." She looked around the busy coffee shop. The atmosphere was relaxed and friendly.

"This is a great town!" she said, "And you really aren't that isolated. It didn't take long to get here by plane. Is your friend at the airport always so generous with his car?"

"He usually has a truck or car available. Never lets me do more than fill up the gas tank for him. I don't fly to town too often though, as we drive in at least twice a month to stock up on supplies."

"Why does the name, Durango, sound so familiar to me?"

"Well, they have some good ski runs close by, and Western movies have been made around here. Or maybe you read that Louis L'Amour lived in the vicinity, one of my favorite authors, a fine man."

"You knew him?"

"Only in passing. He used to write in a room at the Strater Hotel. We talked a few times. Never wanted to bother him. People in these parts respect each other's privacy."

The waitress came by to fill their coffee cups again. Caroline talked about some of L'Amour's titles that she'd read. "My favorite was different from his others, *The Haunted Mesa*. Have you read it?"

"I've read all his books, but I agree with you, that one is special. I like stories that involve Indian mysticism. The cliff dwellers that he wrote about, the Anasazi, lived at Mesa Verde, which is not far from here. Historians aren't sure why they abandoned their dwellings. It's the kind of mystery that lends itself to stories like *The Haunted Mesa*."

"I'm sure you've visited the ruins often," Caroline said.

"Countless times. It's on one of my favorite spots. The mesa is a world unto itself. The cliff dwellings are amazing, and the views from the different sites are magnificent." He paused, remembering one particular vista.

"Sometimes, when I'm there," he said, "I feel like I've stepped back in time to a place I remember."

Caroline nodded. "I've experienced that feeling in certain places."

He smiled his appreciation at her understanding. "One day I'll take you there," he said. "But first we have to get Charles out of trouble. Which reminds me, I want to gas up today so I can get an early start in the morning. The weatherman calls for a storm to roll in later tomorrow which could ground me for another few days."

"Snow storm?"

"No, rain, but you never know for sure this time of year. It could turn into ice or snow, and I can't afford to get stranded. The sooner I get back to Odessa and the business at hand, the quicker I can get home." He paused. "And I imagine you're anxious to get back to your life in LA."

Caroline answered, truthfully.

"I'm in no hurry."

CHAPTER TWENTY-TWO

Where the hell are they? Charles wondered. Adam had gone down to the landing field to pick Josh up, and they weren't back yet. He felt impatient because he wanted to send Adam to LA to check on his partners and Brenda, but there was no way he was going to let him go without Josh.

It had been six days since Josh had left. Almost a week at his ranch, alone with Caroline. No matter. He rather liked the challenge of competing with a man who wasn't afraid of him. Most men were. Caroline once said it was because they sensed a ruthlessness in him, but that description no longer pleased him. Since his marriage to Brenda, he had experienced first hand the pain a ruthless person could inflict. On the other hand, he didn't plan to have mercy on his abductors once they were found. If he had his way, they would spend the rest of their miserable lives in jail. However, for that to happen, he had to depend on Josh.

Josh listened as Charles went over the details of their trip to LA. He was instructing Adam.

"I'm counting on you, Adam," he said, "to do a good acting job with Brenda. I want her convinced that I'm dead and that it will only be a matter of time before everything is legally hers. But be careful. She's shrewd. One wrong word or gesture, and she'll catch it.

"Josh, I want you to just stay in the background and watch and listen, especially around my partners. I honestly don't think they are involved in this, but you never know. I'm trusting you to pick up on anything they say or do that is suspicious."

Josh nodded. "And what about Linda? The last word from Thompson wasn't encouraging. The casino is cooperating, but basically, she checked in one night, and the next day her room was cleaned out even though she'd paid for a week's stay in advance. The Las Vegas cops are working with Thompson, but stranger things than this have happened in Vegas, and they don't seem too interested."

"Leave Linda to Thompson and the cops for now," Charles said. "I want you and Adam to take care of matters in LA and get certain files out of my office. I need...."

He paused, obviously unsure of how much to say.

No, by damn, Josh thought. No more hidden agendas. I'm not taking another step until this man comes clean with me.

"Charles, I want to talk to you alone."

"Wait outside," Charles said to Adam, who hesitated, started to speak, then left the room.

"Okay, let's have it," Charles demanded. "We don't have a lot of time. I need for you to get going on this."

"Fine, but I'm not moving a muscle until you tell me what the hell is going on. I want to know what we're up against before I stick my neck out again. If you choose to keep your damn secrets, I'm out of here and heading back to Colorado. I'll keep everyone safe, but I won't lift a finger to help you. Trust me or fire me! It's your choice."

Josh watched the slow burn of Charles's anger. He had him by the balls, and Charles knew it. The minutes ticked by, and the tension in the room grew until Josh finally saw resignation in his eyes.

"All right. It looks like I have no choice, but by God, if you betray me, you'll wish you never rescued me from that mountain."

Josh smiled. "That sounds reasonable to me."

Josh stared out the wall of windows of the conference room. He was tired. They had arrived late last night. This morning Adam was doing a good job of convincing Charles's partners that he was probably not going to return. Brenda sat at one end of the table, unable to hide how she felt about such a possibility. Josh could see why Caroline disliked the woman.

Allowing their voices to fade out, Josh thought about Caroline in Colorado. Thank God, she, Mike and Kate were safe. And that they didn't know the extent of the cartel's plans. He still couldn't believe what Charles had told him. And he wasn't sure how he felt about it.

In one sense, the cartel would be meeting a real need, but what about the safety aspect? Charles didn't seem concerned, but Josh wasn't that sure. Environmental groups would definitely have questions.

Raised voices caused him to look at the people around the conference table again. Brenda's French accent and elegant, feminine appearance hid a will of iron. She had done her homework and was informing Charles's partners exactly how much it would cost them to buy out his shares if it turned out that her husband was dead. Their shocked expressions amused Josh. He doubted if Brenda's demands were negotiable.

It was clear that Jenson and the other partners would be happier if Charles never returned, but Josh doubted any of them would consider murder a good corporate strategy.

Adam, however, he still wasn't sure about. He was a clever son of a bitch. He had these smart businessmen and lawyers eating out of his hand. By the time they left today, Charles would be dead and buried.

Charles sat on the porch, enjoying the silence of the desert. Leroy had driven Caroline's SUV to the motel to get food for their supper. He welcomed the solitude, feeling more relaxed than he had in weeks, mainly because Caroline was safe for the moment.

Caroline. He missed her. He planned to reassure her that their life together would be different this time around. She no longer would have to plan elaborate parties or chair benefits. Except perhaps for her environmental groups. He knew that was important to her.

The last successful benefit they had co-chaired was over ten years ago. He closed his eyes, seeing Caroline in the long red sheath, her dark hair piled high. He had gotten drunk that night because earlier in the day she had given him an ultimatum.

What an ass I was, he thought. All she wanted was a faithful husband. How different the last ten years would have been if I'd just....

Charles opened his eyes. *Wait a minute. That's it! That's the party where I talked about owning a ghost town!*

He remembered people crowding around him, listening to his drunken monologue. After the party, Caroline had complained about several of the people at the benefit. What had she said? Militant. She'd said they were too militant in their beliefs. Shit. That was it. Somehow, the cartel's plans had been discovered by a group of environmental madmen. And he had given them the perfect place to bury him.

Charles reached for his phone.

In the dining room of the ranch house where she had set up her easel, Caroline stepped back, tilted her head and viewed the large landscape critically. The proportions weren't quite right. The valley seen from the mountain should be wider.

Her cell phone rang, and she hurried into the great room to answer it. Josh or Charles? she wondered. Laughery, Charles, the ID read.

"Hi, Charles."

"Caroline, listen carefully. I need some information that only you can provide." The urgency in his voice startled her.

"What is it?" she asked.

Charles described a long-ago evening that Caroline could barely remember. Finally, it came back to her. That had been the evening Charles had gotten drunk and embarrassed her. A few weeks later, she'd left him, and her life had changed forever.

"What I need to know," he said, "is the names of those in attendance, especially those you said were too militant in their beliefs. Does any record exist of that particular benefit? I know what I'm asking, but this is very important."

Caroline gathered her thoughts. Tax records must exist somewhere, even that far back.

"Let me think about it and get back to you. The central office moved to San Francisco, but Gloria Lindsey is still the accountant. I don't know what records she has, but I know she kept track of the extreme faction that broke off from our group. We were very careful not to accept any money from them after they left. Let me see what I can find out."

"Today! I need for you to get on this today."

"Okay. I will. But, why are you looking at these particular people?"

As Charles explained his theory, Caroline wasn't sure what to believe. If the cartel's project had anything to do with endangering the environment, fanatics *might* be involved. But kidnapping? Murder? That seemed unlikely.

From the 737, Caroline looked down at the clouds. The plane would soon be landing in San Francisco.

Gloria had assured her that records for the past twenty years were stored in the basement of their new offices. It was just a matter of finding that particular year. Caroline had decided to search the files, herself. Maybe she could locate the information that would bring this whole matter to a close.

Josh stood on the porch, looking down at Charles. "She what?"

"She left the ranch to track down the records I need. I never dreamed she'd try to check them out herself. I couldn't get through on her cell phone, so I called the ranch house. Kate told me one of the ranch hands drove Caroline into Durango this afternoon where she caught a plane to San Francisco."

"Goddamn it!"

Charles knew exactly how Josh felt.

Adam frowned. "This isn't good. We should fly there right now."

"Do you think you can handle this alone?" Charles said to Josh. Before he could answer, Adam asked, "What about me?"

Pointing his finger, Charles said, "You are going to stay here with me. I was going to send Josh to Judson to register the deeds, but I'll just send Leroy tomorrow. You get to play bodyguard. You do know how to shoot a gun, don't you?"

Adam's brown eyes darkened. "I own a .357 and a .44 Magnum. Does that answer your question?"

Charles turned back to Josh. "I want you to catch up with Caroline in San Francisco and stick with her while she searches the files. Then get her back to Colorado."

Josh frowned. "I don't like the idea of leaving you two alone on this mountain—but then we can't leave Caroline alone in San Francisco either."

"That's right," Charles said. "And I need Leroy to get the paperwork to Judson right away. Whoever is trying to delay our finalizing the land deals must know about our plans. Someone is feeding them confidential information." He looked at Adam.

The room grew silent.

Finally Josh asked, "Do we know where Caroline's staying?"

Charles tossed him a pad of notepaper. "Kate gave me the hotel's address and phone number. Call me when you get there!"

CHAPTER TWENTY-THREE

He stood at the reception desk at the Fairmont Hotel. He had called Caroline from the airport.

"Would you please let Caroline Laughery know that Josh Logan is here?"

The young woman at the desk nodded. In a few minutes, she turned back to him. "Ms. Laughery said to go right up—Room 414." Josh hurried through the lobby to the elevator.

When he knocked on her door, Caroline opened it slightly then undid the safety lock.

"Good morning," she said, smiling.

Wrapped in a terry cloth robe, her dark hair loose on her shoulders, Caroline looked sleepy but relaxed and happy to see him. He wanted to take her into his arms but quickly reminded himself why he was here.

He walked into the room and threw his hat on the nearest chair. "What the hell were you thinking?"

Caroline closed the door behind him, unfazed by his angry question. "I was thinking that you and Charles would never allow me to do this, so I didn't ask your permission. I decided to check out the information myself, because I don't want Gloria involved. I am sorry, however, that I worried you."

Josh sat on the bed and held out his hand. "Come over here," he said.

She sat beside him.

"Promise me you won't take any more chances," he said.

"I promise. I know this was rather rash of me. But now you're here and maybe we can locate the information Charles needs to finally solve this mystery."

She jumped up, tugging on his arm. "Let's get going! I'll dress and meet you downstairs for breakfast. I told Gloria I'd be there around 9:00 a.m. I have a cover story all ready, so just let me do the talking."

Josh rolled his eyes, grabbed his hat and headed out the door.

"Lordy, lordy," Caroline said, staring at the rows of file cabinets. "This could take awhile, but Gloria said her computer base didn't go back far enough, so we don't have a choice but to follow the paper trail."

"Where should we start?" Josh asked.

"She said the files we are looking for would be in the back of the room."

Twenty minutes later, Josh called out, "Caroline, come over here and check this out." He handed her a file that read, "Returned Donation." It contained a copy of a check and a note that it had been returned to the ASE.

"I remember that," Caroline said. "Several members left our organization but later sent us a donation. We had heard they were threatening companies who weren't meeting environmental standards. The board voted to return the check. We wanted to distance ourselves from them. "They called themselves Advocates for a Safe Environment—ASE. I believe some of those members were at the party Charles is talking about. But I don't see any guest lists in these files.

"Wait a minute. I used to keep a guest book of every event. The next day I would look for the names of those who, after a few drinks, had promised me a donation. Rather than admit they didn't remember our conversation, they would simply send a check, even more than promised. I raised a lot of money that way."

Josh laughed.

"Anyway, I have a storage area in my house in LA that I've never cleaned out. I bet I still have those books. Maybe even the one for that very event."

Josh began replacing files.

"Okay. Next stop, LA"

"I can't believe you put this wonderful meal together in so little time!" Josh said.

Mattie beamed at him. It had been love at first sight between Josh and Caroline's housekeeper. After her phone call from San Francisco, Mattie had readied the house for company and had a dinner of steak, baked potatoes, fresh vegetables and chocolate cake waiting for them.

"Josh is right, Mattie. You did a wonderful job on such short notice!"

"I loved doing it, Miss Caroline. It's been too long since I cooked for a man in this house."

Josh looked amused.

"Well, everything was delicious." Caroline pushed away from the table. "We'll have our coffee in the den."

Josh followed her through the hallway and into the den, looking at her paintings on the walls. "I had no idea how good you were," he said.

"Thank you. I've had a few rather successful shows over the past years. These are my personal favorites, however. I'd never sell them."

Josh stopped in front of a smaller painting.

Caroline moved in front of him to straighten the frame.

"I awoke one night with this scene clear in my mind. I got up and went into my studio to work on it, painting what I had dreamed. What does it remind you of?"

"I think you know. It's similar to the view from the mountain at Odessa. Yet you said you had never been there before."

"I never had."

He placed both hands on her shoulders. "Interesting."

At the sound of Mattie in the hallway, he moved away.

"Where do you want the tray, Miss Caroline?"

"On the coffee table would be fine. And Mattie, before you go this evening, I want to give you a check. We'll be leaving tomorrow, and I don't know when I'll be returning, so I want to cover the next few months."

"You'll be gone that long?"

Caroline stole a glance at Josh, who was studying other paintings around the room. "I'm not sure. I'll let you know later. Just stop by periodically and check on the house. And please don't tell anyone where I am. Things are a little complicated right now."

Mattie looked at Josh and back at Caroline. "I understand," she said. As she left the room, she called out to Josh. "I hope you come back again real soon, Mr. Logan."

"I hope so, too, Mattie."

As soon as they were alone, Caroline started to laugh. "I never knew you were such a ladies' man, Josh."

"Only with certain ladies," he said, crossing the room to sit on the recliner. "Now, I have a question. Should I be looking for a hotel room, or am I invited to spend the night?"

"Mattie has the guest room all ready for you. We need to start digging through my storage area first thing in the morning. I'd start tonight, but it's been years since I filed those books away, so it could take awhile."

Josh settled back in the recliner. Caroline was happy that he seemed so comfortable in her home. There had been few men in the house since her divorce, and she had never been completely relaxed having them here. It felt right with Josh, however.

"What are you thinking about?" he asked.

"I was thinking that it seemed so natural for you to be here. I've never felt that way before."

"Charles never came here?"

The portrait of Charles in her studio suddenly filled her mind, as though he were watching her. She shook her head to dismiss the image.

"No," she said. "I bought the house after our divorce. I wanted this place to be my own. Charles tends to take over any space he's in, and I was determined he wasn't going to control my life or my feelings once we were divorced."

"And did it work?"

She hesitated. "I guess that's why I agreed to meet him at Odessa. I needed to find out."

Before she could say more, Mattie walked back into the room, announcing she was ready to go. Caroline was relieved. She didn't want to think about Charles tonight.

"Excuse me a minute, Josh. I need to give Mattie a few instructions."

In the kitchen, Caroline said, "You have my phone number, and I'll leave my Colorado address on the desk for you to forward my mail in case I'm not back by the end of the month. Call me if anything looks urgent before then. Okay?"

Mattie nodded, glanced toward the den and smiled. The two women hugged each other.

Josh looked around the room. He really liked this house, perhaps because it represented the feminine side of the woman he had fallen in love with. Yet she was comfortable in his more masculine environment at the ranch, too.

Hearing Caroline's voice saying good-bye to Mattie at the front door, Josh made a decision. He wasn't going to wait any longer. He was going to find out tonight exactly how Caroline felt about him.

She returned, carrying a decanter in her hand. "Would you like some cherry brandy to spike your coffee, Josh?"

"Sounds good."

He joined Caroline on the couch as she poured fresh coffee and brandy into their cups. They sat quietly, sipping their drinks. There was no tension in the silence. Josh could feel the warmth of Caroline's leg next to his.

Then, in unison, they set their cups down and turned toward one another. When Josh looked into Caroline's eyes, he saw the reflection of his own feelings. She lifted her face to his, opening her mouth to his kiss. Only when he moved his hand to her breast did she tense up then relax again.

She wrapped both arms around him. He kissed her neck, then stopped and waited for her reaction. He was not going further than she wanted him to go. She shifted into a sitting position.

There was a thoughtful look on Caroline's face. He could sense she was making a decision.

When she pushed herself off the couch, he didn't look up, knowing his eyes would show his disappointment. He poured himself a full cup of brandy. Was this his answer? Was Caroline going to return to tell him that she still loved Charles and couldn't be with him? He had imagined several scenarios by the time Caroline reentered the room.

She was wearing a pale green satin negligee, her hair loose and flowing. Her dark eyes smiled at him as she turned to leave again. He crossed the room in a few strides and followed her through the hallway to the bedroom. Candles were lit around the room, and music was softly playing.

Reaching the bed, Caroline turned and placed both hands on his chest. She began unbuttoning his shirt. When she reached the ornate buckle of his belt, she tugged on it and guided him toward the bed where she lay down.

Josh quickly shed the rest of his clothes and joined her.

He propped himself on one elbow, enjoying the sight of the luxuriant hair spread out on the pillow and the contours of her long, slim body. Lifting her hand to his mouth, he kissed each finger until Caroline reached up and pulled him to her.

As he covered the full lips with his own, he began to slide the straps of the satin gown off her shoulders, kissing each bare one. There was a subtle scent of lilacs and an earthy, clean smell of skin. He breathed Caroline in, burying his head in the curve of her neck.

Trembling, she moved his head to her breast, and he kissed the soft mound. They began to tenderly explore each other's body. There was something familiar about their intimacy, as though each knew exactly what the other needed. Josh listened for sounds of pleasure as he moved his hands, slowly, skillfully over her body.

He kissed Caroline's forehead, eyelids, cheek and finally her soft mouth again. She pushed against his chest and moved on top of him, without taking her mouth from his. He enjoyed the full weight of her body until, unable to wait any longer, he rolled her under him again, holding their interlaced fingers over her head.

Caroline's eyes were closed, and the tip of her tongue played over her lips. When she opened her eyes, they were dark with passion, and Josh knew she was ready. A small hand guided him where she needed him to be.

Their bodies fit perfectly together.

Josh lost himself in the fierce passion of the moment, prolonging it as long as possible until the tense, quivering body beneath him arched, and he heard Caroline's husky whisper, "Yes, yes!"

CHAPTER TWENTY-FOUR

In the shower, Caroline washed her hair then stood for a few minutes, enjoying the water on her skin, remembering the feel of Josh's hands. Closing her eyes, she lifted her face to the warm spray for a few minutes before turning off the water.

Last night had been unexpected and unplanned, but on some deep level, Caroline always knew she would have to explore her feelings for Josh. They were too strong to ignore. Their closeness and camaraderie on this trip had somehow made the decision for her.

Or had it been the fear that Charles was pulling her back into his world again, a world she didn't belong in anymore? That being with Josh would somehow protect her from making a mistake?

Two very different men. And she was attracted to them both.

Back in the bedroom, she sat cross-legged on the bed, her wet hair wrapped in a towel, still thinking about last night. She had fallen asleep in Josh's arms, but apparently he had thoughtfully gone to the guest room sometime during the night. There was a light knock on the bedroom door, and she called out for him to come in.

"Good morning," he said, crossing the room to sit beside her.

He leaned forward to lightly kiss her lips. She reached up to touch his unshaven cheek.

Before she could bring up their night together, he said, "I came to tell you that Charles just called. I told him we were going to check out the guest books today, and he wants us to fax him whatever we find. He wasn't too pleased that we hadn't tackled the job last night." Caroline recognized the same unease in his eyes that was beginning to build inside her.

She took his hand and held it to her breast. "I don't know where this is leading, Josh, but we are not going to let Charles make us feel guilty about it."

He stared at her for a moment then nodded and stood.

"Mattie left us cut-up fruit and muffins for breakfast. And she had the coffee pot set to turn on this morning. What a woman!"

Caroline slid off the bed. "Give me two minutes to dress, and then we'll eat on the patio."

Boxes were stacked around them. Only a few remained in the back of the storage area. Caroline wiped her forehead, leaving a smudge of dirt. "I can't believe I kept all this stuff."

"Thank God you did," Josh said. "I just wished you'd written the dates on the outside of the boxes." He yanked open the top of another. "Was this the year of the event?" Caroline pushed herself across the floor to peer into the box. "I think so." She began pulling out papers and small books.

"What time of year do you think the benefit was held?" Josh asked.

"Close to Christmas, because Charles remembers a red dress, a color I usually wore around the holidays."

Six guest books lay on the bottom of the box. Josh handed several to Caroline, who began checking dates. "Here's the one marked December," she said.

As she opened the guest book, several sheets of paper fell out, listing the food served and decorations used. It brought the evening back to her. The memory wasn't a happy one. She'd given

Charles an ultimatum earlier in the day, and he had laughed at her. Then he drank more than usual at the party and flirted with several of her friends. They'd gone to bed in separate rooms that night.

"Well?" Josh said. Caroline made an effort to focus on the list of names in the book. There had been almost 200 people there, and she turned page after page, recognizing some names, not recalling others. She ran her finger down each page, until....

"Oh, my god!"

"What?"

She stared at the name and the notation beside it.

"Caroline, what is it?"

"Oh, Josh, I don't want to believe this, but look!"

She handed the book to him, pointing her finger at one name and her note beside it—'James Hill, Adam's brother, a strange young man.'

Josh got to his feet and left the room. Caroline pushed herself back against the wall. She'd been so sure Adam wasn't involved.

Josh reentered the room, holding the cell phone to his ear.

"Damn, his voice mail. Charles, this is Josh. We've found what we were looking for. Adam's brother, James, was at that benefit. He must have heard you talking about the haunted mine. Call me the minute you get this!"

Caroline got to her feet and held onto the nearest wall for support. What had they done? Charles was alone in the desert with Adam.

"Why isn't he answering his phone, Josh?"

"He's probably just charging it, or he's taking a nap and doesn't hear it. But we need to get back to Odessa as soon as possible. I wish I had Leroy's cell phone number or even Adam's."

"I have Adam's!" Caroline said. "But we don't want to alert him. What would I say?"

Josh thought for a minute. "Just tell him that you need to talk to Charles and haven't been able to get through to him. Be casual about it but insist that he put Charles on." Josh handed her the phone.

Caroline ran out of the room in search of her purse. Pulling her address book out, she found Adam's name and punched in the numbers. She took a deep breath, preparing to hear his voice, but her call went immediately into voice mail. She left a message, asking Adam to have Charles call her. When she finished, she handed the phone back to Josh, frowning.

"Where are they?"

Charles grimaced as they hit a rough spot in the road. Thank goodness for four-wheel drive, he thought. Caroline's SUV had done the job as they climbed the steep, narrow roads over the mountain.

Adam hadn't wanted to go on this trip, but Charles wasn't about to sit around another minute.

He reached for his phone. Another bump jarred him as he searched his jacket pocket. Great, he must have left it by the bed. Oh, well, he'd use Adam's. Then he remembered that Adam had given his phone to Malcolm for charging when they went to supper last night.

Maybe this trip hadn't been such a good idea. So far, no one had been in any of the cabins on this side of the Odessa Mountain. Another small cabin was up ahead, but it looked more like a large shed with a door and one window. Adam turned off the engine in front of the dilapidated building, and Charles waited while he got out of the car. Before he reached the door, however, it opened.

A bearded, older man stepped out carrying a shotgun. Adam started talking fast. Charles couldn't make out what he was saying, but the man finally leaned the shotgun against the side of the building and walked toward the SUV.

Charles lowered the window. "Hello there." He stuck out his hand. "Charles Laughery here."

The man ignored his hand. One cheek jutted out with what Charles assumed must be a wad of tobacco. He chewed for a few seconds, spit and then said, "This is private property, mister. You gotta leave."

Charles retracted his hand. "Okay, no problem. We just wondered if you'd seen any strangers over this way the past few months."

Adam had gotten back into the car and leaned over to murmur, "Let's get the hell out of here." Charles continued to talk to the man, who hadn't responded and was eyeing his shotgun again.

"I tell you what," Charles said, "we'll be on our way, but if you think of anything, we're just over the mountain in Odessa. Or you could tell Malcolm at the motel."

The change in the man's demeanor was instant. "You know Malcolm?"

Charles nodded. "Known him for years."

"You that rich guy that comes to Odessa every once in a while?"

"I guess you could say that." Seeing the sudden interest in the beady eyes, Charles added, "We've had some trouble over there, and we just wanted to know if you've seen any strangers in the area. If you have, and you can describe them, I'd make it worth your while. By the way, what's your name?" He pulled out his wallet.

The old man stared at it then said, "Clarence. And the only strangers I seen was earlier this year... maybe, oh, back around March or so." He glanced at Adam. "There was three of them. One was a skinny, little fella who looked like your friend here. They was changing a tire on the road half-way down the mountain from Odessa. I was on my way to Malcolm's on my monthly run for groceries and liquor. I stopped to ask if I could help. They was rude as hell. Told me they didn't need no help—to go on my way! I says 'screw you' and left. Haven't seen um' since. Is that worth anything to you?"

Charles handed Clarence a hundred dollar bill. "What kind of car were they driving and did you notice the license plates?"

Clarence cocked his head to the side. "Let's see...oh, yeah, it was a black truck, one of those little ones." He chewed, and Charles waited. "I think...I think they was California tags."

"I don't suppose you remember the numbers on the plate?"

"Weren't no numbers, just letters spelling out somethin', don't remember what."

Charles gave Clarence another hundred. "Thanks. You've been a big help. Come see me at Odessa if you remember anything else, especially what those letters were."

Clarence smiled for the first time, and Charles knew he had a new best friend. Adam started the motor, backed up and jerked forward, speeding up the rutted road. He was frowning.

"What's wrong, Adam? This is great news! Our culprits obviously came up here last spring, got into the house, saw the maps and checked out the haunted mine area. They didn't count on running into Clarence. Now, all we have to do is get Caroline up here to draw the faces of the men as Clarence describes them to her, and we'll have composites of my kidnappers." Hitting another pothole, Charles shouted, "Slow down!"

Adam sped up. Charles grabbed hold of the armrest. "Damnit, stop!" Braking to a halt, Adam stared straight ahead.

"What the hell is wrong with you?" Charles shifted sideways in order to face Adam and was shocked to see fury on his face.

"Do you really think that bastard was telling the truth? For god's sake, Charles, you offer money, and he comes up with something—anything—to tell you."

"You believe he made up that elaborate story on the spur of the moment? I don't think he's that swift. Especially the part where he said one of them looked like you. That would be pretty inspired, don't you think? Besides, we don't have much else to go on at the moment, so it's certainly worth checking out. Between whatever Josh and Caroline come up with and this guy's story, we may be on our way to solving this thing."

The look on Adam's dark, brooding face disturbed Charles. Feeling uneasy, he said, "Let's get going. I want to call Josh and see what's happening there."

Adam turned toward him. "I worked for you all those years, followed your orders, kept your secrets, but in the end, you didn't let me in on the biggest deal of your life.

"Now some yokel starts talking about a black man changing a tire. Would you have bought into his story so quickly if those three imaginary men had all been white?"

Charles was too amazed to speak.

Adam continued. "So now we're going to bring Caroline over here to this low-life and start to look for some poor son-of-bitch, because he's skinny and black. I'd say that's taking profiling a bit far, wouldn't you?"

Finding his voice, Charles said, "Adam, that is the worst crap I've ever heard from you. Maybe the old man did make up the whole thing but to accuse me of listening to him because.... Well, that's just bullshit, and you know it!"

Adam's eyes reflected both sadness and resignation. "All I ever wanted from you was respect. But that's never going to happen, is it?" He turned on the engine and pulled back onto the mountain road.

Neither man spoke again.

Caroline stood with Josh outside the Odessa house, looking around. "Where could they be?"

Josh tried to think of an explanation that would satisfy her but could only suggest they go back down the mountain and check in with Malcolm. They were climbing into the truck when a car came into sight. Leroy pulled up beside them in Adam's Porsche. They hurried to the driver's side.

"Leroy! Have you seen Charles?" Josh asked.

"The boss isn't here?"

"No one's here," Josh said. "Have you talked to him today?"

Leroy shook his head. "Left a message on his phone, but he never called me back. Where's Adam?"

"Charles and Adam have gone off somewhere in my SUV," Caroline said. She looked at the dusty Porsche. "I'm surprised Adam let you use his car."

"The boss didn't give him a choice. He wanted me to get to Judson as quick as possible. Good thing I didn't run into any cops. I must have averaged 95 mph and—"

"Leroy," Josh said, "we may have a problem here. Come inside. The three of us need to brainstorm."

Ten minutes later, Leroy was pacing the floor and waving his arms. "I knew it, I knew Charles shouldn't trust him. I told him. I told him a million times that guy was bad news." He sat on the bed. "Charles could be dead."

Caroline had never seen Leroy so distressed. Forgetting her own misgivings, she sat beside him, patting his arm. "We don't know that, Leroy." Sensing his discomfort at her gesture, she started to move off the bed when her hand brushed against something under the covers. Pushing aside the sheet, she picked up a cell phone.

"Well," she said, "now we know why Charles isn't answering his phone."

Leroy wasn't reassured. "The boss don't go nowhere without that phone."

Before Caroline could respond, Josh said, "Listen!" The three of them ran out the door.

"Charles!" Caroline cried out.

"So I've been judged and found guilty?" Adam's face was contorted with rage.

Caroline's throat closed with unshed tears. This wasn't the man she'd known all these years. "What do you expect us to think, Adam?" she asked. "We find out that the one and only time Charles let slip that he owned a haunted mine in an old silver mining town, your brother is there."

"Along with a few hundred others," Adam shot back.

"There were only a few of us standing around when I talked about the mine," Charles said.

Adam shook his head. "No. Jimmy can be extreme in his thinking, but I can't believe he'd do anything like this."

Caroline could hear the doubt in his voice, even as he defended his brother. She leaned forward. "When did you last talk to him, Adam?"

He looked down at clenched hands. "Not since my parents died."

"That's a lie," Charles said. "I know for a fact that earlier this last year, your brother was in our office."

Adam glared at Charles. "Caroline asked when I last talked to Jimmy. It's true he came to see me, but I wasn't there. My secretary expected me back momentarily and let him wait in my office."

Charles nodded. "Okay. Yes, I remember now. I stopped by to tell Alice that I had sent you out of town, and I needed to pick up some papers from your office. When I entered, your brother was sitting at your desk. Said he'd been playing games while waiting for you. I doubted that you had any games on your computer but let it go and just told him you wouldn't be coming in and that he had to leave."

Josh, who had been quietly listening, asked, "Did you have the location of Odessa in your computer?"

Everyone waited for Adam to answer.

"On one file." He frowned. "The truth is my brother has always been a computer nerd. It would have been easy for him to get into my files. Even in high school, he could do things with a computer that I never even understood. My parents were so proud of him." Adam put his head in his hands. Caroline heard the muffled words, "Thank God, they're not here."

She stooped down in front of him.

"Adam, look at me," she said. "In your heart, you know that Jimmy is involved in this, don't you? You really haven't had anything to do with him for years, because you knew he was obsessed and had lost perspective. His neglect of your parents was the last straw."

His stricken look broke her heart. This was the Adam she knew. "How could Jimmy have found out about Charles's plans?" she asked.

Charles answered for him. "The international cartel has offices in every country. The terrorists abroad use our domestic fanatics whenever they can in whatever way they can. The more disruption they can generate the better. If there was a leak abroad, any of the terrorist groups over there could have fed the information to Jimmy's group, knowing that the words 'nuclear power plant' would set them off."

Stunned, Caroline stared at Charles. *Nuclear power plant?*

Adam looked up. "Caroline's right. I broke off from Jimmy, because I couldn't reason with him. After my father died from the chemicals he was exposed to in his plant, Jimmy went a little crazy. Then my mother died from lung cancer, and he blamed the tobacco companies.

"I'm not saying he was wrong about everything. It's just that he carried the role of activist too far. He saw himself as some kind of environmental savior, and he thought the end justified the means."

He turned to speak directly to Charles. "He especially hated you. You represent everything he despises. He thinks the rich and powerful are all enemies of the people. Our conversation always degenerated into arguments about his beliefs. That I worked for the 'enemy' was too much for Jimmy. During our last argument, he told me that unless I quit my job, he could no longer call me brother. That was the last I saw of him." Adam paused. "So I was surprised when Alice told me he'd stopped by. She didn't tell me he'd been in my office, however. For that matter, Charles, neither did you."

"I didn't want to embarrass you. It was clear the guy wasn't all there. So I just didn't say anything. Now I wish I had. We might have had a heads-up on all this."

Caroline could see the tension between Charles and Adam begin to ease.

"If Jimmy's group is really behind this," Adam said, "I'll do whatever I can to bring them to justice. That is unless you believe I'm a part of it, too. I know my actions have been suspect, but I swear to God that I would never be party to this kind of thing." The room became quiet, everyone lost in their own thoughts. It was Charles who broke the silence.

"This could turn nasty, Adam, and your brother is going to be caught in the middle—innocent or guilty. Are you ready for that?"

"If you had known my father," Adam said, "you would understand that honesty and justice were the tenets he lived by. Jimmy carried those beliefs to the extreme, and I didn't adhere to them closely enough. I'm willing to help find those who did this to you, whether Jimmy is involved or not."

"Then we have work to do," Charles said.

CHAPTER TWENTY-FIVE

"Well, that was an interesting experience!" Caroline said. "You handled Clarence beautifully, my dear," Charles said. "Of course, he was fascinated, watching his description of the men take form on your sketch pad. I don't know how you do that."

Josh and Adam gave appreciative nods as she laid out the three sketches. "He was amazingly specific, considering he only saw the men for such a short time. The man with the goatee, of course, would stay in your mind—and Adam's brother." She caught herself but saw from Adam's expression that he was resigned to the fact that the man she had drawn was indeed his brother.

"But the younger man was not as clear, so I hope I got him right. His appearance is rather nondescript. It could be any man with sandy hair, in his twenties, and that's not much help."

Charles grabbed the picture off the table. "I'll be damned!" he said. "No, it can't be!"

Everyone stared at him.

"I just realized who this looks like! There was someone with me when I left Vegas, a son of one of the members of the cartel. This is Stephen!"

"What!" Josh said. "Goddamn it, Charles, you swore to me that my source was mistaken. That you left the Bellagio alone. What the hell were you thinking? This is vital information!"

"I know. Or at least I know now. Then, I was sure that Stephen had just been in the wrong place at the wrong time, and I didn't want to drag him into this mess. I also was protecting his father. Giving out the name of one of the members is grounds for... well, let's just say, we never divulge one another's name."

Caroline spoke up. "So you out and out lied to all of us and tried to make us believe that poor Kate was hallucinating about seeing a man in the desert that night. How could you, Charles?"

He ignored her outburst and studied the picture in his hand.

"I can't believe Stephen is involved," he said.

"But you had no problem believing I would betray you!" Adam said.

"Cool it, Adam," Josh said. He turned to Charles. "Tell us more about this Stephen and exactly what happened, starting in Vegas."

Charles sat on the bed. "I ran into Stephen as I was leaving that day. I'd last seen him a year or so ago in England. I was paying my bill when he came up and asked for my help. I thought it was a happy coincidence. He said he was living in the states now and had just lost a bundle at the craps table. He didn't want his dad to know and asked if he could catch a ride with me to Los Angeles. I explained I wasn't driving all the way to LA, but he asked to ride with me as far as I was going. Said he'd hitchhike the rest of the way. Now his father, Leonard, is not a particularly reasonable man, so I agreed to help him out. I thought he could find someone at Malcolm's motel who would give him a ride. Well, you know the rest of the story.

"It was obviously a setup, and I fell for it. I remember going to the men's room and when I returned, Stephen had ordered another round of drinks. As soon as I finished mine, we left the casino. He seemed in a hurry. Shit. He must have put something in my drink. That's why I felt dizzy when we got to the car. The last thing I remember is Stephen offering to drive. I must have passed out soon thereafter. Stephen probably drove like crazy across the desert to get me to Odessa and lost control, thus the accident."

Charles reached for the glass of water on the table beside him. The eyes of everyone in the room were riveted on him.

"When I was rescued and taken to the hospital, I called Leonard and was surprised to hear him say that he'd just talked to his son and that he was doing well. Not wanting to get Stephen in trouble, I didn't say anything about Vegas.

"I assumed the boy must have been hurt and wandered off into the desert. I based that on Kate's story. I did wonder why he hadn't gone to the authorities when he woke up. Or why he didn't see Kate. I decided he must have gone back to the road and been picked up by someone, that he probably saw the empty car and assumed I'd been taken to the hospital. I knew he would be afraid to tell his father that he wrecked my car. What never occurred to me was that he might be involved. I know how that sounds, but I watched this kid grow up, for god's sake!"

"Why would his buddies leave him behind when they snatched you?" Adam asked.

Charles thought for a moment. "When we didn't show up at Odessa, they probably came looking for us. When they found the car with just me in it, they grabbed me and ran. Later that night, they must have gone back, looked around, saw Kate on the ground and quietly got Stephen, erasing all traces that he'd been there."

Josh sat beside Charles on the bed and looked at the sketch of Stephen. "Do you realize," he said, "that we've just identified two of your kidnappers?" He looked up. "Okay, listen up, everyone. Leroy, Adam and I can handle things from here on. I'm going to take Charles and Caroline to Colorado where they will be safe while we wrap this thing up."

In the great room of the ranch house, Caroline adjusted the blankets covering Charles. He was exhausted after the plane trip from Odessa. Mike, Kate and Josh had gone to bed.

"I hope you'll be comfortable on this couch tonight," she said. "Josh said he would set a bed up for you down here tomorrow since all four bedrooms upstairs are full."

She yawned. "Are you as tired as I am?"

"I'm bushed, but before you go upstairs, I want to ask you something. How much do you know about Josh Logan? I thought he was just a small rancher, scratching to survive by working as a P.I." He looked around the large room. "But no P.I. makes enough money to run a spread like this. Who the hell is this guy? Have I put our lives into the hands of the wrong man?"

"Oh, for Pete's sakes," Caroline said. "You're suspicious of Josh now? Who's next, Leroy? Me?"

Charles laughed. "I'm just trying to figure this out. If Logan's got this place to run, what's he doing taking on cases like mine? What I'm paying him wouldn't cover his feed bill, so why is he spending so much time and energy on it? Even turning his ranch over to us. Which he might eventually regret, because from the looks of Kate and Mike, I think he has permanent guests."

"There's your answer," Caroline said. "If Kate, Mike and I weren't in danger, I don't think Josh would be on this case."

"Which is pretty much what he told me," Charles conceded.

Caroline stretched. "Okay, now that we've got that straight, I'm going to bed. Is there anything I can get you before I go upstairs?"

Charles assured her he was fine. As he watched her climb the stairs, he made a mental note to get his people to check out Logan.

The plane circled above them then headed west. Caroline waved until it was out of sight, feeling strangely bereft. Charles stood beside her.

"I wish Josh could have stayed longer," Kate said. "It doesn't seem fair. We're here enjoying his home, and he's off risking his neck to protect us." Caroline knew the comment was aimed at Charles.

"If all goes well, little girl, he'll be back for good very soon," Charles said.

Caroline waited for the explosion that was sure to come.

"Excuse me, Mr. Laughery, I'm a woman, not a girl." Kate stalked off.

"I guess that puts you in your place," Caroline said.

"I don't think the young lady likes me very much," he said, with a chuckle.

At the ranch house, Caroline suggested they relax on the porch for a while and sat on a large wooden chair. Charles chose the wide railing.

"I'd forgotten how you can almost taste mountain air," he said, breathing in deeply.

"I know what you mean," she said. "And like Odessa, the night sky is packed with stars."

"You really love it here, don't you?" He paused. "Is the ranch all you love?"

She lifted her eyes to Charles's piercing gaze. She doubted he was really worried about Josh, only challenged. He enjoyed competition, because he always won. Well, things were different now.

"Caroline?"

"You're asking about Josh and me. How far our relationship has gone, and where you and I stand."

"Only if you're ready to tell me," he said.

Caroline hesitated. Was she ready? They would have to talk about it eventually, but....

A shout from the barn saved her from responding. Mike was headed toward them on a frisky Pinto named Hunter, with Kate not far behind on her more docile horse, Brandy.

"Want me to saddle up Peaches for you, Caroline?" Mike yelled. "We're going with Tom to check on some cattle. He says a snow storm is coming in tonight."

Mike's excitement was catching. A brisk ride was just what she needed. She looked at Charles, who said, "Go on, enjoy yourself."

Who is this new, considerate man? Maybe he really has changed. Maybe....

She jumped to her feet. "You're sure you don't mind?"

"I'm perfectly capable of entertaining myself for a few hours. Have fun!"

Charles watched as Caroline hurried toward the barn. It had been wise not to force the issue about her relationship with Josh. He needed to reestablish the bond that had always been between them while Josh was off working with the LA and Nevada authorities. He also wanted to find out more about Logan.

Charles reached into his coat for his phone. A few calls to the right people, and he would have his answers.

Two hours later, as he sat alone in the library area of the great room, Charles's phone rang. He listened and took notes. "Good job. No, that's all I need right now. I'll let you know if I want more."

He looked at the figures in front of him.

Josh wasn't quite in his league, financially, but close, too damn close. This was no cowboy. Josh was a player. He wouldn't quietly disappear into the background after all this was over. Neither would he be intimidated.

Charles smiled. Interesting.

In the renovated saloon at Odessa, Adam paced back and forth, as Leroy cleaned his gun. Josh was restless, too, waiting for the phone to ring. When it did, he grabbed it.

"Josh here."

He listened to Charles, feeling more and more frustrated.

"How can he not know where his son is staying? When you called him from the hospital, didn't he say that he'd recently spoken to him? Hasn't he talked to him since?"

"Apparently not," Charles said. "He says he and his son often don't communicate for long periods of time."

"What about the boy's mother? Doesn't she keep in contact with him?"

"I'll have someone contact her, but I doubt she talks to any of her children often. After the divorce, she married three more times. That tends to keep you busy, especially when you are as self-involved as she is."

"So where does that leave us?" Josh asked.

"Well, I told Leonard that we were close to solving the case, and that I would be able to comply with his request to interview Stephen for a job. He sounded happy at the prospect and promised to get back to me as soon as he located him. Now, what about the other two? Any information about them?"

"Not yet," Josh said.

There was a silence on the line. "I know you're feeling as frustrated as I am," Josh said. "Well, it's just a matter of time. I'm sure we'll be hearing from our sources soon."

"Damn." Charles laid down the phone.

"They still haven't found them?" Caroline asked.

He shook his head. "It makes no sense. I was sure it would take no longer than twenty-four hours, given what we know."

"I know this waiting is hard," she said, "but try to relax. Let Josh and the others do their jobs."

Charles settled back into the couch. "You're right. Everything's basically under control. And this is a pretty comfortable hideout. By the way, I heard a weather forecast. We may be snowed in by morning."

The fire danced from gusts of wind down the chimney. Caroline could hear Kate and Mike laughing as they played cards in the dining room. She curled up in the corner of the long couch, stroking Shadow, who sat close by her. She could hear Cody snoring in the corner. If only Josh were here, she thought.

"What are you thinking about?" Charles asked from the other end of the couch.

"Josh."

She didn't have to look at him to know his reaction to her honesty. Maybe the time had come to clear the air. She moved off the couch to the hassock in front of Charles, searching for the right words.

"I have to tell you I find it very ironic," she began, "that at exactly the moment you reappear in my life, I meet someone else."

Charles cleared his throat. "Am I to assume you're about to tell me that you have an intimate relationship with this man you basically just met?"

Caroline took a deep breath before replying. She wasn't going to let Charles make her feel guilty about Josh. Not with his history with women.

"You know," she said, "it always amazed me that you took for granted that I would be faithful to you while we were married, yet I was not supposed to expect the same fidelity from you. Even now, your tone of voice suggests that I somehow belong to you and have behaved inappropriately."

"And have you?" His voice was cold.

"If you must know," she said, "we were the soul of propriety while you were missing and for weeks after you were found. However, while we were in Los Angeles, yes, we *were* together. I'm sorry if that hurts you, but you and I have been apart for ten years. You have no right to question me about this."

Charles leaned closer to her, his eyes dark with anger.

"I invited you to Odessa, and you agreed to meet me, knowing my marriage to Brenda was over. Don't pretend you didn't understand the implications of my invitation!"

Caroline bit her lip. She couldn't deny the truth of that. A log fell in the fireplace. She stood, walked over to the fire and held her hands out to its warmth. When she finally turned, she was shocked to see the stricken look on Charles's face. He clearly hadn't expected this. I've hurt him, she thought. I've hurt him badly.

"Is this pay-back time?" he asked, in a low voice,

She barely recognized the voice full of pain. Without thinking, she went to sit beside him on the couch. "I'm sorry. I didn't do it to hurt you. It just...."

"So this is how it feels."

"What?"

The anger had drained from his eyes, leaving only sadness.

"This is how you felt years ago while we were married."

He looked devastated.

Caroline pushed herself up and off the couch, knowing she couldn't stay close to him another minute. Her every instinct was to hold him in her arms and tell him how sorry she was. The desire was so overwhelming that she could only stumble away— across the room and up the stairs.

"Caroline!"

She didn't look back.

CHAPTER TWENTY-SIX

Kate carried a tray laden with tea and cookies up the stairs and into the room. Caroline was standing at the window, looking out at the snow that had been coming down steadily during the night.

Turning, she smiled. "Good morning. What's all this?"

Kate was shocked to see how tired she looked. Charles had appeared the same way at breakfast. What was going on?

Setting the tray on the bed, Kate said, "I made us a midmorning snack. You didn't come down for breakfast, and I thought you might be hungry. Hope you like cinnamon tea. Sugar? Honey? Milk?"

"Here, I'll do it," Caroline said, joining her. "This was very sweet of you." Stirring in the honey, she carried the cup back to the window and sipped the hot tea.

Kate sat on the bed, poured her own tea and bit into one of Lottie's oatmeal raisin cookies.

"What are Mike and the men doing today?" Caroline asked.

"They're in the barn. I guess they save certain work for days like this, although Mike says they'll ride out later today to check on things. He'll probably go along. I've given up trying to slow him down."

Caroline stretched out on the chaise lounge in the corner of the room.

"These cookies are really good," Kate said. "Don't you want one?"

"I'm sure they are. Josh has a wonderful cook in Lottie. Maybe I'll have one later."

Kate knew she was being dismissed.

"Caroline," she said, "Is there anything you'd like to talk about?"

The falling snow seemed to wrap them in a cocoon of silence. Finally, Caroline said, "Maybe it would help to talk."

Kate grabbed another cookie and moved to rest her back against the headboard.

"I don't know how much you know about my relationship with Charles," Caroline said.

"I know you were married for a long time but didn't have any children."

Caroline nodded. "That's true. And just about the time we decided to look into adoption, we separated and divorced—which was my decision. I foolishly thought that if I left, Charles would change his wandering ways and come after me. Instead, he went to France and came home a few months later with his French mistress, who became his second wife."

"And we know how that turned out."

Both women laughed.

"This tea is delicious," Caroline said, looking more relaxed. "I think I'll have a cookie now."

Kate jumped up and carried the tray to her, sitting on a nearby chair. She loved having Caroline confide in her. Charles was such a jerk to have hurt this wonderful woman. She was about to say as much, but what Caroline said next shocked her into silence.

"I've never stopped loving him, you know. He was the only man I ever loved and that doesn't just end, even when your mind tells you it must. Oh, I dated off and on, but it was mainly just to socialize and get out of the house. My painting is really what sustained me over the years, that and my friends. Don't misunderstand, I've had a good life since our divorce, but I never met another man I was seriously attracted to."

"Until Josh," Kate said. Seeing Caroline's startled look, she said, "Sorry. I shouldn't have said that. I was just thinking that you and Josh have gotten close."

Caroline looked down, her face pale and drawn. "I admit that I'm attracted to Josh, but the emotional pull toward Charles is still there. When I told him last night that Josh and I...." She stopped, realizing what she had just admitted.

Kate clapped her hands. "That's great. I hoped that you and Josh would...well, I mean, you know...."

Caroline laughed. "Yes, I know. And it was wonderful! By the way, how are you and Mike getting along?"

Kate felt her face getting warm. "We haven't quite gotten to the place you and Josh have. Mike is being patient, and I haven't wanted to do anything that would hurt his recovery. But back to Josh and Charles—is it possible to be in love with two men at the same time?"

"You don't know how many times I've asked myself the same thing. I'm afraid I may end up hurting both of them." She sighed. "I did hurt Charles last night, and now he's trapped here, angry and upset. And I feel terrible about that."

Kate shook her head in amazement. "Why? You weren't the one unfaithful in your marriage. And you aren't his wife anymore, so where does he get off trying to make you feel guilty about being with another man?

"And while we're talking about Charles, I have to tell you I don't appreciate his lying about being alone in the car. I knew I saw a real, live man that night, a man that looked like my husband. But Charles just let everyone think I was crazy."

Caroline reached over and touched her hand. "I am so sorry about that. I suspected that one of his cartel friends might have been with him, but he convinced me that none of the cartel was involved. Of course, no one knew about Stephen. It just goes to show that we're way over our heads where Charles's wheelings and dealings are concerned.

"And now Josh is out there somewhere risking his life to protect us. Charles doesn't understand why Josh is so committed, but I do. He wants this to end, so he and I can move on. But how can we if I still have feelings for Charles?"

Kate understood Caroline's confusion, because her feelings for Mike didn't make sense either. Danny had been a sweetheart, so easy to love, while Mike could be a pain, and they argued a lot. But she did feel something special for him.

"Kate?" Caroline said, tilting her head. "What are you thinking, honey?"

"I was thinking about Mike. These past few weeks with him have been great." She smiled. "I don't think he ever wants to leave here. He really loves it."

"I can see that, and I know that Josh would love for him to stay. Would you like living here?"

"I don't know. Adam thinks I should see more of the world before I settle down."

"Really? And did he offer to show it to you?"

"I don't think Adam is interested in me that way. I mean he's sophisticated and smart and—"

"A very complicated man," Caroline finished for her. "Katie, dear heart, I think you and I both have decisions to make. Thank you for encouraging me to talk about everything. I do feel better."

Hearing Mike at the front door, Kate rushed from the kitchen into the great room to meet him.

"You are soaking wet. Get out of those clothes, immediately."

"You mean right here, right now?" Mike asked.

"I'll go get a robe and socks for you. I can't believe you were out all afternoon in this weather."

Mike walked over to stand in front of the fireplace. He took off his shirt, socks and shoes and stood shivering in the large room that was dark except for the light from the fire.

Kate hurried back down the stairs and across the room to him. He wrapped up in the heavy robe she handed him and stripped off his pants from underneath it. Sitting on the leather hassock close to the fire, he pulled on the new socks while Kate started to dry his hair with a towel. "Enough already," he said, taking it from her and rubbing his head briskly. He then tossed it aside, reached out and threw another log on the fire.

Kate sat beside him on the large hassock, and they stared into the fire that had flared higher around the new wood.

Mike put his arm around her and buried his face into her auburn curls. He whispered, "What did you do today, Katie-girl?"

She leaned against him. "Caroline and I talked about Charles and Josh—and you."

She moved away to look into his eyes. What she saw made her catch her breath.

Mike pulled her backwards on the hassock, and they started to kiss when a voice from the doorway of the dining room brought them both to a sitting position.

"Oh, excuse me," Caroline said.

Kate slid across the hassock to the closest chair, and Mike moved to the couch.

"Come join us," Kate said. "Mike was just getting warmed up."

"So I noticed," Caroline said, smiling. She sat beside him on the couch.

"Is supper ready?" Kate asked.

"Just about. Have you seen Charles?"

A sudden cough made everyone turn toward the far corner of the large room, where Charles's bed sat.

"Shit, were you there all this time?" Mike asked.

"The dogs and I were napping." Charles got out of bed, stretched and called out, "Come on, boys, let's go see what Lottie has for you in the kitchen." Shadow and Cody ran ahead of him through the room.

"See you at the supper table," he said, chuckling.

Kate covered her face with her hands. "I can't believe we didn't see him over there."

Mike stood and wrapped the robe around him. "This room is too damn big." He headed toward the stairs. "I'm going to put some clothes on. Didn't realize I had an audience while I stripped or when…."

Kate and Caroline burst out laughing.

Kate waited impatiently. Mike and she had agreed that he would come to her room as soon as everyone in the household had gone to bed.

Finally, she heard the knock she'd been waiting for. Crossing the room, she opened the bedroom door. Mike stood in the doorway, holding two beers in his hand.

"Come in. Everyone else asleep?"

"I hope so. It's damn hard to get privacy around here. I thought we might have to go out to the barn."

Kate giggled. "Now that sounds like fun. We could still do that."

Crossing the room and sitting beside her on the bed, he said, "With our luck, Tom and the whole crew would check on the horses in the middle of the night."

Kate pulled her robe tighter around her. She *had* invited Mike to her room but was beginning to feel a little nervous.

He handed her a beer.

She placed it on the bedside table, where a decanter of wine and two glasses sat. "I did some smuggling tonight, or rather, Caroline did—said Josh wouldn't mind. Apparently he's got a big wine cellar." She poured herself a glass.

"I'll stick to beer," Mike said. He quickly drank one can then reached for the other on the table.

He's as nervous as I am, Kate thought. Somehow knowing that made her feel better. She slid back and patted the comforter. "Come get comfortable."

Mike finished his beer, moved farther onto the bed and rolled onto his back, an arm behind his head.

Kate sipped her wine and glanced toward the dark window. "I love being snowed in. It's cozy."

"Real cozy," Mike said. Smiling, he closed his eyes.

Kate finished her glass of wine and felt the warmth of its effect. She looked at Mike's lean body from the broad shoulders and chest to the tapered waist. He had taken off his boots.

She touched the flannel shirt covering his ribs. "Do they still hurt you?" she asked.

He opened his eyes but didn't move. "No, everything's healed, Katie. You don't have to worry about that."

She could feel the tension in the muscles under her hand.

Glancing up, she said, "I'm not very experienced, Mike. Danny was the first, well the only man...."

He took her hand and pulled her alongside him. "I understand. It's all right."

She snuggled closer, aligning her body to his and resting her head on his shoulder. Mike turned slightly toward her and whispered, "Katie." She lifted her face to his, and he kissed her, first lightly then....

She didn't want the kiss to end. This was the Mike she had come to love—strong but tender, intense in his feelings. She moved into the embrace, feeling every muscle of his lean body as it strained to get closer. He moved his hand down her side and under her robe, touching bare skin. Kate guided it to her breasts. Her robe fell open.

She trembled. Needing him closer, she grasped his shirt in both hands and tugged until he lay on top of her, enjoying the feel of his clothed body on her bare skin and the slow, deep kiss until he shifted and.... "Oh!" she cried out. The cold buckle of his belt brought the intimate moment to an end.

"I think you'd better get out of those jeans," she said, laughing.

"I also need to get something."

Mike rolled off the bed. Kate slipped completely out of her robe and under the covers. She had no more reservations, no more fears or doubts. She knew exactly what she needed now and what she wanted to give to this man, who had healed her pain and led her into a new life.

Joining her under the covers, Mike said, "You feel so small in my arms." He touched her mouth then ran his finger slowly down her throat and between her breasts to her stomach. He buried his face into her softness. She grasped his head tightly, feeling vulnerable, unsure.

He glanced up, and she tried to smile but her mouth began to quiver. Mike immediately shifted upwards until he was face to face with her. Holding himself over her, he stared down in concern. "You know I would never hurt you, Katie. Never do anything you didn't want me to do. Protect you. You know that, don't you?"

And she did. She knew she could trust this man. This beautiful, sensual man. She reached up to him. She didn't want tenderness anymore. She wanted his passion, his hard body.

And fiercely, skillfully, Mike took her where she wanted to go.

Caroline walked down the steps, Shadow following close behind. She didn't want to wake anyone up. The clock by her bed had read 2:09 a.m., and she'd tossed and turned for another twenty minutes. Knowing that a cup of tea was the answer to her insomnia, she reached the bottom of the steps and started across the great room toward the kitchen. From his dog bed, Cody raised his head and looked at them. "It's okay," she whispered.

"Caroline?"

The slight glow from dying embers in the fireplace allowed her to see well enough to make her way over to Charles's bed.

"Can't sleep either?" he said.

Caroline sat on the end of the bed, hugging her knees to her chest. Charles shifted to a sitting position. She waited to take her cue from him. They had made the necessary small talk at supper last night then gone their separate ways for the evening, both knowing they would eventually have this conversation.

"Well," Charles began, in a cool, controlled voice, "I've been thinking about you. I think we need to clear the air. Then maybe we both can sleep again."

Caroline waited.

"I need to know how you feel about Josh. I knew he was attracted to you, but I didn't know how serious things had gotten. Just spell it out for me, Caroline."

"I wish," she said, "that I could tell you exactly what I'm feeling about everything. This is the first time since we divorced that I've had strong feelings for another man. But you have to understand how unreal the past few months have been. First your disappearance, then all the rest. Josh has been there for me every step of the way. I'm grateful to him for so much. I don't know if...."

Charles leaned forward. "Gratitude is one thing, love is...well, you and I had the real thing for many years. I believe we still do. Even before my experience in the mountain I knew that I wanted our life back. Being alone in that damn mountain only deepened my commitment to a future with you. Surely, you can sense that. You've always known me better than anyone."

The coldness of the room made Caroline shiver, and she pulled one of the several bed covers covering Charles around her.

"You know," she said, "that I will always love you in some part of my heart. And I believe you when you say the last ten years and the horrible experience in the mountain has changed you." She stopped, unsure how to explain her feelings.

"Go on," Charles said.

"But I guess I don't really trust you, emotionally. Your marriage to Brenda shocked me more than you can ever know. I felt as though I was replaceable, that your love for me was not as deep as my love for you.

"Eventually the pain went away, and I saw you more clearly. I realized that the life you kept secret from me was more important to you than our marriage. When I gave you an ultimatum, you chose that life. I know you came to regret that decision later, but it *was* a choice."

Charles had listened without interruption. Now he cleared his throat and said, "You're right. About everything. There was a time when building my business empire and enjoying the perks that went with success were all that mattered to me. I took your love and our marriage for granted. When you called me on it, I thought you were trying to control me. So I ran the other way, right into the arms of the most controlling person in the world."

Caroline appreciated his honesty. "Thank you," she said. "I know that was hard for you to admit."

After a few minutes of silence, Caroline moved the covers aside and got out of bed. "I think I can sleep now," she said. She leaned down, kissed Charles on the cheek and walked toward the stairs.

Charles called out, in a tone she had never heard before, "I love you."

CHAPTER TWENTY-SEVEN

Josh sat at the makeshift desk in the saloon and listened to his messages, first Charles's instructions and then Caroline's reply to the message he had left her. There was something in her voice....

This was taking too damn long. He turned to the papers spread out in front of him and studied the sketches of their three suspects. Adam had filled in details about his brother. Jimmy appeared to be a screwed-up idealist. Josh found it difficult to understand how a man from such a fine family could have gotten so far off-track.

Then there was Stephen. According to Charles, his parents had provided a rich playground growing up but little attention or love.

Which hardly explained becoming a kidnapper and murderer.

He looked at the third sketch. They had no profile on the man with the goatee. He appeared Caucasian with a narrow face and hooded eyes, balding and probably in his late thirties or early forties. He was an enigma.

Josh tapped his fingers on the desk. For days he'd been anticipating leads from his different sources. Detective Anderson at the L.A.P.D. was waiting for him to provide a possible address for Stephen. His father would hopefully come through with that information.

Adam walked into the saloon. "No, not yet," he was saying into the phone. "No, I'm not coming back any time soon." He listened, frowning. "I only take orders from Charles, and until I know for sure he's dead, I intend to continue to follow up on leads."

"Jerk," he said, as he turned the phone off.

"Problems?"

"Nothing new. Jenson wants me back in the office. I don't know how much longer I can put him off. With Charles gone, they're in something of a bind. Maybe we should head back to LA."

"Maybe, but first I want to get a few things clear in my mind. Sit down, we need to talk." Adam pulled up a small, wooden bench.

"I'm sure Charles told you that I know what he's been up to, in general," Josh said, "but lay it out for me, chronologically and in detail. When did this project get underway?"

When Adam hesitated, Josh repeated the threat he'd made to Charles. "I refuse to work in the dark. If you don't want to end up working this case by yourself, you'd better tell me what you know."

"Okay, okay," Adam said, "this is what I've been able to piece together. In the mid-nineties, Charles received confidential information from a friend at the Bureau of Land Management who owed him a favor. He told Charles that the government was searching for a safe place to build the largest and most productive nuclear facility in the country."

Josh nodded. "So how did the cartel fit in?"

"That's where it gets interesting. A member of the cartel has the patent on a new technique of water recycling. As you know, nuclear power plants generate large amounts of electrical energy but use vast amounts of water. This new technique eliminates the need of constant replenishment of river water. The cartel realized that with the patent and the right location, they would be in a great bargaining position."

"So Charles finds the perfect location," Josh said.

Adam got up and began to pace the floor. "Right. Judson, Nevada is isolated and not close to any fault lines. Even more importantly, it sits on top of natural underground caverns— capable of holding vast amounts of coolant water, which can be recycled and replenished by a pipeline to the Colorado River. This means the plant could provide inexpensive electricity to the western states in an almost inexhaustible supply."

Josh pushed back in his chair and propped his boots on the table. "Which puts the cartel in a powerful negotiating position."

"Right, but they also had to get their political ducks in a row. So, in California, they supported unsuspecting politicians behind deregulation, and the energy crisis developed exactly as they hoped, pushing the state deeper into debt. Between water concerns and laws prohibiting construction of plants anywhere near a fault, California was now out of the picture, leaving Nevada as the only viable location. All that was left to do was buy up the land. Then they could begin negotiations with the government." Adam stopped pacing. "Damn, I wish Charles had cut me in."

"Oh, yeah," Josh said. "Then you would have ended up inside that mountain with him."

Adam ignored the comment. "Charles started quietly buying up land between Judson and the Colorado River. It took time, money and persuasion, but finally, the cartel was almost ready to deal. If the Bureau of Land Management and the Atomic Energy Commission approved the site, they planned to sell the land in Judson to the government plus easements to the Colorado River and then bid to construct the plant. They would offer to provide the innovative technology and engineers with the expertise to manage the new recycling system."

Josh finished the scenario for him. "And by now they had the backing of the right people in the right places, both in

Washington and Nevada. They're ready to finalize the deal and—Charles disappears."

"That's right," Adam said, "years of planning, and everything stops cold."

Josh sat quietly, going over everything in his mind. He wasn't sure how he felt about the project in regard to the environmental impact. But he did know how he felt about people who took the law into their own hands, and he was determined to put those responsible for Charles's kidnapping behind bars.

As Charles stood in the library area of the ranch house trying to decide on a book, the cell phone in his pocket rang.

"Laughery here."

"Charles! I didn't know they were murderers. I swear I didn't know. I wouldn't have taken their money if I'd known. You've got to believe me!"

"Linda! My God, are you all right?"

"I'm okay, but…." He heard the fear in her voice. "I'm calling to warn you. They know where you are, and they're coming after you. They're crazy, really crazy. I overheard them talking last night, and they were bragging about getting into your ex-wife's house and finding an address on her desk. Jimmy and Victor took off this morning. Stephen is still here with me. This is the first chance I had to call you. He went to the grocery store, but he'll be back soon. I'm scared, Charles!"

Charles began talking in a calm voice, trusting Linda would do exactly what he told her to do. She always had. "Listen carefully. Get out of there and go to the nearest police station. Ask them to contact Detective Richard Anderson, the LA detective working with us on this. I'll let him know you're coming. Now give me your address. The cops will be waiting for Stephen when he returns."

The silence went on too long. Charles could hear her weeping. "Linda, you have a choice. You can spend years in jail as an accomplice or help us catch these guys and get a second chance."

Finally, in a quivering voice, Linda said, "I'm sorry, Charles. Please forgive me. Victor insisted they planned to get you out of the mountain eventually. He explained they were just trying to save the environment from a nuclear disaster. I don't know why I listened to him, but he's so charismatic, so—"

"A last name, Linda. We need Victor's last name." There was a pause; then in an embarrassed voice, she confessed, "I don't know. He never told me. Just talked about his goals and how he was going to make a difference in the world. The young guys hang onto his every word, and…well, I did, too. Until last night."

"Are you sure they don't know you overheard them?"

"I'm sure, or Stephen wouldn't have left me alone today. I tried to sneak out around 1:00 a.m. to call you, but Victor woke up. He bought into my story about being hungry. I was afraid to try again. I didn't sleep all night. Victor and Jimmy flew out of LAX to Colorado early this morning. Oh, my God, Charles, I'm so sorry about all this. I…."

"Linda, give me your address and get out of there. Cooperate with the cops. We'll sort out the rest later. You're going to have to trust me. I'm the only hope you have of getting out of this mess!"

Charles took down the address and called Anderson, who promised to send his men immediately to pick up Stephen. His next call was to Josh, who listened to the news without interruption.

"So how soon can you get back here?" Charles asked.

"Not soon enough, but that's okay. Time should be on our side. Depending on how early the two left this morning, they may not have landed yet, and the police might be able to catch them at the airport. I know this is a bit hairy, Charles, but it's the break we've been waiting for. Just keep everyone calm on that end."

"I'm not worried. We have plenty of men around for protection and only one road out of here. As long as we stay put, we should be safe. Shit! Caroline. She went with your manager, Tom, to Durango this morning. Needed art supplies. No problem. I'll call and tell them to get back here right away."

A few minutes later, Charles's call to Caroline went to her voice mail.

CHAPTER TWENTY-EIGHT

Caroline paid for the art supplies and checked her watch. She still had almost an hour before she had to meet Tom and head back to the ranch. Maybe she would check out the bookstore on Main Street. She breathed in the brisk Durango air, enjoying the sight of the snow-covered San Juan Mountains. Mike was right. This would be a great place to live.

She walked slowly, window-shopping. A block before Main, a car pulled up beside her, and a man jumped out. Caroline immediately recognized the slim, handsome face. Jimmy was a slighter version of Adam. He smiled, and she forced herself to smile back.

"Well, this is a surprise, Ms. Laughery. We haven't seen one another for quite a while, have we?"

"Jimmy Hill. How nice to see you. Do you live in Durango now?" Caroline's heart was beating wildly. Then she saw the police car down the street. *Thank God.* The car moved closer but turned into a parking lot and disappeared from view.

Caroline slid her hand into her pocketbook and pulled out her cell phone. "I'll take that, Ms. Laughery," Jimmy said, grabbing it from her. "Now, come along with me. I want you to meet someone." He opened the car door and motioned for her to get in.

Caroline saw an older couple approaching. The gun that Jimmy had taken from his jacket was hidden from their view. He saw them, too. "You don't want to endanger anyone else now, do you?" he said, his eyes narrowing.

She crawled into the back seat, and the man behind the wheel turned around.

"Hello, Ms. Laughery. Jimmy's told me nice things about you. I'm sure we're going to get along just fine." He continued talking as he pulled away, watching her in the rear view mirror. "Isn't it amazing how fate solves our problems for us? We were trying to figure out how we could flush your ex-husband out of his hiding place, and—there you were! Now just relax. We're going to a special place and see what the world was like before bastards like Charles Laughery began destroying it."

"Tom, I need to talk to Caroline," Charles said. "She must not have her phone on."

"I'm not with her, Mr. Laughery. We're supposed to meet up downtown. I'll tell her to call you when I see her."

Charles wiped perspiration from his forehead.

"Listen carefully, Tom. The men who kidnapped me are on their way to Colorado. I want you to find Caroline and go straight to the Police Station. Josh is talking to the Chief of Police right now, and his men will escort you back here."

"This isn't good. I should have stayed with Caroline."

"Never mind that now, Tom. I thought we were safe here, too. Just call me as soon as you find her."

"I'm on my way."

Charles stared at the phone. *Come on, Caroline, check your messages and call.*

The sudden sound of Mike and Kate's laughter on the porch calmed him. Everything was going to be okay. Caroline would be back soon, and all of them would just hunker down and wait for reinforcements. Josh was right. The police would probably intercept the men at the airport.

Kate stomped the snow off her boots before entering the front door of the great room. "Charles, you've got to go outside. It's a gorgeous day. Isn't it, Mike?" Crossing the room, she said, "I'm going to make us lunch. Want a sandwich?" Charles shook his head. As soon as Kate left, he turned to Mike.

"We've got a problem."

Charles quickly explained what was happening.

"The Durango police are going to escort Tom and Caroline back here?" Mike asked.

"Right. What I want you to do is round up a few men and station them down the road as look-outs. Who knows, we may just wrap this up today, and we all can go home."

Seeing Mike's face, he revised his statement. "Well, Caroline and I can leave. You and Kate may want to stay awhile."

"That's up to Josh," Mike said. Hurrying out the front door, he called back over his shoulders, "First, we need to catch these guys."

As soon as the door closed behind him, Kate walked into the room. "Lottie insists on making.... Where's Mike?"

Charles walked over to the couch. "I asked him to do something for me. Come sit down, Kate. I need to talk to you."

She hesitated then joined him, curling up on one of the chairs. Charles glanced at his watch. He'd give Caroline and Tom a few more minutes to call. No need to frighten the young woman who sat staring into the fire.

"You don't like me much, do you, Kate?"

She looked uncomfortable and didn't answer.

"Look," he continued, "I'm sure Caroline has told you about our history together. But that's in the past. I'm not the same man I was ten years ago. You don't have to worry about me hurting her again."

Kate glanced at him then away.

I've embarrassed her, he thought. I must be more anxious than I want to admit if I'm wasting time trying to.... His phone rang. It was Tom.

"Yes!" he shouted then listened in dismay. "Where was she supposed to meet you? You've checked every store? Have you called the...? Oh, okay. Be sure the police cover every inch of the town. She has to be somewhere. Just keep looking. I'm going to call Josh and tell him to fly directly into the Durango airport rather than here. Call me the minute you find Caroline."

Kate was staring at him, wide-eyed. "What's wrong? What's going on?"

Before he could answer, Mike came through the door.

"Okay, the men are on the road and stationed around the house."

He saw Kate's face and hurried over to her. Charles let him explain the situation.

When his cell phone rang again, Charles was relieved to see Caroline's number. Before he could speak, however, a male voice said, "I have someone here who would like to speak to you."

Caroline came on the line. "Charles, I'm okay. I'm sure they won't hurt me—"

"Don't count on that, Laughery," the male voice said. "How this turns out is up to you. All we want is a simple exchange. We'll be waiting for you at Mesa Verde. Take 160E out of Durango to Ruins Road. Chapin Mesa Road will take you across the mesa to the Cliff Palace ruins. I'll keep in touch with you by phone. Wouldn't want you to get lost.

"One more thing, Laughery. If you bring the cops into this, things will not turn out the way you want them to. Do you understand?"

"I understand. I'm on my way."

There was a brief pause.

"Remember what I said. Don't involve anyone else. And come without weapons!"

"Don't worry," Charles assured him, "I intend to fully cooperate. I won't notify anyone. Just promise me you'll let Caroline go."

The line went dead. When Charles looked up, Kate and Mike were staring at him. "I have to get going," he said.

Kate's eyes were full of fear. "You can't do this by yourself. You've got to call Josh, the police. Get help!"

Charles leaned toward her. "If I don't do exactly as I've been instructed, Caroline could die. Do you understand? As long as I don't involve the authorities, she'll be back here by tonight, safe and sound."

"What about you?" Kate asked.

"I've talked myself out of difficult situations before."

Mike put his arm around Kate. "Charles is right. We have to do it his way. If we do, this could all be over very soon."

Kate turned back to Charles. "Can you at least tell us where you're going?"

He shook his head. "I can't risk the plan going awry. You can't tell anyone what you don't know.

"Mike, I want you to come as far as Durango with me. I'll drop you off at the Police Station. Josh is on his way there. As soon as Caroline is safe, she can call and let you know our exact location."

"Sounds like a plan to me," Mike said.

The men hurried out the door.

The winding road seemed to go on forever. Charles gripped the wheel tightly as he raced toward the mesa. He saw a sign ahead that read, Ruins Road. At the gate to the park, he double-checked the directions to the Cliff Palace ruins with the attendant and began the climb to the top of the mesa.

Maybe I should have brought a gun, he thought. No, too dangerous. Undoubtedly Caroline's abductors have guns, and she might get caught in the crossfire.

He was going to do this by the book and whatever happened to him happened. He didn't intend for anyone else to pay for his mistakes.

CHAPTER TWENTY-NINE

Josh, Mike, Adam and Leroy stood in the hallway of the Police Department. "Let me get this straight," Chief Weaver said, "Charles Laughery has taken off to rescue his ex-wife. But we don't know where he went. Is he out of his mind? He could get both of them killed."

Leroy looked distraught and shaken. "Why didn't he let me go with him?"

"He's protecting Caroline," Josh said. "She'll be able to call us as soon as they let her go, and then we can move in and help him."

Josh knew he would have done exactly what Charles was doing—get Caroline out of harm's way first.

"I don't like it," Chief Weaver said, "but there's nothing we can do about it. Here's what we know. James Hill and a Victor Harrison arrived several hours ago at the airport. They rented a dark green Ford Taurus, and I think it's safe to say they won't be returning it. We have an APB out on them. All we can do now is wait for the lady's call." He turned and left.

Josh sat on one of the long wooden benches along the wall. He understood the Chief's frustration. The last time he'd felt this helpless was when the doctor gave him Hannah's prognosis. Now another woman he loved might die.

And then there was Charles. *I've let him down.*

Adam joined him on the bench. He had said little on the plane ride to Durango.

Knowing your brother is threatening the lives of people you care about must be devastating, Josh thought.

As though reading his mind, Adam said. "He won't hurt them, Josh. Jimmy might go along with some crazy schemes, but he's not a murderer."

Josh raised one eyebrow. "He left Charles to die in that mountain."

Adam shook his head. "We don't know that for sure. I think he would have eventually let someone know where Charles was." He stared down at the floor. "I have to believe that."

Josh didn't agree, but even if Adam was right about Jimmy, there was still Victor, the third man, the unknown element.

Victor leaned back against the stone wall of the ruins cut into the cliff. "Your ex-husband should be here soon," he said.

Caroline turned away from him. The late afternoon sun glistened off the snow in front of them. A few tourists walked leisurely around the far side of the large ruins. *If I called out, would Victor shoot me and innocent people? No, I can't take the chance. But what about Charles? If I wait until he arrives, what chance will he have?*

She had tried to establish a rapport with Victor by agreeing with his environmental beliefs, but he was too savvy. She glanced over at Jimmy. Maybe she could reach him.

"Jimmy," she said. "I'd like to help you stop Charles's project. You know how I feel about the environment. I mean, look at this place. Victor is right. This is how the world once was. We have to find a way to protect it."

Jimmy was staring off into the distance. When he finally spoke, his eyes were wild. "Don't you understand that it's too late? Haven't you kept up with the statistics? Our efforts didn't stop men like Charles Laughery from destroying everything they touched. This isn't about saving the planet anymore. This is about justice!"

Caroline quickly changed the subject, hoping to calm him down. "Do you know the history of Mesa Verde?" Seeing a flicker of interest in his eyes, she continued. "The Anasazi Indians built these cliff dwellings."

Jimmy didn't respond. "They successfully grew crops, hunted and stored food. Made lovely pottery and were masters at basket making. No one knows why they left around the end of the 13th century."

"I know all about the Anasazi," Jimmy said. "They built hundreds of kivas in these ruins."

"Kivas?" Caroline repeated. She knew what they were but if it got Jimmy talking....

"Kivas are underground rooms, some small, some really big with small openings at the top. They used them for workshops, leisure and their religious rituals." Jimmy closed his eyes, apparently visualizing it in his mind. "There's a round space in the middle of the floor of the kivas that represents the spirit entrance to the Four Worlds below, where the Indians believed they came from."

He smiled and opened his eyes. They were bright and clear now.

What happened to this intelligent, young man? Caroline wondered. How did he get so lost?

When he didn't continue, she prompted, "That's fascinating. Please, tell me more about—" "There he is!" Victor said. He pointed toward the path leading from the parking lot.

Shielding her eyes from the bright sun, Caroline saw Charles walking down the path, scanning the ruins.

"Wave to him," Victor demanded.

Trembling, she held up her hand, and Charles immediately looked their way.

"Now," Victor said to Caroline, "as soon as he gets here, you can leave. There's just one more thing that I want you to do. Tell the media that we stopped Charles Laughery and his cohorts from a nuclear disaster. I want the world to know that we're heroes. Do you understand?" Caroline, her mouth too dry to speak, could only nod.

When Charles reached them, Victor said, "Jimmy, check him for weapons and phones." Jimmy frisked Charles, tossing his cell phone to Victor.

"Check out his vehicle." He looked at Charles. "What are you driving?"

"An orange Chevy truck. I left the keys in it."

Jimmy ran across the ruins and up the path. Ten minutes later, he was back.

"Nothing there," he assured Victor.

"Good. You did good, Laughery. Now, dear lady, get out of here."

Caroline quickly reached out to hug Charles.

"Under the tire chains," he whispered. She stared at him, until Victor shoved her forward.

"Get going. And remember what I told you."

"It's going to be all right," Charles said. "Go on."

Stumbling away, she looked back at him. He seemed strangely composed. Resigned. *Dear God, he's accepted that he's going to die.* Victor motioned her on, and she continued walking. When she turned again, Charles, Victor and Jimmy had disappeared.

In the parking lot, Caroline understood Charles's cryptic message. In the bed of the truck was a pile of tire chains. When she spread them out, she found another cell phone entangled in the bottom chains.

Her hand shook as she called Josh's number and gave him the location.

In a voice filled with relief, he assured her that the Durango police were on their way.

"We'll also alert the park rangers at the mesa. They'll come get you. Someone will bring you to the Police Station. Leave the truck there. I'm going to fly to the mesa, and we'll need it. It's going to be all right, Caroline. We're going to find Charles."

Too weak to stand, she leaned against the truck.

"Hurry, Josh. Hurry."

The men stood at the back of the ruins behind a wall. Victor had been ranting for several minutes about his father.

"John Harrison's son," Charles said. "I thought your voice sounded familiar. It's been almost twenty years, but I can still hear you threatening me on the phone—that is, until the authorities tracked you down. Your father begged me not to prosecute. And I didn't."

The sneer on Victor's face reminded Charles of the one time he'd seen him. Then he'd had long hair and no goatee. After all these years, he still hates me, Charles thought in amazement.

"You actually came to my college," Victor said, "and lectured me on the illegality of harassing phone calls. I should have killed you then!" The hatred in his eyes was chilling. He's not just an environmental advocate, Charles thought. There's something more going on here.

"You killed my father! He didn't only lose his company, he lost his will to live. I tried to get him involved in a new business venture, but he basically retired and gave up. He was a broken man by the time you got through with him!"

Charles tried to remember the details of the deal, but he'd been involved in so many corporate takeovers in the eighties.

"I'm sure your father got full market value for his company. It was a tough business environment, but I always played fair." Charles didn't mention that he tried to target those CEOs who appeared weak and vulnerable.

Victor leaned forward, pushing his face into Charles's. "You bastard, you don't know the meaning of fair. But you are about to learn, because I intend to be fair with you. I left you alive in the mountain, and somehow you survived. So now I'm going to give you another chance. Only this time...."

He called to Jimmy, who was standing guard a short distance away. "Let's get going, James."

Charles watched the conflicting emotions on the young man's face. He stood in front of Victor, kicking at the hard-packed ground. "I've been thinking, Victor. Kivas are sacred places. I don't know if we should use one for...." He looked at Charles. "The Anasazi thought they were gateways to...."

"Will you shut up about those damn Indians! They left 700 years ago, and I don't think their ghosts are going to give a shit if we use one of their stupid kivas. Now come on. We need to get out of here." He pushed Charles forward.

They climbed the steep incline to a maintenance road, where Victor shoved Charles into the back seat of the Taurus.

He began to breathe easier. He was still alive.

A few minutes later, Victor pulled off onto a side road and around a "closed for winter" sign. He continued down the road until snow stopped the car. Yanking Charles out of the back seat, the men trudged through snow toward an undeveloped area. Reaching the ruins, the men sat on the rock-strewn floor, breathing hard.

Victor smiled at Charles. "A friend of mine worked here years ago and showed me some of the areas not yet renovated. I decided this would be the perfect final resting place for you." He turned to Jimmy. "Go find a suitable kiva for our friend here."

Walking around the ruins, Jimmy yelled, "Over here!"

Victor yanked Charles to his feet and across the ruins floor.

Jimmy was on his knees staring into what appeared to be a room below the surface. Charles could feel his chest constrict.

Not again. Dear God, not again.

CHAPTER THIRTY

The men searched through the Cliff Palace ruins, but there was no trace of Charles or his abductors.

"I still don't understand how they could have escaped without us seeing them," Mike said.

"Goddamn it to hell!" Leroy exclaimed. "Where did the bastards take him?"

"Is there another way out of here?" Josh asked.

The ranger standing beside him pointed to the steep terrain that surrounded the ruins.

"Up top, there are a few small utility roads, but most are closed during the winter. Let me check with the rangers at the other sites."

As they waited, Mike said, "I can't believe you landed your plane on the main road, Josh."

"Neither can I," Adam complained.

"Well, you do what you have to do," Josh said.

The park ranger returned. "No sign of a Taurus at any of the other sites or on the main road."

Josh shook his head in frustration. "Damn. Well, the Durango police will be here shortly. Between them and you guys, we should be able to come up with a search plan. We'll find Charles. I just hope it's in time."

"You can climb down or we can give you a little help," Victor said to Charles.

Jimmy was pulling a wooden ladder across the ruins. He lowered it into the kiva and nervously looked around. "We need to go, Victor. They could be right behind us."

"Stop whining. I want a few more minutes with our friend here. It's not often that you get to bury your enemy twice."

Charles looked into the opening of the kiva and then into Victor's eyes. He knew he had no choice. If he cooperated, Victor probably wouldn't shoot him. The madman wanted him to suffer—as he had in the mountain.

He turned and started moving downward into the darkness, one step at a time, until he reached the bottom. He looked up into Victor's grinning face.

"I didn't get a chance to say good-bye last time. I can't tell you how satisfying it is to know that the last face you ever see— is mine!" With those words, Victor pulled the ladder out of the kiva, and he and Jimmy slid a sandstone block over the opening.

Caroline was surprised to see Kate rush through the front door of the Police Station.

"Kate! Josh said you were safe at the ranch."

"I told the men they could either drive me to town or I'd ride Brandy. Where's Mike?"

"Let's find a quiet place to talk." The women went into a small, adjacent room.

Kate tugged on Caroline's arm. "Is Mike in danger?"

"Everyone is on their way to the ruins to help Charles. The men have plenty of backup. Mike will be okay." Tears unexpectedly filled Caroline's eyes. She looked away.

"But you aren't that sure about Charles, are you?" Kate said, touching her shoulder.

"I'm sorry." With both hands, she wiped away the tears that had spilled down her cheeks.

Kate put an arm around her.

"Did they hurt you?" she whispered.

"No, no. Just scared me. If it had only been Jimmy, I think things would have turned out differently, but Victor is a very disturbed man. He has some kind of vendetta against Charles."

A presence at the door made both of them look up. "Mrs. Laughery, I have a call for you. Can you come to the front desk?"

Caroline didn't correct him. In some ways, she still felt like Charles's wife.

The desk clerk handed her the phone, and she was relieved to hear Josh's voice.

"We haven't located Charles yet," he said, "but we will. I wanted to let you know what's happening. And I needed to know if you were all right."

"I'm fine. Kate's here with me."

"Kate's at the police station? How did she... oh, never mind, as long as she's safe. Promise me that you both will stay there until this is over."

Caroline agreed, looking at Kate, who was gesturing in front of her.

"Is Mike with you?" she asked.

"He's right here, but we have to go now. I'll call you as soon as we know anything."

He was gone before Caroline could say goodbye. She felt fear and a sense of helplessness. The men were out there somewhere with potential killers. And poor Adam. His brother was one of them.

Adam looked out over the darkening mesa as purple shadows moved over the vast expanse of snow. Chief Weaver and Josh walked over to stand beside him.

"We're ready to go, Adam," Josh said.

"When we find them, let me talk to Jimmy first," he pleaded. "I know I can reason with him. Give me a chance to save Charles without bloodshed!"

Josh turned to the Chief. "It's your call."

"If your friend here can negotiate Laughery's release, great, but I won't endanger any of my men, so we'll have to see how things play out." He turned to Adam. "Understand?"

Adam nodded, sure that Jimmy would listen. He'd be able to reach him. Or at least distract him long enough for the others to deal with Victor.

He listened as the men worked out a search plan. The park rangers knew the mesa best. Chief Weaver told Josh, Leroy and Mike to go with the rangers then beckoned to him. "You come with me and my men. If we find your brother, you can take a stab at talking to him as long as the only life you risk is your own."

"Fair enough," Adam said.

Although he had never been involved in Jimmy's schemes, he felt responsible for his brother's actions. Maybe he could redeem himself by saving Charles.

Trapped in the dark again. Was this to be his fate? To escape from the mountain, only to die here?

The darkness of the kiva was not as black as that of the mountain. He could see a sliver of twilight at one edge of the stone slab blocking the entrance. Soon the sun would set, however, and all light would be gone.

Although the opening was small, the kiva, itself, was large. He could barely see the far wall in the dim light.

He felt strangely calm. What had Jimmy said? Kivas were spiritual places. Was he feeling the presence of those who had once prayed here? If he prayed, would he be heard? Would Caroline hear him again?

Or would he join the spirits of the Anasazi?

Charles rubbed his arms briskly against the increasing cold. No, he'd survived the mountain. He would survive this!

Josh and Mike stared through the windshield of the ranger's truck as the wipers swept away the lightly falling snow.

The ranger stopped the truck and jumped out, looking up into the sky. Josh heard the sound of the helicopter before he saw it. He rolled down the window and stuck his head out. "Lead us to the bastards," he shouted.

Victor cursed as he pushed the car while Jimmy gunned the engine. The tires spun. He thought they'd be out of the park by now, but every side road they'd taken after dumping Laughery into the kiva had led to a dead end. Or, like now, the car couldn't get through the snow.

The car door opened, and Jimmy climbed out. "We're never going to get out of here!" he said, panic in his voice.

"Shut the hell up! Come help me find more rocks to throw into this blasted hole."

The men began digging through the snow by the side of the road. An unusual noise broke the silence.

Victor stood still as the whirring sound grew louder. "Holy shit," he muttered.

"Get in the car!" he yelled to Jimmy.

Running to the driver's side, Victor climbed in and floored the gas pedal. The car jerked forward slightly, slid back then moved ahead again. Jimmy had jumped into the passenger seat. The Taurus lurched forward and picked up momentum as it started down the narrow road.

Jimmy laughed. "Good job."

The idiot doesn't know what the hell is happening, Victor thought. Reaching another, smaller road that branched off to the right, he turned the wheel abruptly and plowed through the snow.

"What are you doing?"

"Are you deaf? Can't you hear the helicopter?"

Perspiration broke out on Victor's forehead but then he saw it—another site straight ahead. If they could get the car close enough, they might be able to hide. Reaching an outcropping of rock in the cliff dwelling, Victor pulled the car underneath, cut the engine and jumped out. Jimmy followed, and they stooped behind a small wall, watching as the helicopter drew closer.

"Won't they see the car?"

"Not if we're lucky."

The men watched as the helicopter flew right, then left, and over the road where their car had been stuck.

"The Indian spirits must be protecting us," Jimmy said. "They would have seen us if we hadn't gotten out of there."

"Will you cut out the Indian crap?" Victor said. "*I* got us out of trouble. Now all we have to do is lay low until the copter is out of sight."

"What's going to happen to us?" Jimmy whimpered.

"You know the plan. We have plenty of money left over from selling Stephen's Corvette, and Linda still has most of the stash we gave her. We'll just disappear. We'll be gone, and Charles Laughery will be dead!"

Jimmy stared straight ahead. Victor could see he was spacing out again. I should just leave him here, he thought. But if I do, he might have second thoughts and lead them to Laughery, and that's not going to happen. By god, this time the son of a bitch stays buried.

"It's leaving! It didn't see us. We're safe!"

"Not yet," Victor said. "But we soon will be! Let's get the hell out of here!"

"Say again." The ranger listened then turned to Josh. "The helicopter hasn't located them yet. The pilot's going to make another sweep over the area. He'll use his search light now that it's getting dark."

Josh nodded and walked back to his truck. He leaned against the hood and stared up into the twilight sky, the same sky the Anasazi had gazed into so long ago.

"Want some coffee?" Mike stood beside him, holding a thermos and two cups.

"Sure. Thanks."

"I talked to Chief Weaver on the radio," Mike said. "His men, Leroy and Adam are feeling as frustrated as we are. You'd think the helicopter could spot a moving vehicle in all this open space. Where the hell can they be?"

"Just about anywhere," Josh said. "There are almost 4000 sites here and over 600 of them are cliff dwellings. They could be in any one of them. It could take days to flush them out."

"But they've got to know we're on their tail. They wouldn't stick around here, would they?"

"Not deliberately. My guess is they haven't been able to find a way out yet. The snow came earlier than usual this year. The car they rented would have a hard time getting around. I don't think this was a well thought out plan. It probably developed as things went along. It's possible they just stumbled onto Caroline in Durango and went from there. If so, they're probably regretting their decision to come to Mesa Verde."

Mike drank his coffee in silence for several minutes.

"I'm just so damned relieved that Katie and Caroline are safe. I was surprised they let Caroline go. They actually did just want Charles. Why would anyone hate him so much?"

Josh had wondered the same thing. What had Charles done to warrant this kind of vengeance?

The kiva was totally dark now. No more twilight to soften the blackness. Charles sat on the sand-packed floor and wrapped his arms around his knees.

This is what Victor calls justice. I destroy his father's life, and he destroys mine.

How would Caroline see it? She insisted there was a reason for everything. He remembered yelling at her one time during an argument, "Can't something ever be just an accident?" She had just laughed and said, "No."

Caroline also believed that when an event happened over and over in your life, there was something you weren't getting.

So why was he alone in the dark again?

He rolled onto his knees and pushed himself up. He wasn't about to sit here all night, philosophizing. With both arms extended, he moved through the dark until his knees hit a ledge and his outstretched hands touched a wall.

He followed the smooth, rounded wall. Feeling his way, step by step, he continued walking around the kiva. His fingers curved—empty space.

What the hell? He waved his hand through the air until, reaching farther to his right, he once again touched a wall. Without hesitation, he knelt and crawled into the tunnel.

In the back room of the police station, Caroline tucked a blanket around Kate then lay down on her own cot and closed her eyes. She felt guilty for even trying to sleep while those she loved were in danger. Turning on her side, she pulled the blanket over her shoulder. Her last thought as she fell asleep was of Charles.

The fog surrounded them as they stumbled along, holding tightly onto each other. Voices were calling to them, but she couldn't make out what they were saying. "We're lost," she said to Charles, but he didn't answer. He held her hand tightly, pulling her along.

Then he let go. "Charles," she called out. "Wait for me. Don't leave me." As she ran to catch up with him, the ground beneath her disappeared, and she began to fall—down, down....

Caroline opened her eyes. The sense of falling was still with her, a sinking feeling in the pit of her stomach.

Shaken, she threw off the cover and sat up. Was the dream meaningful? Was Charles dead? Or alive and trying to contact her as he had in the mountain?

She looked over at Kate, who was peacefully sleeping. Would this nightmare ever end?

The snow had stopped and a half-moon appeared and disappeared between the scurrying clouds. The men waited at the Sun Temple area for the helicopter to land. Adam watched as it circled lower. When it touched down, Josh grabbed his arm and pulled him forward. Chief Weaver was right behind them. The three of them ducked their heads and ran to the open door. As soon as everyone had climbed in, the pilot took off, flying over the mesa toward the site where the Taurus had been spotted.

Adam could see the lights of the trucks below them heading in the same direction. Mike and Leroy were riding with them. He looked at the gun that Josh had thrust into his hand. Apparently they would have to jump from the hovering copter. *I hope I don't shoot myself. I'm not cut out for this commando stuff.*

Ten minutes later, the pilot pointed toward the ground. Following the spotlight, Adam saw a car stranded in the snow and two figures running from it. The helicopter started down. The men unbuckled and prepared to jump. Adam was the last out the door. The landing was harder than he expected, but what really knocked the breath out of him was the sight of Jimmy in front of him.

The brothers stared at each another. Adam saw Jimmy mouth something but the noise of the helicopter made it impossible to hear his words. The copter moved higher overhead, its spotlight illuminating the area. Jimmy stood, transfixed. Adam struggled to walk through the knee-deep snow to his brother. There was a sudden shout behind him.

"Look out, Adam," Josh yelled. Too late he saw the gun in Victor's hand.

Following his gaze, Jimmy turned and shouted, "No!" throwing himself toward Victor. Two shots rang out. Jimmy sank slowly into the snow, and Victor writhed in pain as he held his bloody hand. By the time Adam reached Jimmy, the snow around him was no longer white.

He stared into his brother's sightless eyes.

CHAPTER THIRTY-ONE

The desk clerk handed the phone to her. Caroline felt almost too weak to hold it.

"You caught them? Is Charles all right?'

She listened, first disappointed then horrified, as Josh described the deadly encounter. "Jimmy's dead? Oh, dear God, poor Adam."

"He's taking it pretty hard, but once he gets over the shock, it's going to mean something to him that his brother saved his life.

"Listen," Josh continued, "it's going to be daylight soon. The search party will go through every ruin until they find Charles. Mike and Adam are going to stay with them, and I'm heading back to Durango with Chief Weaver. We have to take Victor to the hospital. He has a superficial hand wound. So far, he's refused to tell us where Charles is, but he'll eventually crack."

He won't, Caroline thought.

"Are you there, honey?" Josh asked.

"Yes, I was thinking about Victor. I don't think he's going to talk. He has nothing to lose by keeping quiet. If Charles is dead, he certainly isn't going to confess to his murder, and if he's left

Charles somewhere to die, he doesn't want us to find him until it's too late."

The silence on the other end of the line told Caroline that Josh agreed with her assessment. "I'll meet you at the hospital," she said. "I'd like to talk to Victor. In some peculiar way, he seems to respect me. At one point, he complimented me on my wise decision to leave Charles years ago. I tried to convince him that I hated Charles, too. Maybe he believed me."

She waited for Josh's response. Finally, he said, "Okay, you might be right. But don't come to the hospital. We'll bring him to the Police Station after they treat his hand."

Two hours later, Kate and Caroline waited in the interrogation room. They had gone out for breakfast, and Caroline felt stronger, better able to deal with Victor. Josh's last phone call had confirmed what she'd known all along. He wasn't talking.

Kate jumped up and began pacing the room. "I hate this waiting," she said. "And I'm not sure it's a good idea for you to talk to that awful person after what he put you through. Do you really think he'll tell you anything about Charles?"

"Not directly," Caroline said. "But maybe inadvertently. He's smart but very arrogant. While I was with them, he kept preening for me, bragging about the turmoil he'd caused for those who weren't obeying environmental laws. I pretended to be impressed, and he seemed to buy into the idea that I admired him for his actions. Maybe I can get him to slip up. Anyway, I have to try. Josh and the police haven't been able to get anything out of him."

The sound of voices penetrated the room, and the door opened. Victor walked in, handcuffed and escorted by a policeman on both sides, followed by Josh, Chief Weaver and several other men. A smile played around Victor's lips when he saw her, sending a shiver through Caroline. *He's done something to Charles that has brought him great satisfaction,* she thought.

Dear God, help me get through this.

Kate joined Josh and the other men at the back of the room, where they talked while keeping an eye on Victor. As Caroline sat across the table from him, she breathed slowly in and out. Somehow she must use his madness against him.

"Hello, Victor," she said, looking him straight in the eyes. Mustering a display of compassion, she asked, "Does your hand hurt?"

Surprisingly, he responded to her overture. "It hurts like hell, but I don't care. I've had one goal for twenty years—to make Charles Laughery pay. And I've achieved that goal. They'll never find him."

"Good," she said, smiling encouragingly. Would he believe her? Had he bought into her story earlier that she hated her ex-husband and disapproved of his environmental decisions?

Victor glanced at the men in the corner of the room and lowered his voice. "Jimmy told me how he treated you, screwing around with other women. He really is a son-of-a bitch!"

"You are so right. He deserves whatever happens to him. So, tell me. Is he dead?"

Victor leaned forward. "Not yet, but soon. In the meantime, he's probably wishing he was with you right now, not dying like some trapped animal."

Oh, dear God, he's alive. Charles is alive. But where?

She hid her trembling hands under the table.

"I've been wondering about something. How did you know I would be in Durango?"

Victor pushed back in his chair. "That's the beauty of it. We were looking for a place to ask directions to the ranch when Jimmy spotted you. And I immediately knew the perfect place to lure Charles."

"The Mesa Verde ruins," she said. "Such a beautiful place. I wish we could preserve more areas like the mesa."

"I know. I visited there years ago and thought the same thing." Victor gazed out the window for a moment and then, as though talking to himself, added, "I remembered there were hundreds of kivas and...." He stopped, and his demeanor changed when he realized what he'd just said.

Caroline nodded, enthusiastically. "Of course, a kiva. But it must have been difficult to find the right ruins. You couldn't go to any of the big ones because of tourists. And some of them are closed because it's winter. No wonder you got stuck, you had to go to an isolated area."

Victor averted his eyes, and Caroline knew he wasn't about to say more.

Josh walked over to her. "Chief Weaver wants to take over now."

She got up, resigned to the fact that she had gotten all she was going to get out of Victor and left the room with Josh. Once through the door, her legs gave out from under her, and Josh helped her to the nearest chair. He stooped down beside her.

"Josh, Charles is alive. He's in one of the kivas."

"I heard Victor mention them, but why are you so sure that...?"

"Because Jimmy referred to kivas several times. And it fits into Victor's warped way of thinking. Put Charles in a kiva and leave him to die and hope no one finds him this time."

"Do you know how many kivas are out there? It could take us months to find the right one. But most of them are large and open from erosion, and this would have to be one of the smaller ones, still enclosed, with an opening that could be blocked."

"And we know they started from the Cliff Palace ruins," Caroline said. "And where they ended up. So it would have to be within that area. Right?"

"True. Let me talk to Chief Weaver." He stood, leaned over and looked into her eyes. "We're going to find him."

Mike groaned and stretched as he sat upright in the cab of the truck. His watch said 8:30 a.m. so he'd gotten a few hours sleep. He peeked through the back window at Leroy, who was still dead to the world in his sleeping bag in the truck bed.

Stepping out into the parking lot, Mike looked up into the cloudy sky. At least, it had stopped snowing. Eager to join the search party, he walked into the museum at the Spruce Tree Ruins where the rangers had set up a command post.

The first person he saw was Adam, off by himself. He obviously hadn't gotten any sleep. You had to feel sorry for the guy. To have your brother gunned down in front of your eyes…. Adam looked up, his eyes vacant, and Mike walked over to him, trying to decide what to say. Sorry your terrorist brother is dead? He grabbed a chair.

The two men sat, without speaking, until Adam said, "Josh called. Caroline talked to Victor, and she's convinced that Charles is in one of the kivas in one of the more isolated ruins."

Mike grimaced. "In some black hole again, after all that time in the mountain. The guy can't catch a break."

"If only I could have talked to Jimmy," Adam said. "I know he would have told us where they put Charles. He was screwed up, but I don't believe he would have let Charles die. At least the brother I knew wouldn't have." Adam sat up and rubbed the back of his neck. "Did you get any sleep?"

"A few hours," Mike said. "But I'm going to need some coffee to get going this morning. Can I get you a cup?" Adam nodded and leaned back against the wall.

The day shift of rangers and police officers were new faces to Mike. They were examining maps of the mesa. He introduced himself, listened to them for a few minutes, then poured two cups of coffee and walked back to Adam. Handing him a cup, Mike said, "Why don't you go to Durango? It's been a tough night for you."

Adam shook his head. "I'm not going anywhere. There's nothing I can do for Jimmy anymore, but maybe I can help find Charles. What's the search plan?"

"From what I just heard, they're going to fan out in all directions. There are more men and trucks on the way. We know where Victor and Jimmy ended up, so somewhere between there and the Cliff Palace ruins, they dumped Charles. Unfortunately that covers a large area."

Adam got to his feet. "Then we should get going."

Charles's first thought on awaking was, I've made a mistake. I should have stayed in the kiva. He'd fallen asleep on the hard floor of the tunnel. His back and legs ached from crawling. What he'd assumed to be a short tunnel leading to another kiva had only led to other tunnels, and each of them had led to a wall of rock.

The Indians must have dug these passages by trial and error, he thought, mostly error.

Now, he had no idea which tunnel led back to the kiva. Fear that he'd been able to keep under control began to creep into his mind.

What was worse? Dying in the tunnels or the partial light of the kiva?

He pushed himself to a sitting position. He had to keep going.

The plane dipped down, waggled its wings and flew low over their heads.

Mike laughed and waved at Josh, then watched as he headed toward one of the main roads.

"Let's go," he said, jumping into the truck.

Adam shook his head in disbelief. "The man lands that plane anywhere he damn well pleases."

By the time they reached Josh, he had pulled the plane to the side of the road, allowing other vehicles to squeeze by. Mike brought Josh up-to-date on the search.

"We've found several places where Victor and Jimmy obviously got stuck but most of those led to dead ends. One went to an undeveloped site, but we checked out every kiva there. All of them are large and wide open. Leroy's with the rangers now checking out another area. This could take awhile."

"I hope not. Charles isn't in great physical shape after the mountain experience. We need to find him as soon as possible." Josh looked at Adam. "Caroline and Kate wanted me to tell you how sorry they are about your brother."

"Thanks. I still can't believe what happened."

The men walked back to the truck, and Adam climbed into the driver's seat. As they drove away, Mike turned to Josh. "Why is Caroline so sure that Charles is still alive?"

"Victor told her when she talked to him at the Police Station. And she believes that Victor would get great satisfaction in finishing the job the way he originally planned it—Charles buried alive, dying a slow, painful death."

"Nice guy," Mike muttered.

"We're dealing with a sociopath." Aware that Adam was listening, Josh chose his next words carefully. "The two younger men were confused and misguided—way over their heads. I believe either one of them would have eventually cooperated with us. Actually, Stephen is talking his head off right now back in LA. Apparently, his father has refused to send his high-powered lawyers to help him, so he's throwing himself on the mercy of the court.

"And as for Jimmy, Caroline is convinced he would have told us where to find Charles, had he lived." Out of the corner of his eye, Josh saw a look of gratitude on Adam's face.

"What's that up ahead?" Mike asked.

Josh squinted. Far down the road, men were milling around several trucks.

Pulling up beside the group, Josh rolled down the window and called out to the closest ranger.

"What's going on?"

The ranger walked over to the truck. "Are you the guys Chief Weaver told us about?" He stooped to stare into the truck at Adam. "You must be the brother of the man who...."

Josh stuck his hand through the open window. "I'm Josh Logan, and this is Mike and Adam. What's happening?"

"One of our men followed the road over there to one of the undeveloped ruins. The snow's too deep to get far. But he thought it looked like several people had walked the rest of the way, so he radioed me. I told him to wait for the rest of us before checking it out. Want to…?"

Josh, Mike and Adam were out the truck before he could finish his sentence.

Had he taken another wrong branch? This tunnel should have led somewhere by now.

Charles stopped to rest, rubbing his sore knees. Sitting, his head almost grazed the roof of the tunnel. Needing to lie down, he stretched out his hand and touched something—a slim, oblong stone. He ran his hands over the tubular-shaped object. It had a perfect, round hole near the end. Man-made? A tool of some kind?

He grasped the artifact in his hand for a few minutes before laying it down. It was a confirmation that another human had been in the tunnel.

He closed his eyes, resting before moving on. Now, at least, he knew these passageways led somewhere.

Someone in the far past had followed the same path.

CHAPTER THIRTY-TWO

K ate stepped out of the shower in the motel bathroom, wrapped herself in one towel and dried her hair with another.

It felt good to be clean again. Lottie had sent clothes and toiletries in from the ranch. She quickly put on jeans and a bulky red sweater and joined Caroline, who was watching the news. The local channels were reporting Charles's kidnapping. CNN and Fox had picked up the story.

Kate ran her fingers through damp curls and sat beside her.

"I guess we don't have to worry about keeping Charles's whereabouts a secret anymore," she said.

"I would love to see the faces of Brenda and Charles's partners right now," Caroline said. "They were so sure he was dead. Of course, if the men don't find him...."

Kate took her hand. "They're going to find him. It's not the same as when he was lost in the mountain. This time we know he's out there someplace. It's just a matter of time."

Caroline squeezed her hand. "I'm so glad you're here with me."

"I just can't believe it's happening again. Poor Charles."

Caroline turned off the TV

"When they find Charles, I'm going back to LA with him."

Kate didn't respond. She knew her voice would betray her disappointment. She'd been rooting for Josh.

"Do you understand?" Caroline asked.

Kate got off the bed, walked over to the window and stared out. The beauty of the snow-covered Colorado landscape filled her mind and heart in a way no other place ever had. She knew this was her home now, hopefully with Mike. But she'd wanted to share her new life with Caroline, too.

"I guess I'm being selfish," she said. "I hoped that you and Josh would end up together. That the four of us could.... But, you have a right to choose the man you want to spend your life with."

"Thank you, Kate, for understanding. I just can't let Charles go back to LA alone. If he survives this, he'll have to deal with the press, his partners and Brenda. I know Adam will do whatever he can to help, because he feels so guilty about everything. But after losing his brother the way he did—well, he's going to need support, too." She paused. "And I feel guilty. If it weren't for me, Charles wouldn't be going through this again. He was willing to sacrifice his own life for mine."

Kate started to argue, but Caroline held up her hand. "I know, I know. But it's how I feel."

She grabbed her purse and coat and walked toward the door. "I can't bear to sit around waiting another minute! Let's rent a car and go to Mesa Verde."

"Over here!" Mike yelled. Josh and Adam ran quickly across the ruins to where he stood, looking down at a large sandstone slab covering a hole in the ground. Josh helped Mike push the heavy stone aside.

Several rangers had joined them. One handed Josh a flashlight. Aiming its light into the kiva, he stuck his head through the opening and looked around then backed out. "Shit, I thought we'd found him."

"Nothing down there?" Mike asked.

Josh swept the floor of the kiva with the flashlight again. It was empty.

"Well, this is just one of many," he said. "Let's check out the rest."

For the next hour, the men combed every inch of the ruins, finding other small but empty kivas. It was now well past noon, and they decided to return to the museum, meet up with the other search groups and decide on their next move.

Trudging through the deep snow to their truck on the main road, Josh and Mike were surprised to see Kate and Caroline waving at them.

Mike ran, leaping through the snow, and pulled Kate into a bear hug. By the time Josh reached them, she was peppering Mike with questions.

"Have you found anything? Have you checked every kiva? This must be the place! You can see how they drove as far as they could then walked the rest of the way."

Caroline was staring at the ruins behind them.

"I want to see the kivas," she said.

"We looked in every damn hole," Josh said. "They were empty. All but one was uncovered and most were full of debris. These ruins haven't been renovated."

Ignoring his words, Caroline started toward the site. Josh looked at Kate and Mike and said, "You two go on. We'll join you in a minute."

By the time he caught up with Caroline, she was sitting on one of the broken walls, gazing toward the cold, white horizon. Once the trucks drove out of sight, silence filled the ruins. Josh sat a few feet away, giving her the space he knew she needed.

The vistas on all sides of them were awe-inspiring. Josh had planned to share this special place with Caroline one day but under much different circumstances. Could there really be a man lost under all this beauty? Did Caroline feel Charles's presence? She seemed so far away. Josh began to feel uneasy.

"Caroline," he said.

She shifted her gaze toward him. "He's here, Josh. He's here somewhere. I can sense it." She stood and looked around. "Show me the kivas you found."

Josh took her arm and led her around the ruins, pointing out small and large kivas. When they reached the one that had been covered by the stone slab, she asked, "You went inside?"

"No, but I stuck my head in. It's empty."

Caroline glanced around and then pointed to a wooden ladder close by.

"I need to go inside."

Josh dragged the homemade ladder to the kiva opening, lowering it into the hole. Before he could stop her, Caroline turned and put one foot on a rung of the ladder. Knowing there was no point in arguing, he handed her the flashlight.

"Take it slow," he said. When her head disappeared, he followed through the opening, hoping the rungs wouldn't break. By the time he reached the bottom, Caroline was flashing the light up and down and around the room. On the far side of the kiva, she stopped.

"Josh!" she called out, excitedly.

He could only see what appeared to be a hole in the wall. Or was it....

Caroline ran across the kiva floor. Before she could enter the tunnel, however, Josh grabbed her arm.

"Not another step," he said. "From this point on, we get help." As she tried to pull away, he held on tightly. "I mean it, Caroline. We do it my way or not at all."

He took the flashlight from her and, in its light, he could see determination in her eyes. *She has no doubt that Charles is in there,* he thought. *The connection between them is that strong. How do you fight something like that?*

He led her back to the ladder. "We'll have the men search the tunnel," he said. "Just be patient a little longer."

Caroline said nothing and began climbing upward—and away from him.

Charles stopped crawling. He needed to rest his back and knees that ached unbearably. His strength and hope were fading, and a pressure in his chest was increasing. Stress or his heart?

Did it really matter? A quick death versus a slow one. As he wiped away the cold sweat from his forehead, the pressure lessened, and he began moving forward again. After a few feet, however, his hand touched something. A rock? Another artifact?

He reached out to pick up the object and ran his hands over the smooth stone. *Oh, God, no.* There was no doubt in his mind that it was the same stone object that he'd left behind earlier.

He had been going in circles.

Wait a minute, he told himself, think. He had gone right where the tunnels branched off. He should have turned left. He laughed at the pride he felt that his exhausted mind was still functioning.

He held onto the artifact, pushed himself to his knees again and crawled forward.

Kate stomped her feet and walked around the ruins to keep warm. The men were searching the tunnel. As Caroline sat beside the kiva opening, she didn't seem to notice that the sun was sinking lower in the west, and the sky was filling with snow clouds.

Maybe Caroline is wrong, Kate thought. Maybe Charles isn't anywhere near here.

"I know he's close by," Caroline said.

Kate stooped beside her. "Why don't we wait in the truck? It's really getting cold."

Caroline pushed herself off the floor of the ruins. "Listen," she said.

Kate heard the voices, too. She and Caroline knelt beside the kiva opening. Within minutes, the first man stood at the bottom of the ladder. He looked up and said, "Sorry." One by one the men climbed out of the kiva. Josh, Adam and Mike were last. All three gathered silently around Caroline.

Josh said, "We went through every tunnel. Most only led to dead ends. One simply led us in a circle. We doubled back many times to make sure we'd covered the area. Only one tunnel led to another kiva, but that was empty and blocked from the surface."

"Where do you think that kiva is?" she asked.

Mike said, "That's hard to say. You can't tell what direction you're going down there. But my guess is over there." He pointed toward the remains of a half torn down tower in the distance.

Kate felt the wetness of the first snowflakes on her cheek.

Shielding her eyes from the snow, Caroline asked, "Is that tower another site?"

"I believe that it's all one ruin," Josh said. "The floor is just covered with snow between here and those walls. But we checked that area earlier. Come on, honey. Let's go."

Caroline stood unmoving, staring into the falling snow.

Charles didn't know how long he had been lying on the ruins floor inside the tower walls. The snow was blanketing his body, and he sat up, brushing it away. His hands were bloodied from wrestling with the large stone he had pushed over the kiva opening. Why did I do that? he wondered, exhausted from the effort. It had seemed important at the time that no one else get lost in those tunnels, but now he realized it hadn't made any sense, and it had taken the last of his strength.

Then he heard it, the sound of car engines. Were people over there? He staggered to his feet and to the nearest broken wall, leaning against it. He couldn't see through the heavily falling snow but could hear the sound of trucks driving away. "Over here," he shouted. His voice disappeared into the rising wind.

"Wait!" he tried again. "Don't leave!"

Throwing himself over the small wall, he dropped into the knee-high snow. His legs immediately gave out on him. A few more feet of dragging himself through the snow, and his strength failed him again.

Josh could barely see Caroline through the veil of snow. He was worried about her emotional state. She seemed obsessed with the notion that Charles was out here somewhere. When she insisted on checking the tower area they had already searched, he decided to humor her, sending the others on their way.

"Hold on," he called out. She turned and waited for him.

When he reached her, he said, "Caroline, we can come back tomorrow and...."

She put a gloved hand on his chest. "I've got to do this, Josh. Bear with me a little longer."

He reluctantly wrapped his arm around her waist, and they stumbled forward. The twilight had darkened into night, and he turned on his flashlight, directing it toward the broken tower.

Caroline grabbed his arm and pointed.

Josh knew before they reached the dark form in the snow that they'd found Charles.

CHAPTER THIRTY-THREE

In the hospital room, Charles dictated a press release to Adam while Caroline and Josh sat in the corner, talking.

"He insists on leaving for LA later today," Caroline said.

"Are the doctors willing to release him that soon?"

"Probably not, but you know Charles."

Josh hesitated then asked, "Are you going with him?"

He watched as Caroline twisted a crumbled tissue in her hand. She had been exhilarated last night over finding Charles, but this morning, she was unusually quiet. He stood and held out his hand.

Walking together into the hallway, Josh asked again, "Are you going back with him?"

"Let's go to the cafeteria and have some coffee. I didn't get much sleep last night."

Josh understood she was giving him time to prepare for what she was about to tell him. His heart was already beginning to hurt.

In the cafeteria, they sat beside the glass wall that looked out onto a pristine field of new snow. The snowcapped mountains were etched against the deepest blue. Caroline stared out, sipping her coffee.

"This is the most beautiful countryside," she said. "I'm so grateful to you for sharing it with me." Josh braced himself for her next words.

"I couldn't have gotten through these past months without you. Even when my feelings didn't make sense, you trusted me." She reached out and took his hand in both of hers. They looked small and pale against his gnarled knuckles.

She gripped him tightly. "I will never forget our one night together. I really thought—"

"Caroline, you've been honest with me about your mixed feelings." He paused. "But I assume you aren't confused anymore."

Biting her lip, she let go of his hand and clasped hers on the table in front of her. "I'm sure of only one thing and that is I have to go back to LA and help Charles deal with the fallout of these past months. I feel responsible for his last horrible experience. Maybe if I'd fought harder to escape from Victor and Jimmy...."

"Nonsense! That's ridiculous, and you know it. If you had, you might have been killed, and I doubt that Charles would have been grateful to you for that. You kept your cool and did better than most people under those circumstances. Feeling guilty is illogical."

Caroline stared out the window. Josh waited.

Finally, she said, "My feelings for Charles have never been logical." She gave a deprecating laugh. "Apparently, I've been waiting ten years for him to come back to me. Something I've never admitted, even to myself, until now.

"I don't know how much pride plays into it, or if I simply still love him. All I know is that I have to go back and work my feelings out, one way or the other."

Her words sparked a moment's hope. "Does that mean there's still a chance for you and me?"

Caroline hesitated. "You don't know how tempted I am to say what you want me to say, but that wouldn't be fair to you. Or to me. This whole thing is wearing us both down, emotionally, and you deserve better. I need to let you go on with your life, while I figure out mine."

She pushed back from the table. When he did the same, she said, "Don't get up. I need to say goodbye now, while I have the courage.

"I wish...," she began, her lips trembling. She turned and walked away.

Josh sat by Charles's bed. Neither had mentioned Caroline in the past fifteen minutes. They had stayed on safe subjects, going over the last few days' events.

"So your corporate jet is picking you up later today?"

"That's right," Charles said, "Hopefully, we can avoid reporters here, although they'll probably be waiting when we land in California. Caroline won't be happy about that."

Instead of responding to the comment, Josh picked up the stone artifact that Charles had placed on the table beside the bed.

"You had a death grip on this when we found you," he said. Smiling, he added, "Fortunately, not literally."

"You're probably up on Indian lore," Charles said. "What do you think it is? And why the tunnels between kivas?"

Josh studied the piece, turning it over in his hands. "My guess is that it was something used by the Anasazi priests—some kind of pipe. The priests used to blow smoke into the sky mimicking rain clouds. They may have used the tunnels to make unexpected entrances during their ceremonies." He held out the artifact to Charles. "The park authorities should be able to tell you when you give it back to them."

"Well, whatever it is," Charles said, "it kept me going, and I'm grateful to whoever dropped it. I realize how strange that must sound, but...."

Understanding his discomfort, Josh changed the subject. "You'll let me know when the court date is set for Victor and Stephen."

"Of course, but you know how slow the California courts can be. The good news is, since his father refuses to help him, Stephen is spilling his guts. But even if he cuts a deal, he'll spend time behind bars for kidnapping and attempted murder. I hope Victor gets the death penalty for killing Jimmy even though he was aiming at Adam."

"What about Linda?"

"She'll probably get probation. She's basically only guilty of greediness and poor judgment in men. Stephen backed up her assertion that she knew nothing of Victor's real agenda until that final night. And then she did call and warn me."

The men sat quietly for a moment.

"What's going to happen with your project when the public hears about the government's plans?"

Charles frowned. "Well…first, the press will go crazy. Then Caroline and her environmental group will get into the act. The Bureau of Land Management and the Atomic Energy Commission will be besieged by questions. And there's no way we'll be able to answer all their questions satisfactorily, so who knows? It may never get off the ground."

"Maybe not," Josh said, "but the public has the right to know what the government is planning and how it will impact them. Although I'm sure your pals in the cartel wouldn't agree with me about that."

Charles gave a short laugh. "I may never know what they think about all this as I'm persona non grata at the moment. Publicity is not welcomed by the cartel. But to tell you the truth, I couldn't care less. I'm not into ruling the world anymore."

Josh stood. "Mike and Kate are waiting for me." He stuck out his hand, and Charles shook it.

When Josh got to the door, he looked back. "Take care of her," he said.

Caroline hugged Kate and Mike, an arm around each.

"I'm going to miss you two. But I'm glad you've decided to stay at the ranch. It will mean so much to Josh."

"Caroline...," Kate began. Mike shook his head at her, and she didn't continue.

"I'll call you when I get home," Caroline said. "I want you to visit me in LA. And after everything calms down, maybe we can meet at Odessa again."

Seeing Josh approach, she gave Kate another quick hug and whispered, "Take care of him, Katie." Then she hurried away.

CHAPTER THIRTY-FOUR

K ate listened to the sound of the pounding rain. Although it was only three o'clock in the afternoon, Mike had finished his chores and was reading in the chair across from her. The fire crackled and snapped in the fireplace. She was content.

Well, almost. She hadn't heard from Caroline for the past few weeks. For a few months, they had exchanged emails almost every day.

Mike put down his book. "I think I'll work on the plans for the cabin," he said. "Want to help me?"

She set her own book aside and followed him to the library area. Mike's enthusiasm for their new home was catching. Josh was supplying the land and the logs, and the other ranch hands had offered to help Mike build it.

"You're sure it will be ready by August?" she asked, looking at the diagram Mike had unrolled on the desk. "I mean it would be neat if we could move in after we get married. Which reminds me, now that we've decided to take Caroline up on her offer to have the wedding at Odessa, I should call her."

"Have you talked to her lately?"

Kate sat on the edge of the desk. "No, but she's had her hands full helping Charles and Adam with the press. The tabloids have had a field day. I loved the look of fury on Brenda's face in that last article about the divorce." She chuckled.

Mike pushed back in the chair. "I wonder if Caroline will marry Charles again. I guess she must love the guy, but I sure do wish things had turned out differently."

"Me, too," Kate said. "I had this fantasy about Caroline living here and keeping her house in LA so she and Josh could go there for plays and things like that. And the four of us spending time together at Odessa." She sighed. "Oh, well, people have to figure out their own lives. I do feel sorry for Josh though. It doesn't seem fair. He finds Charles, only to lose Caroline to him."

"Who says life is fair?" Mike said.

Knowing he was thinking about his ex-wife and best friend, Kate said, "You have to forgive them, Mike. They didn't fall in love and have a baby to hurt you. I think you should let them know you're okay now. That you've started a new life here."

Mike didn't answer, but Kate knew he was listening. She'd eventually get through to him. She had to, because he needed to let go of his anger if they were to have a good relationship.

She opened her mouth to continue, but Mike held up his hand. "I'll think about it!"

He pushed back in the chair. "I'm more concerned about Josh right now. Maybe it will help that spring's almost here. He can spend more time outdoors, won't be snowbound anymore."

"Where is he right now?"

"In the barn. I believe he sent everyone home early so he could be alone out there."

"Which means we can be alone in here," she said, sliding over the desk top and landing in Mike's lap.

Kate was settling into his arms when she heard the sound of a car pulling up outside.

Josh sat on a hay bale, leaning against the stall door. Peaches chomped on the apple he'd just fed to her. He could feel her warm breath. The quiet shuffling of the horses in the other stalls was the only sound except for the rain on the tin roof of the barn.

Shadow watched him with sad eyes then lay down, one paw on his boot. The dog always seemed to sense his mood. He reached down and rubbed behind his old friend's ears.

He hadn't hurt like this since Hannah's death. It had taken him years to get over the loss of his wife. Would he miss Caroline for that long? Ache for her touch, the smell of her hair? Dream about her night after night?

He leaned back against the stall again and stroked Peaches's velvet nose, as she nuzzled his shoulder.

Damn. I need to get out of here, he thought. Stop feeling sorry for myself. Maybe take on another P.I. assignment. Soon the snow will be gone, and I can fly wherever I want. Odessa. I'm sure Caroline wouldn't mind if I stayed at the house there.

He closed his eyes, seeing her standing in front of the mirror in the bedroom of the small house, lifting her long hair....

Caroline slid open the barn door, tossed her umbrella aside and made her way down the packed dirt aisle. Max whinnied when she passed his stall. The barn smells were pungent. The rain on the tin roof grew louder; thunder rumbled. In the dim light, she saw Josh before he saw her. He was sitting outside Peaches's stall. He leaned over and ran his fingers through his graying hair. The gesture brought tears to Caroline's eyes.

"Josh." He didn't hear her above the pounding rain.

"Josh," she said, louder. He looked up. She couldn't read his expression.

Unsure what to do, she called out to Shadow. The German Shepherd stood, wagged his tail, glanced up at Josh, then ran to her. Relieved to have something to do, Caroline rubbed him briskly and whispered in his ear, "I'm glad to see you, too."

When she looked up again, Josh was standing. For a moment, neither of them spoke or moved.

She said, "I hope you don't mind my just showing up like this. I was going to call you, but I wasn't sure if you.... I didn't want you to tell me not to come. Because I needed to see you, talk to you. I needed to...."

In a few, long strides, Josh reached her and took her into his arms.

"I thought they'd never go to bed," Caroline said, sitting beside Josh on the couch. "After Mike and Kate joined us in the barn, we couldn't really talk, and I have so much to tell you."

"I still can't believe you're here."

Caroline laid her head on his shoulder and stretched her legs out on the leather hassock. "I can't tell you how many nights I envisioned this scene. The two of us here in front of the fire."

He leaned slightly away and looked down into the brown eyes. "Really? But you never called or wrote."

She reached up and touched his face with her fingertips. "I couldn't," she said. "I promised myself I wouldn't intrude on your life again until I was sure, really sure about my feelings."

She shifted sideways on the couch to face him. "Things fell into place for me a few weeks ago. Charles and I were having dinner in his penthouse. He was telling me about the latest visit to his lawyers regarding his divorce. Actually, I'd had lunch with Adam that day, and he'd told me Brenda would have to eventually agree to the proposed settlement."

"How is Adam doing, by the way?" Josh asked.

"Better than I expected. He's come to terms with Jimmy's death. He even visited Stephen in jail and learned about the last few years of his brother's life—a bizarre story of obsession and fixation on men like Charles. Adam understands now that he couldn't have helped him. He's just grateful that his parents never lived to see Jimmy's downward spiral."

"Okay, so much for Adam," Josh said. "Let's get back to you and Charles. Go on with your story."

"All right, but listen carefully, because you're the main character." She smiled then turned serious.

"Charles and I didn't have a lot of time together when we first got back to LA. He was still recuperating, and he had to deal with the press and his partners, who were in the midst of a nervous breakdown over his reappearance. He finally promised he would sell his stock to them if Adam could have a place on the board. Somehow, he and Adam have bonded again, something I don't completely understand but I'm glad, because they need one another. Of course, good old Leroy is still glued to Charles's side."

"What about Brenda?" Josh asked.

Caroline turned to stare into the fire. "Brenda, well, she's fighting tooth and nail for every penny but, like Adam told me, Charles will win in the end. There was a morality clause in their pre-nup. Apparently, however, she's now trying a new tactic. I ran into her on Rodeo Drive one day, and she made it clear that she hoped to get Charles to change his mind about the divorce." Caroline laughed. "Good luck with *that*."

"Where's her young lover?"

"He disappeared after his fifteen minutes of notoriety."

Josh smiled. "You certainly haven't had a dull few months. I've been mucking out stalls."

"Sounds like heaven. I'll help you tomorrow. But, seriously, the last time I felt as lost and miserable was ten years ago when Charles and I divorced. No matter how hard I tried to focus on Charles and my own life again, I couldn't stop thinking about you. You were the first thing on my mind when I awoke each morning and the last thing before I fell asleep at night. I tried to talk about it to my friends, but they didn't understand why I wasn't thrilled to have the new, improved Charles back in my life. And Charles didn't understand why I couldn't be intimate with him. I even talked to a counselor, but it always came back to you."

She moved to lean against him again. They sat for a few minutes, without speaking. Josh didn't rush her. He'd already heard what he needed to hear.

"Anyway," Caroline continued, "by the time Charles and I talked at dinner that particular night, we both knew my heart was with you.

"He was gracious about it and made it easy for me. He said he loved me enough to let me go. I'll always be grateful to him for that."

"So will I," Josh said.

They watched the dying embers spark as a log shifted in the fireplace. Caroline sat up and turned to him.

"I just realized I left out the most important part of the story."

Josh smiled, his mind and heart content. "I know," he said, softly. "I love you, too."

EPILOGUE

Caroline watched as the first stars appeared one by one in the Odessa sky. She stood at the edge of the cliff at the old ghost town. The minister had left, and Mike and Kate were on the way to Vegas to spend their honeymoon. She and Josh had chosen to spend theirs in the small house behind her. In a few days, the four of them would return to Colorado.

Behind her, Josh walked out of the house, carrying two glasses of champagne. Caroline took her glass and said, "This is where it began."

"And where it begins again," Josh said, touching her glass with his.

Holding one another, they gazed up into the star filled sky.

The night was still. The silence was complete.

ACKNOWLEDGEMENTS

So many people have encouraged my writing efforts. I never marketed any of my work over the years until the members of my critique group, past and present, read it. Thanks Tim S., Rich, Brenda, Hong-My, Cindy, Jim K., Jim G., Harvey, Bethany, Mary, Marilyn, Andrew, Arman, Millie, Sue, Judy, LizBeth, Tim C., Darlene, Dock, Dominic, Bob, John, Vickey, Delores, Teresa, Will, Susan, and the original creator and facilitator of our group, Carlene Jones.

Thanks, also, to all my writing friends in the Inland Empire Branch of the California Writers Club. Special thanks to Laura Hoopes, Kay Murphy, Millie Hinkle, Tim Sunderland and Barbara Bailey, who took the time to read the final draft of my manuscript.

Writing would be a lonely endeavor without friends like these.

I would also like to acknowledge the historical ghost town of Calico, California, located off Interstate 15 in the high desert for providing me with the inspiration for the fictional locale of my story.

ABOUT THE AUTHOR

Libby Grandy lives in Claremont, California with her husband, Fred. Her next book, *Promises to Keep*, the first of a trilogy, will be available in the Fall 2013. She can be followed on her website/blog, www.libbygrandy.com and Twitter, @LibbyGrandy.

Made in the USA
Charleston, SC
07 July 2013